A NOTE ON THE AUTHOR

TOBIAS HILL was born in London. In 2003 the *TLS*
nominated him as one of the best young writers in
Britain. In 2004 he was selected as one of the country's
Next Generation poets and shortlisted for the *Sunday
Times* Young Writer of the Year. His collection of
stories, *Skin*, won the PEN/Macmillan Prize for
Fiction and was shortlisted for the John Llewellyn
Rhys/Mail on Sunday Prize. His most recent novel is
What Was Promised.

www.tobiashill.com

Skin

Tobias Hill

BLOOMSBURY

LONDON · NEW DELHI · NEW YORK · SYDNEY

First published by Faber and Faber Ltd in 1997
This paperback edition published 2015

Extracts from *Noddy Goes to Sea* (in the story 'No One Comes Back from the Sea')
are reprinted by permission of Gillian Baverstock, Enid Blyton Limited

'Skin' was a winner in BBC's First Bites radio script competition; an adaptation was
broadcast on BBC Radio 4 In 1995, and a short version of the story was published
in the *London Magazine*. 'A Honeymoon in Los Angeles' appeared in *Cascando* and in
the anthology *Cold Comfort* (Serpent's Tail, 1996). 'Losing Track' won an Ian St James
Award in 1996. 'The Memory Man' first appeared in *Quadrant* (Australia). 'Brolly'
won the Sheffield Thursday Prize in 1994 and appeared in *The Printer's Devil*. 'No
One Comes Back from the Sea' appeared in *Quadrant* (Australia) and in the *Richmond
Review* (internet magazine). 'The World Feast' appeared in *Nieuw Wereldijdschrift*
(Holland). An adaptation of 'Zoo' was broadcast on BBC Radio 4 in 1997.

Bloomsbury Publishing Plc
50 Bedford Square
London
WC1B 3DP

www.bloomsbury.com

Bloomsbury is a trademark of Bloomsbury Publishing Plc

Bloomsbury Publishing, London, New Delhi, New York and Sydney

A CIP catalogue record for this book is available from the British Library

ISBN 978 1 4088 4417 5

10 9 8 7 6 5 4 3 2 1

Printed and bound in Great Britain by CPI Group (UK) Ltd, Croydon CR0 4YY

For Victoria

Contents

Skin

1: Pictures

His name was Tomoyasu and he was twelve in the year Japan invaded six countries. He had a photograph of an American spy. Kozo hugged himself when he saw it, thin arms tight around his greed. He didn't smile. A day later he offered Tomoyasu his softball, straight swap. The softball smelt of crushed leather and cut grass and it was made in the USA. Tomoyasu kept the photo. They swapped shoes, to show each other they were still friends, and no one realised for three days. Tomoyasu stole the softball anyway, from Kozo's school desk. Kozo had others. Tomoyasu hid it in the bamboos above Seven Stone Children Cemetery, buried under two blue-green rocks. When he came back a week later, he couldn't find the rocks. He walked home along the train track, singing the Red Dragonfly Song, not questioning his happiness.

His father had sent the photo from the Japanese state of Manchuria in a brown box sealed with hard wax. There were other presents in the box: a letter to them all in father's fine 'grass-writing' script; an American coin with an eagle on it; a necklace of blue stones for Tomoyasu's mother, and a plastic comb for his sister Natsuko.

There was a tiny hole in the comb, perfectly round, like the doorways weevils made in some grains of rice. When Tomoyasu put his eye to the hole, focusing carefully, he could see the skyscrapers of America. Under the picture it said Empire State in English. The last word was stained a rusty brown where something had leaked into the pinhead lens. Tomoyasu looked up 'Empire' in his classroom English dictionary. Sugihara-sensei, the Languages master, had brought the book from England. It was bound in inkstain-coloured card. 'Supreme and extensive political dominion. The approximate population of the British Empire is now 321,000,000 – Whitaker's Almanack,

1887'. Tomoyasu asked his mother if the British Empire was an enemy. She was writing the farm accounts and she stopped to laugh. 'The British Empire? Honey fungus is an enemy, and June drought. Write to your father. He knows about Outsiders.' He took the comb apart and found he couldn't put it back together.

Natsuko had died in the silkworm factory. That was after the European war but before the box came. She had worked there every winter with the other town girls, when there was no fieldwork to do. She had lost a little finger cutting open cocoons. She had shown the stub to Tomoyasu because he had asked her to. He thought it made her look like the Yakuza, the Gangsters, who cut off their little fingers as pledges of loyalty, wrapping them in red silk. Her hands became clumsy, as if they had been knocked off balance. She couldn't eat with chopsticks properly, dropping food like a little girl. After that she couldn't spin the raw silk into even thread. She brought some home for Tomoyasu, but it looked ugly and he threw it away.

The owners beat her with rice flails, but they didn't kill her. The spinners slept on the damp floors of the silkworm rooms. The cold killed her, moving up into her through the packed earth and matting. The owners brought Tomoyasu's mother a full kimono made of black silk. She thanked them; she was grateful. When they were gone she took her clothing scissors and cut the bright black dress into rags. Tomoyasu knelt, put his tongue to the paper doors and watched her through the moisture's transparency. The scissors sighed brokenly down their long, notched blades. The silk covered the floor like hanks of hair.

Tomoyasu got the photo and the comb. Sometimes he missed Natsuko. He got the coin, too. He took it from his mother's camphor-wood jewellery-box when she was laying food at Natsuko's grave. She had forgotten about it. Once, when he broke a writing brush and cried, she laughed. She said it was harder to care for a dead child than a living one. Her hair was falling out. She forgot lots of things. Sometimes she would come into his room at night and shout that he didn't deserve

2

love. Then for days she wouldn't talk to him or look at him. If he didn't step out of her way, she would walk into him. Later she would say sorry and try to cradle him. Tomoyasu didn't care about any of it. It gave him more time for himself. He took the coin with him when he played baseball.

The coin was slim and bright, shinier than Japanese sen and yen currency. Tomoyasu's father wrote that he'd got it from a spy. The spy had been captured flying a night plane from Korea. The photograph was of the spy and a boy with light hair. The spy and the boy sat on stools in front of a glass counter. There were burgers and slices of fruit pie inside the counter. Tomoyasu knew the colours of the fruit; blue and red, like the shells of lobsters. He tried to imagine all the colours in the photo but couldn't. He didn't know the shades of the boy's eyes or the spy's hair or the sky outside the wide windows.

The boy had a glass shaped like a jasmine flower, full of dark ice-cream. The spy didn't have a glass. He had one hand on the boy's light hair and the other raised in a fist. His smile was very bright in the dim photo. The boy was raising the glass over his head, crook-armed, a trophy. Both of them were wearing baseball whites. There was English on the baseball whites but Tomoyasu couldn't read it, even with Sugihara-sensei's magnifying glass. He was the only boy in his class who owned a photo of America.

He put the photo between the stiff yellow pages of his Japanese History text, put the book into his satchel and tugged the strap tight. He put on his baseball whites and left the satchel by the door, where he could pick it up after training. Every schoolday he played sport, then helped in the fields before lessons. He ate a quick breakfast of red beancurd soup. The dog scratched at the door for food. He gave it a wedge of beancurd but it wouldn't eat it.

It was nearly five o'clock and the frogs were groaning in the flat green tide of the rice paddies. It was still half-dark, so that the rice was really grey, Tomoyasu could only see it was green if he stared at it and narrowed his eyes. His mother had

3

already made him rice-parcels for lunch. There was a dab of pickled plum in the middle of each parcel. He could smell it, sweet and salty, a hidden treasure, even through the dry musty odour of the rice ration. He slid the door shut and ran to baseball practice through the white gloom of waterlands.

'Fall out! Now, please. Line up by the windows – good, Kokichi. Quickly, all of you. Immediately!'

They were practising slow pitches and low swings, 'grass cutters', when Niimi-sensei came into the gym and began to shout. Tomoyasu had paired with Kozo, whose uncle had one eye like a carp's and who ran a water-trade dockside bar. 'Water-trade' meant low-life, Tomoyasu knew. His mother had told him. Kozo threw, pacing it gently, and Tomoyasu struck, moving from the shoulders. They were the tallest boys in the class, already looking down on Niimi-sensei. The Sports master was too old to be a soldier. He had the permanently hunched shoulders of a rice farmer. Sometimes he wouldn't teach them sport at all, but Confucian ethics; respect, obedience, subservience.

'Kozo, Tomoyasu!'

They ran for the line. Niimi-sensei began to cuff stragglers. The hall became quiet, draining of echoes. Niimi-sensei was looking at the damp morning light filling the high windows. His head shook as he spoke.

'So slow, mm? It is not enough to be skilful if you lack obedience. Do you understand?' They straightened their backs, shouted, 'Yes, teacher!' in almost perfect unison. He waited for silence again. The shaking had spread to his arms and he folded them tightly across his ribs.

'If you cannot obey you are not a team. You lack team spirit! You lack spirit!' His voice had risen from an undertone to a bark. His thin arms unfolded and he began to point out grimacing faces. 'It is as if you are not Japanese boys at all. It is as if you are American boys!' The old man was screaming. He stopped abruptly and turned away. He picked out a wooden kendo sword from the rack behind him. He stabbed it against the mats as he spoke, punctuating the sentences. A first ray of sunlight struck him, illuminating his anger. Retorts boomed like the fireworks in the harvest festivals.

'Baseball, eh? Why should you learn baseball? Does it teach you about the Japanese spirit? Baseball is foreign in spirit!' The Sports master's voice was rising again, stretching his features into a bony grin. 'A game for Americans. For their inferior allies. There will be no baseball in the Greater Asian Empire. There will be no more baseball in this school. The team has been dismissed, by order of the government. Now we will sing the national anthem.'

They sang, not understanding the archaic words, only shivering in the cold gymnasium, astounded, too old to cry. The school team was disbanded. Tomoyasu went and stood with Kozo. The other boy wouldn't look at him, he concentrated on strapping up his bag.

'What are we going to play now?' Tomoyasu whispered.

Koto shrugged. 'There are plenty of great Japanese sports. My father will teach me. Maybe you, too. This is the right thing. Baseball's shit.'

He hefted his bag and left quickly. By the time Tomoyasu came out, his friend was running to catch another group of boys, Upper School students. The first schoolgirls were arriving on their heavy-framed bicycles, skirts flying. They stopped in groups to watch the playing fields where workmen were erasing the baseball diamond with long brooms. Tomoyasu passed them with his head down, avoiding the whispering of the girls and the dirt-seamed faces of the workmen.

He walked home along the railway track, mechanically following his daily routine. In the deep shadow of cedar trees he waited for the seven o'clock munitions train. He was very early. The sweat on his uniform cooled against his chest and armpits and he shivered, tucking his hands into the pockets of his trousers. In the left-hand pocket he felt the knurled edge of the American coin. He took it out and thought about baseball.

It was the most beautiful thing he knew. He dreamed of baseball as a dance sometimes, but more often as a stylised battle with two heroes at its centre. Batsman and pitcher, rival

5

champions, as there were in some of the kabuki dramas his grandfather loved. Tomoyasu loved baseball because it was American, the country beyond the end of the world. The enemy. He felt a wave of guilt that left him giddy and wide-eyed. Squatting on his haunches, he balanced the coin on the silvery curve of the track. Carefully, so that the train would catch it dead centre under its galvanised wheels.

When he bent and put his head against the track, Tomoyasu could hear the train far off, a sound no louder than the trickle of water from a tap. He dozed like that, his shaved head on the cushion of warm steel. He dreamed of his father in Manchuria, seeing with abrupt clarity his sternness, the Mongol features of a northerner. His father was standing on a construction site, speaking into a telephone. He was building the Greater Asian Empire and catching American spies at night. Tomoyasu tried to remember if his father liked baseball.

The train blared its horn and he stood up quickly and ran alongside the track towards it. The first carriage was newly painted. At one sashed window was an officer. The officer was wearing a Japanese sword in a simple wooden scabbard. His face was waxy and quite motionless. Tomoyasu wondered if he might not be a decoy. Behind the carriage came batteries of anti-aircraft guns, hooded under tarpaulins. They looked like the bulks of sleeping dragons. Intelligent and powerful. He turned to wave at the sappers in their military khaki, stretching his hands above his head. He felt a moment of joy, without guilt. The sappers laughed with him or at him. He ran back up the track, to the cedars. One of the sappers threw him a cigarette and he tried to catch it.

When he looked down at the coin it had already left the track with a sound like a startled bird, the thrum of wings. It caught him under the chin, a slim silver pain. He felt his skin indent and pressure against his windpipe. When he swallowed he recalled an instant of summer, ice-water sliding against his gullet. He fell, choking. Lopsidedly, he watched a sapper jumping from the train. Pine needles crushed their overpowering scent against his cheek. He tried to blink. The rhythm of the train and the rhythm of his blood became too loud and he was deafened.

He awoke in a Western-style bed, one of many in a long room full of sunlight and dry air. The linen sheets had been tucked in so tightly and the smell of starch was so powerful that he couldn't feel his torso at all. He lay, disembodied, moving his head carefully to watch a young nurse hold a syringe up to the light, testing pressure. She was talking to a patient, smiling; her teeth were white and very small. She brought the syringe down and uncovered a man's stomach. On the stomach was a yellow carp. She injected the needle into the carp's eye. Tomoyasu yelled at her to stop and blacked out at the force of his own voice.

Later the doctors came to see him. They spoke with a foreigner in a foreign language. Tomoyasu knew it was German; all doctors worked in German. His father had told him it was the language of medicine. Medicine was good, so the Germans weren't enemies. This German had black hair just like a Japanese, but his eyes were a dark blue, the colour of temple roof tiles. The German bent close to Tomoyasu and said something that made all the doctors laugh. His breath smelled of pig meat. He gave Tomoyasu back the American coin. It was pinched on one side, like clay, defacing the eagle's feet. Tomoyasu felt its knife-edge and watched the man in the next bed while the doctors talked.

The man had a tube in his arm and his eyes were covered with a wet cloth. His mouth moved as if he were crying. He wore a hospital shirt, but it had come half-off, tangled with the bedsheets. There were pictures in his skin. His skin was a picture.

A dragon coiled around his right arm, folded against the cables of muscles and ligaments. It had a green moustache and a jewel in its forehead. Golden birds flew round the dragon like comets. The dragon grinned at the man's chest, where a boychild rode on the back of a giant golden carp. Waves fell away from the carp towards the man's ribcage. In the distance, where his heart must be, Tomoyasu could see Mount Fuji,

7

rising out of the horizon like an arrow-head. There were words written there, too, but the characters were difficult and Tomoyasu couldn't read them. A small berry of blood stood out on the face of the carp, becoming encrusted as it dried.

'Who is he?' Tomoyasu asked one of the nurses. She was the one he'd seen giving the injection, and she was very young, only a few years older than Tomoyasu. Her hair was braided into pigtails. She spent a lot of time over the man with pictures in his skin. Now she was replacing the compress on his eyes.

'He's a carpenter from Kobe. A skilled man.'

'Is he dying?' said Tomoyasu.

It wasn't what he'd wanted to ask, and the nurse's eyes widened. 'Don't say that! It's bad luck. Please, just lie back and don't talk so much.' She moved over to Tomoyasu's bed and made him drink some water without moving his neck. 'He fell from scaffolding. Now he's hurt, inside. It's hard to tell how well he's healing. If anything's still broken. But he's an honest worker, a real craftsman, not a criminal. He deserves to live. And he's so young.'

She touched the man's arm, one finger pressing insistently against the wings of a golden bird.

'Why would he be a criminal?' said Tomoyasu.

The nurse looked at him, surprised, and then laughed with one hand to her mouth. It made her look like a schoolgirl. Tomoyasu turned away. He had known why. The Yakuza wore tattoos, the gangsters who swore oaths with fingers wrapped in silk. He had known. He'd wanted to keep talking. He wanted to touch the man's skin or the face of the nurse. There was a cicada's empty husk, clutched to the windowsill. It was fragile as rice-paper. He watched it until lights-out.

He dreamed of the nurse. She offered him drink. Milk trickled from her lips and forked across her small chin. He woke to the sound of her crying. In the curtained darkness he couldn't see her, although the room was full of people. Someone had opened a window and the curtains billowed inwards and spread apart. The carpenter was being taken away. The body sagged between two men, one arm trailing on the ground, palm upwards. The tattooed skin caught the small light from the window, colour peeling away from it. Tomoyasu watched until it was gone. The empty bed beside him terrified him. He curled up against his nakedness.

2: *Exhibits*

National Police Force of Japan
Canal District Sub-Office, Otaru City 446, Hokkaido State

Interim Investigative Report (Capital Offences). Page 11. Report completed by Constable Yasuhiro Abé. Dated: 14 September 1993. Initial report completed by: Y. Abé. Dated: 6 September 1992.

NOTES – (1) *Iconography of deceased's body-tattoos.* Chief Constable Murasaki's convictions on this matter have been borne out by the expert analysis of Dr Jun Tanigawa (Lecturer specialising in Organised Crime in Japan, Sapporo College of Law Enforcement). Her opinion is that the symbolism of the various tattoos suggests an affiliation with the extremely widespread Yamaguchigumi criminal organisation. The tattooist's signature, three characters near the deceased's right armpit, was rendered largely illegible by swelling and decay. The first character, 'Hori-', is apparently common to the trade names of many tattoo artists.

The second extant portion of tattoo, on the deceased's right thigh, is a floral design of chrysanthemum and almond blossom. The outline of the far-right blossom is executed in micro-calligraphy. The twenty-four characters are too small to be read with the naked eye, and were only noticed when the skin was forensically examined. Possibly the deceased was unaware of the script himself. Micro-calligraphy is particularly difficult to carry out with tattoo needles. This suggests that 'Hori-' is or was an exceptional artist. There is some probability that he is well-known in his field. I am currently making efforts to identify the tattoo artist's work through other 'skin-diggers'

9

in the northern isles and on the mainland. The micro-calligraphy is a sutra, written in Sanskrit. The sutra translates as 'God is just. God is all-seeing. God forgives.' Efforts to identify the deceased through Yamaguchigumi contacts and interns over a period of nine months have revealed no relevent information.

The last surviving portion of the tattoo is a section of chest skin. The illustration is damaged, but the colouring is primarily red. According to Dr Tanigawa, until recent years Japanese red tattoo ink was made from cadmium. Toxic shock and fever from the ink were common, and occasionally victims would die. However, forensic tests, (see [4]), have shown that the deceased was in his late fifties or early sixties. Fading and corruption suggest that the tattoos are at least forty years old. If it had occurred, cadmium poisoning would have set in immediately after the tattoos were inscribed. No other useful portions of the body-tattoo have survived.

(2) *Mr Kim Sugihara, witness.* (Sugihara is a tenant farmer in Long Headland District, near Yoichi town, and rents 14 hectares rice paddy/barley field owned by Morinaga Ltd, land adjacent to the trailer home where he found the deceased on 2/9/1992.) Since confirming to police that the trailer home had been inhabited prior to the incident, Mr Sugihara has become less cooperative. He has implied (but will not state) that he has been visited by Yakuza employees since the incident. Mr Sugihara's health has also deteriorated since the incident, and unfortunately (or coincidentally) he has now been diagnosed as suffering from Alzheimer's disease. Mr Sugihara has been unable to give any description of the occupant whom he never formally met. Most crucially, he has not been able to identify the deceased as the last occupant of the trailer. Other members of the Sugihara family have been unforthcoming. No other witnesses have come forward. House-to-house questioning has been attempted twice in a five-kilometre radius.

(3) *Personal seal.* (Used on land purchase documents for a cash transaction between Morinaga Ltd, the Seller, and Hikari

Basho, the Buyer, signed and agreed on 8/2/1992; 1.2 hectares undeveloped land and contents, one General Motors trailer home.) Investigations last year showed that the name of the Buyer and his personal seal were not officially registered. Since then three leading Otaru City seal-makers and a professional calligrapher have confirmed our belief that the Buyer's seal is not Japanese; that the two characters printed by the seal are Hong Kong Chinese; and that the design is archaic and abstract to the point of incomprehensibility. There is no consensus among the experts on the meaning of the characters. Two of the Sapporo seal-makers have suggested that the seal-mark is an amalgam of two characters, 'Basho' and one other.

Forensic studies suggest that the seal was made of a hard impermeable material such as onyx, agate, etc. The style of the characters is not attributable to any of the well-known Hong Kong seal-makers. The ink used was standard Japanese charcoal-based congealed ink, matched to samples from the Morinaga offices.

(4) *Forensic identification of the deceased*. As previously noted, acid damage to the upper head, face, hands, chest and upper back was extensive. It was also 12–13 days before the deceased was discovered by Mr Sugihara. Photographic files, dental records and fingerprinting have been less than accurate. DNA samples of hair and sperm have not matched any of those few available on record. The remaining molars and wisdom teeth, and a segment of print from the base of the left ring finger, have positively identified 32,455 convicted Yakuza, including 2,600 who are currently serving penal sentences. A majority of these criminals are affiliated with the Yamaguchigumi organisation.

Blood samples taken from the deceased's clothes and body have tested as B Positive (moderately uncommon, 20 per cent of Oriental males). Overall physical condition suggests a large, muscular man in late middle-age. Unfortunately only a minority of convicted Yakuza in this age group were blood-tested when they were criminally active 'on the streets'. Many have been promoted to honorary positions of authority within the criminal organisations, and it would be problematic to request they answer questions at this time. As noted above (1), other inquiries among Yakuza with Yamaguchigumi connections have produced no new information.

The deceased suffered slightly from piles and stomach ulcers, suggesting an unhealthy diet and, possibly, stress. In his late teens the deceased contracted chicken-pox and shingles. Callouses on the hands and feet point to an active lifestyle. The head hair was long, though much of this growth may have occurred after death. The deceased had recently eaten a large meal of beef, fish, soya beans, rice and beer. There were no gunshot wounds on the deceased (see [5]).

(5) *The trailer home.* On 4/1/1993, the area of land on which the trailer home stood was leased freehold by Morinaga Ltd to StoneRiver Industrial Laboratories. The trailer was transported to Otaru Police Station, and was stored in a rented warehouse until August of this year. At that time Chief Constable Ezo Murasaki judged that no more could be achieved by continuing to store the vehicle and I arranged its sale as scrap on 28/8/93.

The trailer consisted of three rooms – a bedroom/lounge, a mini-kitchen and a bathroom. Initial fingerprinting of the vehicle last September produced limited results; those found in the bedroom and the mini-kitchen were extensively defaced by mildew and moisture. Blood samples found on the exterior of the wok above the cooking range matched those of the deceased, B Positive. In the rear wall of the mini-kitchen were two small bullet holes. The bullets had been fired from inside the trailer. One bullet has since been found embedded in a eucalyptus tree by Route 5, 120 metres from the trailer. The bullet is 9 mm and matches the exit holes in the mini-kitchen.

The trailer stood on four brick-pilings, and had moved slightly prior to the discovery of the body. This, and the internal destruction of fittings and furniture, may indicate a violent struggle.

The fragments of industrial ceramic in the mini-kitchen and outside the trailer bore traces of hydrochloric acid. A further two ceramic bottles marked HCl were found empty in the badly damaged front area of the mini-kitchen. All four bottles appear to be standard industrial acidware, made in Japan by Nikkei Laboratory Products. With the permission of Chief Constable Murasaki, I have kept the acidware (#42–50) and a sample of calligraphy found in the bedroom/lounge (#127) for further examination.

The tyre tracks found outside the trailer have been identified as all belonging to one car, probably a Mercedes (though in the 12–13 days before the deceased was discovered, it rained at least three times). The car was parked within 1 metre of the trailer door and damaged a crop of recently harvested soy bean plants as it reversed out of the enclosure. A shovel (#242), pruning saw (#243) and hoe (#244) have been tentatively identified by Mr Kim Sugihara as the property of a previous occupant of the trailer, a Korean farmworker called Kim Mori who lived in the trailer during the rice harvests of 1987–9 (this individual is not officially registered to work in Japan and has not been located). Along with the farming implements, a Toshiba microwave oven (#112), a Sanyo rice steamer (#113) and four fireblankets (#114–17) were found stored under the trailer base.

The body of a large yellow, female dog was found beside the trailer, killed by a single blow to the neck with a hard object. Time of death matched that of the deceased to plus/minus 48 hours. The remains of the animal were incinerated on 20/9/1992 on the instructions of the Police Coroner.

RECOMMENDATIONS – I have been advised by Chief Constable Murasaki that the resources available to pursue this investigation are finite, and that an exhaustive study of previously convicted Yamaguchigumi-affiliated Yakuza is not practicable.

It is now a year since I began my investigation into the cause of death and the identity of the deceased in this case. In that time the case, and this officer, have been relocated from Otaru

City Head Office to the Canal District Sub-Office. The case has consumed much of my time and there have been suggestions that my commitment has been excessive. I have been advised to close the case at this time.

I must recommend that this case remains open. This form may also be taken as a letter of resignation, although I would like to make clear that I hope to continue serving as an active police officer, and I submit my resignation only since I am disobeying an advisory order and it is my duty to do so.

The primary reason for my recommendation is that I believe the evidence suggests premeditated murder of a retired Yakuza by his organisation. 'Washing the feet' is the phrase used to describe a Yakuza who attempts to leave the organisation. This is punishable by death within the Companies, on the principle that a Yakuza may not withdraw from the blood oaths he has made, even in old age. Execution of this kind is a capital offence under Japanese law.

According to my study of police files, Yakuza attacks on retired members have never occurred in Otaru City – a surprising statistic. During the course of my investigations, I have been told repeatedly by fellow officers that the punishment of 'washing the feet' is a Yakuza duty, not police business. Among certain officers there is an element of respect towards the strong martial organisation and traditions of the Yakuza. I am disturbed to think that if this investigation is closed, a capital offence may be pardoned as capital punishment.

Additionally, I believe that there is sufficient evidence to warrant keeping the case open. It is unfortunate that due to the time-scale of the incident and acid damage, more than 90 per cent of the body-tattoo has been destroyed. However, what remains of the design is as unique as a fingerprint. More effort could be made to locate the tattoo artist since this would provide a direct lead to the deceased. Furthermore, and despite the premature decision to scrap the trailer, several dozen partial fingerprints remain on police files. Composite computer reconstructions could provide a more accurate shortlist of Yamaguchigumi criminals.

Also worth investigating further, in my opinion, are: the personal seal (#302); the sample of 'grass-writing' calligraphy (#127), which appears to be a haiku poem; and the dog (#9), which had distinctive coloration and markings. I also recommend door-to-door questioning over a wider area, specifically to determine where the inhabitant of the trailer bought food and supplies.

Report completed on 14 September 1993.
Please consider me favourably,
SIGNED: Constable Yasuhiro Abé.

3: Designs

'Come *on*, before someone else gets it, stupid, don't you see it? Catch me that one!'

She wore a small blue-and-white summer kimono and miniature wooden clogs. The summer kimono was belted overtight and the clogs clacked against the asphalt as she wormed through the crowd, clutching an older boy in a Lower School uniform. 'The one that looks like a little banana. Qui-ick!' She had small, raised eyebrows and round eyes. Tomoyasu could see the boy adored her, but he was too indecisive with the rice-paper scoop, following one lithe goldfish as it swam along the cool bottom of the tub, dipping the scoop too often so that it became flabby. He sighed and the girl clicked her tongue against her teeth, her face comically dismayed. Finally the gunge of wet rice-paper dropped off into the pool with a plop. Bronze, black and gold minnows swarmed up towards it and were caught by a laughing man with a scoop in each hand and two grown daughters. 'How's that, eh?' He pointed the scoops at Tomoyasu, fish jack-knifing languorously in their soft traps. 'Fast, ain't I? Too fast to see, weren't I?'

Tomoyasu stuck his cigarette in his mouth and grinned back. He nodded, not answering anything in particular, just watching the girls. They were a year or two younger than Tomoyasu but that didn't make so much of a difference anymore. One had

15

a ponytail, like an American girl Tomoyasu had seen at a gambling nightclub in Tokyo. The other wore a summer kimono, brightly coloured for the Star Festival. They moved together to one side of their father, whispering, smiling at Tomoyasu and at each other. The smoke from the Lucky Strike was hot in his eyes and he concentrated on getting the man's three fish into an oilpaper bag.

He filled it with spare water from a canister under the stall and shucked the fish in. They were metallic-skinned, lethargic in the heat. 'Congratulations. Three golden treasures.' He handed the bag to the girl in the summer kimono and watched them go until they were lost in the crowded festival market. The girl with the ponytail looked over her shoulder just once. He waited for it, smiled when she did it, bowed at her as he smiled. He imagined her face at the point of orgasm. It was the most beautiful thing in the world.

'Tom. Hey! Tom!' He looked up. Kozo was at the next stall, grilling ruddy tentacles of octopus on a broad iron skillet. Sweat sheened his tanned face, darkening his happi coat and pouched money-belt. 'I'm sick of the smell of this junk food, Tom. Will you swap for a while? What time is it?'

He looked like a farmer, thought Tomoyasu, with his bandanna and red face. But below the short, wide sleeves of the happi coat, the skin was illuminated with pictures. On the left arm the tattoos were already almost complete. Cherry- and plum-blossoms discoloured the skin, symbols of courage and quick, beautiful death. Two months' work for the tattoo artist and four months' wages for Kozo, except that his father the bar keeper had paid half the fee. He'd introduced Kozo to the tattoo artist, too. Between the flora there were outlines in charcoal-blue, still scabbed and puckered.

The crowd were less rowdy by Kozo's stall. The children stood behind their parents' backs or held on to their legs, wide-eyed. The men used a respectful level of language. The other stallholders called Kozo by his family name, Ishikawa. Many of them knew the family. Tomoyasu felt his stomach tighten with envy.

He glanced at the cheap American watch on his own pale wrist. 'Only three o'clock, we've hardly started. But of course, let's change, eh? I'm hungry, anyway. Smells good.' He moved to the octopus stall, took a square of red cotton from his apron and rolled it to make his own bandanna. The heat from the skillet seared his breath. He picked up a small curlicue of flesh and chewed, enjoying the sweetness. From here he could hear the mah-jong players in the park, the clatter of bamboo pieces loud as the plotch of frying meat. He concentrated on turning the octopus tendrils and allowing time to pass unnoticed. It was August and the shadows grew long and well defined between the street-trees and shopfronts.

Some time before midnight they packed up the stalls, washed the last of the canister water over their heads, scrubbed at the smoky grease on their faces and necks. After packing away, they sat with the other stall-holders on upturned crates, drinking chilled rice wine in the warm night air. There were few townspeople left in the streets, drunk men singing and lurching home. The stallholders collected in their takings and drank quietly. Besides Tomoyasu and Kozo, only two or three were local. Most spoke gruffly with the strong accents of Osaka and the southern island of Kyushu. One man came from the far northern prefecture of Aomori. He cursed in his rough dialect and scratched his tattooed chest.

'Before was better. I mean it. People had money then.' There was a beautiful woman tattooed across the man's ribcage. Tomoyasu watched how the woman moved as the man scratched. Someone passed him his day's wages and a bottle and he hung his head to listen.

'Shit. Before was better, of course, but not because people had money. They had no money.' That was the festival foreman, Kawai-san, one of the Osakans. 'Because they were open-handed, it was better. Now it's tight fists everywhere we go. Everything we do – Star Festival, New Year Festival, the whores and the gambling, damn it, even the hospitals we run bring in less than before. Maybe some of you young men should go and break a few arms, no? How about you,

17

Ishikawa-san?' Kozo grinned, teeth white against his greasy, sunburned skin. 'Then we'll make a bit more money.'

'Before what?' Even as he said it, Tomoyasu knew he had lost face. He felt himself blush in the warm dark. The Aomori man swore and from the corner of his eye, Tomoyasu saw Kozo smile, eyebrows raised. Kozo understood Company talk. It wasn't just that he knew names and faces. He understood what the other men left unsaid, the important things. Tomoyasu only followed conversations, puzzled, trying to learn.

'Before the war, boy. Or aren't you old enough to remember the war? Anyway,' he stood up amidst the laughter, 'it's late and I have to deliver the takings. Goodnight to you all, mm? Long day tomorrow. Oh, and son' – he pressed money into Tomoyasu's hand – 'cover your skin.' He hawked and spat into the gutter. Tomoyasu watched him walk to where a black Chevrolet waited. He folded the money into his shirt pocket. Kozo offered him a cigarette. They shouldered their packs and walked home without speaking. Not enemies, but entirely different. Enjoying their solitudes.

It had been a hot year. Much of the rice had been cooked dry in the hard fields long before the Star Festival. The docks smelt of baked salt. Kozo had teased Tomoyasu about the farmland, how the rice would be dry as old birdshit. In May he had sold the fields and the house he'd lived in as a child. His mother had cried. The two paddy-fields had been clogged with rubble and shrapnel from the war, and the house sagged at its southern end where a bomb had dislodged the foundations. Five years after the Americans arrived, the last of the old farmworkers had been killed by an unexploded bomb while planting rice. Tomoyasu had sold it all and bought an uptown apartment for his mother. It was expensive but small, a bed where she could sweat and drowse, and a calm, quiet street, full of the sound of birds and cicadas. She spoke about her husband whenever Tomoyasu stayed with her, how he was missing, nobody could say he was dead yet. Only missing. He tried not to think of his father. He thought of the coin instead. Its hard edge and simple, bright design.

Sometimes Tomoyasu's mother confused him with his father and tried to kiss him passionately, her bony hands shockingly strong on his arms. On other days she would ignore him, refusing to look at him. It made him remember the farmhouse, his mother looming in the bedroom doorway, a dark shape shouting. He'd left her alone with two servants and enough to pay them. She'd died when one of the maids left a window open. A black solitary wasp had blown in, looking for a place to nest. She'd died trying to kill the wasp.

He'd buried her in Seven Stone Children Cemetery. It had been a very hot day, air rippling over the new gravestone, so that Tomoyasu had been unable to cry. No one had cried, but then there hadn't been many people. So many had been killed in the war. He was the last member of his immediate family.

He had taken what money was left and moved into Kobe. It came to two years' wages as a Company labourer. Kozo had told him it would be enough for a complete tattoo. He gave Tomoyasu the tattoo artist's address: 'Tree-Flower Street, opposite the noodle-stand, next to the stone carver.' Many days he did nothing but sit at the noodle stall, watching the tattoo artist's workshop. Horicho the Third was successful enough to sit outside most days, playing mah-jong and eating eel with his neighbours, a jeweller and a temple sculptor. The man was heavy, not like a sumo wrestler but like a thug. On the dog-days of July he would leave the door of the workshop open during appointments. Tomoyasu would crane to watch him straddling the bodies of clients. Leaning into his incisions like a fisherman gutting tuna.

It was almost the end of July before he'd visited Horicho for the first time. The wad of money had lodged uncomfortably against his chest. The door had been wide open. He'd called out to announce himself, ducked in and taken off his shoes. The long workshop had been deserted. It was an old building, well-made, the wooden beams and tatami mats impregnated with the pungent smell of Japanese ink. He'd called out again,

'Excuse my rudeness ...' When no one had come out he'd turned to go. Standing behind him in the doorway had been Horicho. The heaviness of his epicanthic folds made his eyes appear strained tight with some emotion: anger, pain, calculation. Tomoyasu had bowed clumsily.

'Please excuse me, I thought you must be inside.' The tattoo artist had said nothing. He hadn't bowed either, and Tomoyasu had been confused by his rudeness. 'I would like a tattoo. A complete tattoo. I have money.'

'Is it good money?' The man's voice was deep and flat, so that Tomoyasu hadn't known if he was angry or sullen. 'Yes, yes of course. Good money.' He'd reached into his jacket and taken out a white envelope, sealed with ornate ribbons and fat with banknotes. He'd held it out automatically. The tattooist had made no move to take it.

'Why is it good money?' Horicho had said. He'd shouldered past the younger man, switched on a radio; Japanese folk-music. 'What?' Tomoyasu had taken a step back into the work-shop. Horicho had been pouring himself a glass of plum wine from an earthenware bottle. He'd spoken with his back turned.

'Did you steal it?'

'No!'

'Did you earn it?' He'd turned round, watching Tomoyasu without blinking, glass in hand.

'I – no.'

'Then why is it good money?' He'd swigged the wine. A woman had come out silently from the back of the house and kneeled beside him without acknowledging Tomoyasu. 'What's your family?'

'The Kurasakis, outside Kobe, towards Kakogawa. Rice farmers.'

The tattooist had shrugged, disdainful. 'Not Company.' The woman had disappeared into the backroom again with Hori-cho's glass. He'd sat down on the raised edge of the mats and taken off his socks.

'I know you. Friend of the Ishikawa boy, Kozo, ain't you? You've done a bit of Company work with them I suppose.

But the Ishikawas, ah' – he'd grinned, wide mouth revealing gold dog-teeth – 'Company for three generations. Four including the boy. He'll do well, like his father. Good business they do in that dock bar, loyal too. Not proud like you, farmer's boy. Loyal.'

He'd stretched, pulled a packet of cigarettes out of his navy-blue happi coat, lit up. Tomoyasu had stood at the door. He'd realised his thighs were trembling with the effort of standing straight. Briefly, he'd remembered the day at school, the Sports master screaming in the cold, half-lit hall. Then the tattooist had been getting up and coming forward, blocking off the room. 'My grandfather worked here, did you know? Horicho the First. Tattooed the Tsar of Russia. King George the Fifth of England, too. A dragon on the king's left arm. Only the best foreigners. That was long before the war, of course, so he didn't know any better. Me, I don't like the feel of foreign skin. But "only the best", that I like. Only the best Japanese. He was an artist. So am I. What makes you think I'd tattoo you, farm boy?'

He'd been too close to Tomoyasu now, proximate enough to threaten. Tomoyasu had felt his composure giving way, his anger growing out of proportion to events. He'd stared back at the shorter man and bowed again, stiffly. 'I must apologise for wasting your time, sir. Please excuse my extreme rudeness in leaving now. Goodbye.'

As he'd come back out into Tree-Flower Street, he'd heard the radio being turned up behind him. The sound of wooden flutes had followed him across to the noodle stall. He'd sat down, ordered a beer and a bowl of chilli-ramen. The smell of pine sap had been very strong from the street-trees, and cicadas had begun to hiss in the high branches. He'd eaten slowly to accompany his thoughts, watching the doorway.

He worked wherever the Company needed him; as a bouncer at the Ishikawas' dockside bar, as a stallholder at the festivals. The pay was bad but he took pleasure from belonging. Sometimes he would wake abruptly in his narrow bedsit with an image in his mind of the foreman, Kawai-san, who they called 'Older Brother'. The image came with a feeling of total security. It was like the warmth from a hot bath in winter. It seemed to fill him and radiate outwards like steam, he could almost see it in the dark. He would lie on the mattress, feeling the heat through his skin. Some nights there would be earth tremors, and the ground's quick shudder would make him feel even safer, like watching rain through a closed window.

On the day after the Star Festival the shopkeepers were out in Tree-Flower Street, clearing up the debris of toffee-apple sticks, bottletops, paper flowers, bunting inscribed with love poems. A banner leaned against a stone Kannon figure outside the temple sculptor's house. On the white board were painted a princess and a peasant, Vega and Altair, the Star Lovers. Horicho was holding the placard steady while the sculptor pried out the last nails. Tomoyasu stood under the pines, watching. When the sculptor nodded to him and grinned he took up one end of the painting, held it firm.

'Good, isn't it? Don't you think? I was just thinking I might put it away for next year. It's so fine.' The sculptor was a talkative man. His wide-set ears, teeth and tanned skin made him look like a Japanese monkey. 'My daughter's, it is. Pretty girl. Talented too, as you can see. Makes bean-paste cakes that're just, mm' – he closed his eyes and grinned, eyebrows raised, then laughed infectiously. He wore the baggy blue dungarees common among artisans, and a Cartier watch with a wide steel band. 'About your age, too. Perhaps they should meet, eh? Horicho-san? Don't you think they'd make a couple?' The tattooist grunted an affirmative and stood back, dusting his hands. He bowed fractionally to Tomoyasu. 'Kurosaki-san, good morning. I saw you at the stalls last night. Working hard, hm. What can I do for you?'

'I was hoping you would do me a favour?'

'A favour? That's a pity. My friend Kawai-san told me you'd be wanting a tattoo. If you want a favour, go to the favourist. Eh?'

A joke; Tomoyasu smiled carefully. The tattooist smiled back, a bleak, flat expression.

'I would like a tattoo, sir.'

22

'Good. Better.'

'I have some ideas, for the designs. I saw a carp-boy once, can you do that? Then, there was a Company man last night with a woman on his chest. I like dragons, too –'

Horicho swore, shook his head. 'You're an idiot, boy. If it was up to me, I wouldn't work on you. I don't think you've got what it takes to be a Company man. There's a selfishness about you, things you keep to yourself, you don't share your feelings, I don't like that. Maybe you don't feel at all. And you're an idiot, like I said. But Kawai-san wants you tattooed, he has plans for you. So listen.'

He pointed at a block of small-grained granite, uncarved, which stood next to the Kannon. 'What do you see? Quickly, too. I've got another customer this evening.'

Tomoyasu shook out a cigarette, looked at the block as he lit a match. He drew in the smoke and sighed it out, suddenly dizzy and confused. 'A rock. A grey one.' He shrugged.

Horicho nodded at the sculptor. 'What about you?' The man sat up straight, as if a schoolmaster had just asked him a trick question.

'Me? Oh well, I wouldn't know. Unless you really wanted my opinion, yes, but I'd need to look at it again, mm?' He scratched his temple, tugged at his nostril hairs, squinted with his head on one shoulder. 'Well, if you really wanted my opinion, I'd say it was a tortoise. Thick-legged, rough-carved. Nothing too slick and polished, maybe for a shrine, you know? A nature god. Nice with a bit of moss on it, you know the kind of thing? A tortoise, sure.'

The tattooist leaned back against a stone lantern, gazed at Tomoyasu. 'Well then. This is what I see. No carp-boy. One dragon, maybe. You don't have the brains for two. A lot of carmine, less green or gold, so it'll take at least a year, this – if I work faster you'll get cadmium fever from the red ink. Some bodies die from that.' He pushed himself upright, glaring at the younger man. 'And on the chest or the back, something big. Not too clever, not too pretty. Something that doesn't give up. Stubborn. But today we'll start on the left shoulder. Then if the

pain's too much, you can hide it away under a workshirt. Go
back to your potatoes and rice.'

He turned to go. Tomoyasu stood in the sunlight. The chant
of the cicadas and the nicotine smoke filled his consciousness
and for a moment he felt outside himself, unable to move. This
is fear, he thought. The tattooist turned back sharply. In his
hand he held a bunch of bamboo needles, hollow and stained
the colours of rust, verdigris, charcoal. 'Are you ready?' Tomoyasu nodded. He followed the tattooist into the workshop.

Outside, the sculptor walked around the unworked block of
stone. Then he went to the door of his shop. Tools hung from
rice-twine thongs on the inside of the door. The sculptor took
down a heavy hammer and a wide-bladed chisel. He went back
outside and stood over the block. He sang for a while to help
him think. Then he stopped singing. He squatted down beside
the rock. The sun was hot on the fine grain of the granite. Sweat
made his face bright and fierce. Angling the blade, he began to
cut away at the design inside the stone.

4: Snapshots

Keiko Yamada
4-11-2 Forest Heights
One River District
Kobe 7   1 October 1993

Dearest Yasuhiro,

I'm so sorry, my love. Ken rang this morning and I've been
trying to get you all day but there's no answer. Are you all
right? Have you been fishing and walking? But please call me
when you get this. I want to come up, if you want me to. Do
you want me to? Please don't be ashamed of this. They are
wrong; you were right. They should be ashamed. You are a
better policeman than any of them and you always will be. Ken
says so, too. He says they were scared of your courage.

Mother and Father are very shocked. Father says he will talk to our district councillor if you want him to. I wasn't sure if you would – what shall I tell him? And Mother wants you to come and stay. She says she feels as if you are family and she wants to make sure you are all right. I want to, too. You were trying to identify the Trailer Man for so long, I know how much it meant to you and the job and everything. Will you come? Yohei is at boarding school now, so there's plenty of room and it's so quiet! We probably couldn't sleep in the same room, with my parents here, but there's lots of nice fields here (I don't make much of a chaste Japanese maiden, do I? Oops. Oh well) and the sea's warm even in autumn. I think you'd like it. Maybe it would be good for you.

Also, I have an idea(!). Do you remember my friend Akiko, who will work at the new Kansai airport? She says there are vacancies for six security officers, and that she could arrange for you to get an interview, if you wanted it. And, if you worked as security for a year or so, you could get training as a customs officer! Would you like that? If you want me to, I can find out more from Akiko (she's so kind). I know it won't be the same as being a constable, but it's sort of the same, isn't it? Yasuhiro, please ring. I have all these questions and I want to hear you talk.

Do you think you should tell someone what's happened? Like a journalist? Because you were right all along, weren't you, about the police respecting the Yakuza, letting them use their own laws. I think even journalists from abroad would be interested. I've got it – you can be a famous Yakuza expert! Except then we would have to go abroad too. Do you think it's safe for you now, Yasu-chan, to stay in Hokkaido? Maybe it would be better if you stayed here. Just for a while, if you don't want the airport job.

It's so beautiful here, now. Don't you miss the Kansai autumn? When I get the train to work, the hills are all pomegranate-coloured with autumn trees, and the sun is hot too. The way it shines through the leaves is like the stained glass in the Protestant churches here in Kobe, do you remember them? And yesterday Mother bought Osaka-noodles and

25

we cooked them with spring onions and chicken from the garden – tasty, huh? Come down, Yasuhiro – and ring me soon!

Love,
Keiko XXX

*

(Message recorded on the answerphone in Flat 622, Azabu Mansions, Otaru City, Hokkaido, belonging to Yasuhiro Abé. The message is undated, the eleventh on a full tape.)

[Tone.] Hello Yasuhiro? It's me, Keiko, are you there? I think you are, I bet you're listening to that horrible traditional music again and drinking *beer*! So I'm just going to talk and hope you pick up the phone. So, are you OK? I wrote to you but you probably haven't got it yet, I only sent it yesterday and I think I missed the post. I was just ringing to, you know [pause] talk. Anyway. I'm fine. Actually I'm not. It's been two weeks now since you called me, since we spoke, did you know? And with everything that's happened, too, I mean the Yakuza might have followed you and I wouldn't know, you could be lying there right now with blood and ... [rising voice; pause].

So I'm feeling worried. It would be really nice if you picked up the phone ... [pause; sigh]. Well anyway, let me tell you about today – maybe you're just on your way home from somewhere now, yes? So I'll keep talking.

Well, today was really boring! Except that at lunchtime I went to the international library and read the newspapers in English. Princess Diana is coming to Japan soon. I know you're not so interested in that. What else? Um. Did you get the earth tremor last week? So many this year! I was in the bath, just soaping myself down, I'm sure you can imagine... and the water just *shook*, you know like when you put down a mug of tea too hard? Like that. So many, people hardly notice them. They say there'll be a big one round here soon, though ... an earthquake, I mean, not a mug of tea! Will you ring me,

26

Yasuhiro? Please? I'll be at home all night. Don't worry about the time if it's late. Just ring. Bye. [End of message.]

*

Keiko Yamada,
4–11–2 Forest Heights,
One River District,
Kobe 7   6 October 1993

Dear Yasuhiro,

Ken will leave this in your hall. So you'll see it when you get back. He had your spare key, and he phoned me and we talked about what to do. No one has seen you for a week, Yasu-chan, we're all so worried. You didn't answer my letter or messages. So I called Ken. I don't know what he'll find. That scares me. You're scaring me.

Ken said call the police straightaway. I know you'd hate that. If we called the police and then you were hiking on Rebunto Island. Or did you find something out, Yasuhiro? About Trailer Man? You know I want that to happen more than anything. I just need to know you're OK. OK? Anyway, Ken is going to call me when he gets to your apartment and if it doesn't look like you've gone hiking, he's going to call the police. We'd have to, Yasuhiro. There's no one else to call.

But if it looks like you've just gone off by yourself, Ken will leave this by the shoe-rack or on the fridge, with the magnets – he has to work, so he can't wait for you. And when you get home, you must call me. Will you do that? I'm sure you've been hiking. I hope you had a good hike.

Love,
Keiko

*

FAX FROM: Hong Kong Transport Police, 010 53 994 3434. 19 October 1993. ATTN: Chief Con. Murasaki. RE: Missing Person (Yasuhiro Abé). PAGE(S): 1.

Sir,

According to our records, a Mr Yasuhiro Abé, passport number 921277 1, entered Hong Kong via JAL flight Ho177 from Sapporo City at 6.15 a.m. on 2 October 1993. His Japanese passport allows Mr Abé to stay in Hong Kong without a visa for up to three months. We have no record of him having left the country by air. Neither do we have any record of him at any of the registered hotels, and there is no data to suggest he has used a personal credit card, made a collect call, driven a car in Hong Kong City, or dealt with a public bank while in this country.

You imply that Mr Abé may be attempting to travel without interference from you or the Japanese mafia. I should point out, firstly, that Missing Persons are few and far between in this country – citizens are closely monitored. Hong Kong is not a place to lose oneself. I suspect Hong Kong was a stopover for Mr Abé, not a final destination.

You also inform me that Mr Abé's police ID was not revoked until yesterday, and that the Missing Person withdrew savings of almost one million Japanese yen before leaving the north island of Hokkaido. I feel obliged to point out also that with his finances and identification, Mr Abé could travel undercover to almost anywhere in the world if and when he reaches mainland China. Officially, it would be necessary for Mr Abé to apply for a Chinese visa before crossing to the People's Republic. Unofficially, it is far easier to enter China from Hong Kong by sea than vice-versa.

If you wish me to alert the Chinese authorities I would be willing to do so, but I must point out that it will be difficult to trace Mr Abé on the mainland, and should the authorities reach him, he will be treated as an illegal alien under Chinese law. Nor will his nationality incline the authorities to treat him sympathetically. I am sure you understand.

I trust this information is of some use.

Yours faithfully,

Sergeant J. McConnell

*

(Picture postcard, undated, postmarked 'Kunming City, People's [illegible; date illegible]'. The picture is of a lake, flat and empty. Behind the lake are the buildings of a sprawling industrial city. In the far distance are the outlines of sheer green hills. The handwriting is small and crabbed. The last eleven lines are cross-written up the left-hand side of the card.)

AIRMAIL EXPRESS

My love, If you didn't think I was mad yet, I guess you will now: imagine sending you a postcard! As if I'm on a company vacation. But I know how many postcards arrive at the inter-

Keiko Yamada
International Library
Festival District
Kobe 2
Japan

national library, too many for the pinboard, right? This won't get noticed. I wanted to explain myself to you first. Then you can choose who to tell or how much to keep secret.

I worked it out. I'm following Trailer Man. I had it all the wrong way round. But he is a killer. I'm going to bring him back.

Before I was sacked I was checking the tattoo designs, ringing tattooists, trying to ID the artist. First call, the skin-digger asks, Why is the skin so damaged? So I tell him, Acid. He says, Sounds like a removal gone wrong. Turns out half his work is taking off unwanted tattoos. Big ones he does with acid – HCl. He didn't think it would be possible to burn off an entire body-tattoo. He thought that would kill most people. No one lives without skin, right?

I traced the acid seller, Keiko. I've met him. He thought he knew where the man had gone. Trailer Man. He was trying to burn off his skin.

I must catch him, you see? To be just. Please believe in me. Give me time. Then there will still be time for us.

All my love. See you soon!
Yasuhiro

5: The Fugitive

He got out of jail and headed for Hokkaido where the sky is wide. From the bullet-train he watched the stone-pickers bent double in the winter fields, a piano factory in a town of zinc roofs, a colt learning to run to the sound of wheels. In the seat beside him, a young office girl ate raw liver from a polystyrene dish printed with gold leaves.

Under the sea from Honshū to the northern island, the Seikan Tunnel was cold and a faint odour of salt permeated the immaculate train carriage. The tunnel was more than fifty kilometres long, and the train slowed, cautious. Around him, the other passengers became quiet and distracted. The rhythm of sodium lights passing overhead was incessant. Somewhere in the rows of seats a child began to cry loudly. In her lap, the girl's hands were white fists. He found it hard not to reach across and touch her skin at the knuckles, feel the quick, faint pulse there. He tried to sleep, but the motion of the train was too smooth. When he closed his eyes he had the sensation of slipping forward, without control. Beyond the tunnel, the landscape was hard and real and he held it with his eyes.

He telephoned his old office from a pachinko parlour in Sapporo. An extra zero had been added to the code and he had to redial. A machine with no recorded welcome took the call. He listened to his own breathing being amplified by the fibre-optic cable and cradled the receiver without leaving any information. He moved away through the chrome roar of pinball games. There were rows of players in crumpled nylon suits or house-dresses, their faces waxy in the artificial light. At one machine a foreigner with shaggy white hair sat staring at the game, only his arms moving, stabbing at buttons. A career woman in a power-suit and sunglasses paused as he passed, watched his progress. He didn't look back. The air smelt of excitement and boredom. In the street he slipped on the impacted snow, got up and kept going.

There was money waiting for him and he bought land and

set his land in order. He lived in a trailer home on the sour earth of old factory ground. When it rained he stood outside and let it fall against his upturned face. In prison, he had thrust his hands through the window's grille, catching the rain's cold movement on the tips of his fingers.

There were no buildings or mountains to limit the sky here: it engulfed the landscape. He thought of Tokyo, where the city's mass had been a rats'-maze of compartments; hectares of sky between offices, gridlocked junctions, steel elevators, foot-streets, capsule hotels, tea rooms. The scale of cloud formations and the curve of horizons threatened him. He expected walls. Sometimes he felt them to be there and when he looked there was only distance and the cries of flatland birds. He missed the hard certainty of concrete at his back, a prop. On the second day it rained and the sky was reflected brokenly in the fields. He hid from it in the cell of the trailer home. He measured distances in prison cells; three to the paddy-fields, seven to the expressway. He walked with the short steps of the exercise yard.

He waited for instructions. He had become old in captivity, and the emptiness of freedom disturbed him. For weeks he kept to his prison schedules. He woke at six-thirty although he had no clock, and prayed at a miniature plastic house-altar which had been left in the trailer bedroom. He washed in the squat-bath, mechanically scrubbing his hairless chest and thighs. Then he worked solidly until sundown, turfing out broken concrete and rusted iron pylons from the muddy ground with a broken shovel. When it was too dark to see he would go back inside, lie down on the foldaway bed and allow himself to sleep.

Then it no longer seemed necessary to be ordered. He slept in the afternoons and lay awake in bed until morning, his tat-tooed skin flat and colourless in the dark. Often he forgot to eat, sometimes for two or three days. After a month the Company men still hadn't come and he wondered why, until he remembered that he had left no directions for them, nothing but his breath on the open line. It would take them some time

31

to track him down. He still waited. He wondered if they would let him retire.

His hunger returned. In the mornings he ate breakfast outside. There was a striped red-and-white deck-chair stored under the trailer with a jumble of old farming implements and fire-blankets. He set up the deckchair beside the trailer's back door, where there was most sun in the mornings. The noise and dust from the expressway didn't bother him, he liked their vinegary smell. He watched the cars passing as he ate. Their contoured enamels were new to him. They looked like animals or women.

He thought of cooking as a woman's skill. He had never prepared food. There was a microwave oven in the mini-kitchen, and a rice steamer with a digital timer. He unplugged them and stored them under the trailer where the deckchair had been. There was a Chinese wok and two gas-rings. He boiled, fried, steamed and simmered his meals in the wok. The rice he made was always dry and tough, or flabby with excess water. He ate it all slowly and with pleasure, enjoying the freshness, the rich flavours of raw egg and salty miso soup.

He thought about women when he cooked, mostly out of lust, but also from a simple love of their sounds and movements. At night the office girls drove home from the nearby Morinaga caramel factory. He watched them from the unlit windows of his mini-kitchen, leaning his head across his folded arms. The office girls wore Western-style work dresses and high heels. They smoked as they drove, like men.

He tried to remember the last woman he had touched. She had been a prison cook, not much younger than him. Every day she had touched his hand when she passed him his plate, stroking. He couldn't recall her name or face, only her assurance, how complete she had seemed, and the softness of her skin behind her thumb. She had left after a few months. No one came to the trailer home. It lay as if abandoned in a wilderness of rice paddies and warehouses, dwarfed by the monotony of waterland.

For a month he walked stooped, watching the trudge of his feet on the frozen ground. Then spring came and the sun pushed him upright and lengthened his stride. He cleared the last brambles and rubble from his few hectares. He stood on the slight rise at the end of his land and looked at the distance to the horizon. It made him want to shiver, he could feel the tension in his arms and chest. He breathed in and was surprised by the capacity of his lungs. He sighed, watching his breath cloud the sunlight.

He planted soy-beans in the sour earth. Lotus flowers grew in the oily ditches and he dug up their hollow roots and ate them. The flesh was white and sappy. He sliced the tubers open with a long curved fishknife. Sealed cavities radiated from the centres, a flower pattern hidden in the roots. He fried the sliced tubers in chicken fat. He found their bitterness satisfying.

As the lotus flowers died, their heads rotted and turned the colour of wet ash. Cosmos flowers began to appear on the lee-side of the trailer, around the deckchair. Their stalks were thread-thin, covered with green hairs. The buds were taut with papery petals. He weeded them out. He dug pungent eucalyptus seeds from under a stand of the trees across the expressway. He planted the seeds where the cosmos flowers had been. He liked the straightness of the eucalyptus, and the speed of their growth. The way they jealously claimed the sun.

When there was no work, he sat in the deckchair and allowed himself to think. His appetite, the sunlight and the expanse of paddy fields made it feel as if his brain had been stripped down, cleaned to gleaming, reassembled. He was aware of this; he was more aware of himself than he could remember being. Birds came to his allotment, tiny and green with white-rimmed eyes. He found he wanted to know their name and was surprised.

He couldn't draw, so he wrote a description of the birds on the flattened inside of a biscuit box. The standard character script felt clumsy in his hands. The angular blades and staves of brush strokes were like weapons. He bought paper at Circle-K and wrote the description again, letting the characters soften. The strokes were like stems of grass, curved together. He drowsed in the chair and when he woke and looked down at the paper he saw his father's 'grass-writing' calligraphy. He couldn't remember if this was what his own handwriting looked like. The characters were expressions of movement. He began to write a short poem about the birds, a haiku. He couldn't find the correct words. He became angry with himself and threw the poem away.

He ran his hands through his hair to help him think, to allay his growing sense of desperation. He didn't know what it was he feared. The hair was grey and quite fine. He swore at himself and shaved it back to a hard stubble. He washed water over his naked scalp and stared abruptly at himself in the bathroom mirror. In half-shadow, his face looked cruel as a Kabuki mask of anger. There were blue spiders inked indelibly into his forearms. They filled him with a horror of his own skin. He stood under the cold trickle of the shower and scrubbed his illuminated chest, his feet, until his flesh was raw and pinked with capillary blood.

He waited for the Company men. When he had to leave the allotment land, he dressed in his farmworker's clothes and a long-sleeved coat to cover his forearms. He looked like a tramp. He avoided other people. He felt the way they looked at him. As if he were an Untouchable or an outcast. He was ashamed because he understood himself to be both. One night each month, at 2 or 3 a.m., he would walk along the expressway for supplies. He kept his head down, out of the beams of oncoming cars. The road smelt of tar and wheat and the sweet fragrance of benzene. The grit stung his eyes and caught in his mouth and nostrils.

It was twelve kilometres to the outskirts of Yoichi town. Before the first homes was a deserted junction. In between the hard shoulders of roads were several all-night stores: Circle-K, 7-Eleven, Lawsons. He went to them in rotation. They sold frozen foods, computer games, house-sandals, pornographic comics. He bought plastic sacks of Japanese rice, meat, and rice wine in two-litre bottles.

He listened to the yard-dogs barking on their chains. When summer came, bell-beetles filled the dark with a sound like telephones, and frogs sang in the scented warmth of rice paddies. Once a dog on a frayed rope followed him home. It had hair the colour of Chinese noodles. Its forepaws were black, like a crab's claws. He fed it on offal and pork bones. It slept under the trailer in a nest of old fire-blankets.

He didn't allow himself to think any more. Many days he did nothing but look at his tattoos in the gloom of his bedroom The faded illustrations covered him like the clothes of a farm-worker in summer – open-chested shirt, short trousers. A design in Sanskrit characters crossed the bare strip of his withered chest. He couldn't read it, and had never asked the tattooist its meaning. He copied the characters onto paper and stared at them until his fascination turned to rage.

His ribcage was an oasis of flowers. Dwarf-maple leaves fell across his shoulders. Chrysanthemum the colour of birthmarks spotted his barrel-ribbed sides. Carp leapt waterfalls towards his collarbone from thickets of pink lotus. The entire design was edged with a scalloping of peonies. Waves and flecks of spindrift rimmed his thighs, the skin tinged red with rising sunlight. Flowers even broke through the water and crowded at its shore. He didn't think of the flora as feminine. They meant other things to him: death, heroism, the pain of understanding.

On the flat canvas of his back a demon loomed in a flaming gateway. The creature's skin, the skin of the man, had faded from cobalt blue to the colour of arteries. From the gateway a halo of fire flowered out behind the monster towards the man's shoulder-blades and hips.

He remembered the night sweats of cadmium fever, the hot baths he had taken to ease the toxic shock. How the nagging stab of needles would become hypnotic, sending him to sleep as he sat crosslegged on the tatami mats with runnels of blood collecting at his hips. The radio on the workshop floor, a hush of static between programmes. Scar-tissue hardening in lines, following designs like termite-roads.

Near his armpit was the tattooist's signature, 'Horicho III', inked black and thick-lined in a black box. Beside the signature one peony in the tattoo's edge remained uncoloured. He'd asked the tattooist when that would would be finished. 'When you die. I made you a skin. But only God makes perfect skins.' They had eaten together, noodles from the street-stall, green tea from the kitchen. But he had never been introduced to the tattooist's wife or family. A customer, not a friend. He remembered how that had suited him. He thought about going back to Kobe, finding the tattoo artist, or the artist's children. He could ask them about the Sanskrit characters, about how things were on the mainland. He sat in the deckchair and thought about leaving the north island. The imminence of danger made his skin crawl.

The pore system of his skin had been destroyed. In summer he was sweatless, cold to the touch as the belly of a fish. Digging for lotus roots, he would have to stop and gasp for cool air. Once, while he dragged prunings together for a bonfire, a massive weight lodged in his chest and he couldn't breathe. He sat clumsily, legs splayed, head down. Then his heart righted itself and began to beat again and he felt a surge of blood that lit up his head. He lay back and breathed delicately with his eyes closed. Later he tried to work out his age, counting back through the reigns of emperors. He had been incarcerated for twenty years, nearly a third of his life.

The sun tanned his face and hands, stressing the frown lines on his forehead. On his torso and arms it was unnoticeable. He became convinced that his skin had died on him, that nothing would affect it. He repressed the urge to run, to kill himself. One evening, as he was clearing deadwood, the trailer began to jolt on its wheel-blocks. He didn't realise the ground was moving until he lost his footing, a curved pruning-saw still in his hand. He cut himself across one many-coloured forearm as he staggered against the earth tremor. He watched with a kind of joy as blood obliterated the coils of a Chinese dragon. He examined the wound for hours in the bluish striplight of the mini-kitchen. He noted the layers of skin, the shallowness of the ink's penetration. The designs felt foreign as a disease. They were thin as appleskin.

He dreamed frequently, but retained only sounds or smells with clarity. There were a few motionless images, like photographs. Often these were events from his childhood. A Japanese officer standing at a train window. The sigh of friction between the steel blades of his mother's dressmaking scissors. The sizzle and char of octopus meat burning on an iron skillet.

Once he woke crouched under the trailer in the tepid summer mud, the dog barking him awake. He had a kitchen knife in his hand. He recalled running. The demon in his tattoo was hunting him. Its name was Fudo – guardian of hell and justice. He could feel its heat on his back. It roared behind him like a typhoon. He traced the creature's iconography across his shoulder-blades. It held a rope to trap the guilty and an Indian straight-sword immolated in fire. Punishment.

He allowed himself to understand. He was running from the Company. He no longer wished to be a part of it, and he had run to ground. At night he drank Sapporo beer on the trailer steps, the dog curled around his bare feet. Its skin would spasm at the movements of fleas as it slept. He stared at the moon's face, where his mother had shown him the shape of a hare. It had leapt from the arms of a god, she had whispered, her lips warm and ticklish against his ear. It had been running forever.

He allowed himself to remember. The first man he had killed had been a Company employee. His name had been Shinzo – 'Heart'. His family had come from the southern islands and he was dark-skinned like a Hawaiian. He had a quick, kind sense of humour; he would recite short, comic poems when they were on their rounds. They had worked together in Kobe, collecting 'security payments' from small family businesses. One of the businesses was a salarymen's bar. A woman served them strong green tea while the manager fetched their money. Her beauty was Japanese but not Japanese; her eyes were wide-set, the irises tawny-brown. Her hair was a dense, mercurial weight against her back.

She was a Korean woman, a refugee who had been forced to marry a Japanese rice farmer, then divorced. She spoke little Japanese. Shinzo couldn't stop talking about her. He married her and then 'washed his feet' – divorced himself from the Company. They left Kobe with one suitcase and two weeks' savings.

They had found him working in a mah-jong room on the outskirts of Tokyo. It had taken only eight days to locate him. Four of them had travelled up in an American car. They had no guns, only truncheons and a pair of heavy cleavers locked in the car boot. Shinzo had bowed when they walked into the club. He'd walked towards them trying to explain, not scared. The first blow had broken his jaw, cutting off his apology. They had clubbed him to death. After cleaning the room, they had found a bath on the fourth floor, large enough to section the body. They had disposed of the remains in five black plastic sacks on one of the huge Tokyo floating dumps, 'Rainbow Island'.

Sitting on the foldaway bed, he began to cry. At first he wasn't aware of it. Then he felt the coolness on his face. He didn't know how to stop. He rocked gently, pulling himself up into a foetal crouch. He tried to count the people he had killed, but he couldn't be sure. Sometimes they had left people for dead. It was always 'they'. The Company. But he'd been good at killing. Efficient, he could remember someone saying, a man called Kozo. He could remember driving to Rainbow Island five or six times. That had been him alone. Hauling out the rubbish sacks, driving quickly away. Every few years a municipal worker would find a set of teeth or the small linked bones of a foot in the looming mountains of rotting plastic, rubber and fish.

It was two garbage workers who had seen him the last time. They had been Untouchables, cousins in the same underclass family. But in court they had looked painfully honest. Their testimony and identification, along with his record of minor arrests, had been enough for a conviction. Without the

38

influence of Kozo, of the Company, he might have been sentenced to death by hanging. The Company had saved him. The Company had betrayed him.

Towards the end of July it began to rain. For short periods it came down hard, clacking like loose teeth against the trailer's windows. Drumming the roof. Then for days it was a soft drizzle, insubstantial, billowing in the wind like lace curtains. From the trailer, the man couldn't see as far as the expressway. The tundra of paddy fields had disappeared. He stood among the rotting lotus flowers, bare-chested, head back. The water coalesced against his patterned skin and ran down his belly and sides. It couldn't wash him clean. The tattoos itched in him, half a century old.

6: Identification

His constabulary ID had expired. In Rat Buri, outside Bangkok, he bought a new one. The coach from the Chinese border had been freezing in the highlands, the metal armrest too cold to touch. Then as they travelled further south, it had become hot and cramped. His knees ached from the pressure of narrow leg-room. Movement felt good, blood re-entering his muscles, and he walked around the town for the sake of walking, not looking for anyone, just feeling the pain lessen.

He bought a cup of hot tea at a grocery and drank it in the sunshine. An Australian called Pat asked him if he needed a visa. He shook his head. Pat gave him a card anyway. On the card was the address of a jeweller's shop with special printing services for tourists. He took out his wallet. In it were a photo of Keiko riding a pony, a bus-ticket receipt for a Japanese man with pictures in his skin, his own tickets from Kunming City to Bangkok, and his police ID. He looked at the card again. The shop was called Pearl of the Orient. He paid for the tea and walked along the dusty road, looking for a taxi.

Pearl of the Orient sold white-metal anklets, swimming goggles, nine-carat gold earrings and seed pearls threaded with fishing-line. In the outhouse were an Apple Mac, a Grant projector and a colour photocopier. The shopkeeper's wife liked his photo, she grinned with her hands on her hips. She offered him two reproductions for $15 instead of one for $10. Her husband kept the jewellery shop while she worked with the outhouse door locked. He was small and quick, while she was loud and powerfully large. Yasuhiro sat with the two daughters in a courtyard. They wore their hair braided high on the backs of their necks and they pretended to be shy of him. They reminded him of Keiko and for a moment he felt a panic at what he was doing so far from the life he had planned.

There were wicker chairs in the shade of teak trees. One corner of the courtyard was filled with bougainvillea flowers and the entire house was awash with their scent. Yasuhiro bought some postcards of Thai temples from the shop while he waited. Then he went back and sat with the daughters. They watched a Schwarzenegger film on a flat-screened TV. He asked them about buying a new passport, in Japanese, in English. They smiled together and shook their heads; they didn't understand. The shopkeeper brought him a Dragon beer and a paper plate of sticky Thai rice with a plastic fork. He asked Yasuhiro to try the rice, see if it wasn't better than Japanese rice. Yasuhiro asked the shopkeeper about new passports. The man gave him some Bangkok addresses, friends of his, an uncle. He wouldn't let Yasuhiro go until he'd finished the rice.

He went into Bangkok. The uncle sold passports from his festival bunting and calendar factory. The passports were cheap and low quality. Souvenirs rather than forgeries. Yasuhiro drank oolong tea in the uncle's office. The walls were hung with pictures of calendar-girls, topless blondes or Thai women dressed in traditional dancing costumes. He asked about a man whose skin was a picture. The uncle shrugged and pouted. He knew about the Japanese mafia, but he had never met any. Did Yasuhiro want a passport or just information. Why hadn't he said? The uncle wrote down some mobile telephone numbers on the back of the 1974 Ocean Harvest fishing fleet calendar and presented it to Yasuhiro. He told Yasuhiro to keep the calendar. In the street two skinny boys were playing handball against the factory wall. They shouted at Yasuhiro and ran after him. When he stopped and tried to give them money they wouldn't take it. They wrote down their names on a piece of paper and gave it to him. A taxi stopped for him. The boys stood in the narrow street, waving. He waved back from the back seat, heart lifting.

He booked into a hotel where the rooms came with private phones. At night he lay on the bed and let the fan cool him while he listened to the lovers and prostitutes in adjacent rooms. He tried to think of Keiko while he masturbated, the sound of her laughter. In the morning he started trying the numbers on the calendar. Often no one would answer or the line would go dead as soon as he said hello in his accented English. Two of the forgers said they knew the Japanese man with body-tattoos. They had information, but it would cost. One of them told him to ring Nguyen the Vietnamese. She gave Yasuhiro another number. He rang Nguyen and made an appointment.

The passport-maker worked in a bare room above a computer-games arcade. Multicoloured light flashed up between the misfitted floorboards. Through the wire grid of the windows, Yasuhiro could see the Royal Palace, lit up. Nguyen's hands were white and limp with sweat. He muttered to himself in sing-song Vietnamese, rocking his head, as he worked. He plugged a laptop computer into one blackened wall socket. On the computer were records of all the passports he had made. While Yasuhiro scrolled through them Nguyen offered to make him an original, using watered paper bought from government sources in six First World countries. He smiled, his eyes almost shut. He could even do visas, good as the real thing.

Yasuhiro stopped scrolling. The green light from the laptop screen lit up his face as he grinned. The name on one of the copies was Hikari Basho. The photo was grainy, with little contrast between black and white. A thickset face, unsmiling, Japanese or Mongol. The passport was British, valid for ten years. Yasuhiro bought the printout for $500. Nguyen leered at him as he counted through the American currency. 'What's so special about him, mm that you run around the world after him, mm?' Yasuhiro didn't answer. The question put him on edge. He left while the passport-maker was still crouched over the laptop, winding its flex.

He felt packed with adrenaline, as if he'd never sleep again. He went to a disco bar near the university and sat by himself on the terrace. He watched the neon in the narrow street. A blue crayfish with waving claws, a pink dancing girl with vanishing clothing, a champagne bottle with rising bubbles. He thought how unnatural it was for neon to be so colourful, when everything else was grey and white in the darkness. He drank Japanese beer until he felt like a policeman again. It made him very happy. He felt relentless, he was an embodiment of justice. He couldn't stop laughing. A Canadian man with blond dreadlocks down to his waist showed him the way back to his hotel. He had two girls with him, children, no older than ten or eleven. In the lobby of the hotel he tried to make Yasuhiro rent the girls. The hotel manageress bustled the pimp outside while Yasuhiro went upstairs. He locked the door of his room and looked for the telephone in the dark. The net curtains were infused with street-light.

He telephoned the airport. No one answered for a long time, but he let it ring, holding the receiver between his head and shoulder while he packed. He was drunk and he kept knocking the suitcase shut. A staff agent called Terry picked up the phone. He asked for the next flight to England. She told him there was a flight to Heathrow at 6.15 a.m. He could hear the rattle of computer keys in the background as Terry checked seats. Then she clicked her tongue against her teeth in mock disappointment. There were no economy or business class seats left. Yasuhiro asked for first class, feeling the sense of strength again, the conviction of the law. Terry asked him for his credit card details. He told her he would pay in cash, that he would be at the airport in half an hour.

He checked out of the hotel, apologising to the manageress. Her son called him a taxi and she made him a glass of lemon tea. In the car he lay back against the plastic seat and stared at the photocopied passport in the intermittent illumination of traffic signals and discos. The Yakuza's face was emotionless. The features of a killer. The beer and the speed of the journey blurred the city into a montage of night-lights and canals and faces.

7: Naked

He feared pain because he feared death. Before prison, he'd been convinced that he could live forever. Now he was old and modest enough to recognise that he could die harvesting soya beans, or washing clothes, or simply from the effort of sleep. He watched the dog bite at its fleas, then fold its forepaws neatly as a knife and fork. His skin was tight and bruised with designs. He wanted to cut them out, and he feared the pain.

He went back into Sapporo for the first time in seven months. It was sixty kilometres along the busy road. He wrapped strips of fire-blanket around his feet to cushion them, and set out as soon as it was light. The rice had been harvested and the fields were already full of wheat. A mini-tractor moved far out in the large fields, tracks of wind moving through the crop and breaking against it.

On the far side of the road was the sea. It was the colour of bomb-sites after the war. Dust in the sunlight and ash in shadow. Beyond that was another country. The idea filled him with a kind of fearful excitement that reminded him of being young. He tried to imagine the country. He didn't know its name. To the south was Hong Kong, he knew. East across the sea was America. The hard asphalt jolted his legs and blistered his feet. He walked along the shore instead, slipping a little on the brassy stems of sea-grass, following a jagged headland around past Yoichi town and Otaru city. For a while he thought he could see the foreign country, grey cliffs rising steeply in the far distance. He stood and watched it. Then the cliffs broke up and he realised they were only cloud. It began to rain. He walked inland, back to the road.

It was getting dark by the time he came to the outskirts of Sapporo. By the roadside an old woman with a yellow rainhat was selling milk and eggs from a formica trestle. The first high-rises loomed behind her. He stopped and picked up a litre bottle of milk.

'Only 130 Yen.' She spoke without looking up from her hands. The skin was discoloured with liver spots. She turned them palm-up. The flesh was soft and loose against the bones. 'Cheapest you'll find, unless you've got udders.' Her hair was dyed black and fastened at one shoulder with an imitation tortoiseshell comb. 'Real Hokkaido milk from real Hokkaido cows. Ha!' She grinned and pared off one nail with her teeth.

'I don't have any change.' His voice had no strength left in it and the consonants were lethargic. He sounded like a victim of palsy. It had been so long since he had spoken. The weakness shocked him and he thought of the pain and was scared again. The woman looked up at him, squinting from under the rainhat.

'Damn, but you're as old as me. How come I don't recognise you? Do I know you?' He shook his head. The shaking spread to his legs and he realised how close to exhaustion he was. 'You must be something pretty shitty, huh. Not that I care. What are you, an Untouchable? Korean? An outcast? Come on, you must be something.'

He kept shaking his head. His mouth opened before he had anything to say. 'Nothing. I used to be. Something. Now I'm nothing. It's what I want.'

They stood looking at one another. The rain began to fall heavily. Above them, an arched street-light flickered and came on. He turned and began to walk towards the high-rise buildings. Behind him the woman picked up the plastic bottle of

44

milk. 'Wait! I don't care about that stuff. Old man, take the milk. A gift. It's good milk!' He kept walking. A black Mercedes passed, tyres hissing in the rain. He stared past it, towards the city.

Before reaching the centre he turned off Great Street and moved south, downtown. Lamplit airships rolled slowly above the office blocks, advertising Morinaga caramel. The streets became brighter, shopfronts lit up with neon. A man in a tuxedo called out to him from the doorway of the Love Soapland sauna. He could hear singing from the karaoke bars and the thick chink of shot-glasses from basement kitchens. The smell of kebabs and soy sauce steamed from ventilators.

He turned into a side-street. It was darker here, and the pavement was cramped with dustbins and empty vegetable boxes stacked against kitchen doors. He slipped on something, a strip of pickled Chinese cabbage, and fell to one knee. It was hard to pull himself upright. He stood, waiting to catch his breath. At a third-floor window he saw a woman in a red cocktail dress, smiling and talking. She combed back her hair between her fingers. He watched until she moved out of sight.

Between a Korean restaurant and the service doors of a department store, he saw a sign painted with old-fashioned characters, 'Skin-Digger'. The display-window was full of the machinery of the tattoo trade: traditional bamboo needles, electric rotary blades. Designs based on paintings by Hokusai. Beryllium laser tools. None of the items had price tags. The lasers had a small note saying 'Removal'.

There were no opening hours on the door or in the window. He hammered on the door until he heard the sound of a cough and a bolt being drawn back. The skin-digger wore white under-trousers, no shirt or shoes. He smelled of pizza. His face was stubbly, heavy-cheeked as an Inuit. He was an Ainu, the aboriginal people of Hokkaido.

The walk had exhausted him and he couldn't think what to say. The skin-digger began to shut the door. He wedged it open with one foot. 'Shit. What have I done?' The Ainu swore

45

and began to whine. 'There's no money here, if that's what you want. Skin-digging's a slow business, you know? And my business is slower than most.'

'No.' He tried to think clearly. 'I am a customer. I've come to buy something, to be a customer. Those.' He moved back into the street, pointed out the laser tools in the window. 'I need them. How much will you charge?'

The tattooist was watching him from the doorway, eyes steady. 'A gangster, ain't you? A Yakuza. From the mainland somewhere. From Tokyo?' He shook his head and spat off to one side. 'Hell, even your cock's tattooed, isn't that so? And now you want to make it white as rice again, mm? On the run. You must be. And you want to clean your skin with lasers? Hah!' The tattooist turned and went back into the unlit shop. He opened plan chests and cupboards. The man followed him. The shop smelled of ink and fried shrimp.

'Yakuza! You people have got no power now. Just your shame. Don't you feel ashamed? I would. All the things you've done to be what you are. Bad stuff, eh? Robbery, sure. I bet you've killed people. And now you're carrying their bodies around on your back, is that it? Am I right?' The man stood in the diffuse light from the display window. The tattooist flicked a switch as he moved around the room. The man raised his hands to stop the glare of a bare bulb. It hurt his eyes.

'Easy to run away from the Yakuza, though. All you have to do is go abroad. Leave Japan. Easy. Where you going to go? Taiwan? Hong Kong?'

There was a chair behind the office door. He sat down. He remembered Hong Kong from before the war. He had gone there to threaten a Chinese merchant. With his friend, Kozo. Kozo had checked the paperwork and merchandise. A cargo of tiger bone bound for Kobe. He hadn't killed anyone, only threatened. The merchant had given them seals carved from nephrite jade, the characters representing their Company and real names. A show of power. A gift, to signify trust. He had missed Japanese rice and the smell of miso soup.

'I remember Hong Kong.'

'There you go then, lucky you. You can run away. What's left of you, hee! hee! And you think you can pay for my lasers? Really? And if you did, you know how long it'd take to clean your filthy skin?' The tattooist stumbled back, leered up at him. 'Rest of your life, old man. Here, take these.' He pushed four small ceramic flasks into the man's hands. 'Acid. Might work on you, might not, depends how much you want to live.' He pulled out a foam-lined box from under the chair, packed the bottles carefully, sealed the box. He looked up sharply. '200,000 cash, all right? Spread it thin, one smear at a time. No skin, no shame. And you'll heal. Old men heal good, you know that? Now pay me and get out.'

He practised erasure in the long afternoons of August. He tattooed the skins of white radishes, then burnt out the designs. The acid wormed and steamed. The trailer stank of vinegar and burnt radish-skin. Mosquitoes got into the bedroom through rust-holes in the floor. The sound of them filled his dreams with images of blood. He wondered if it would be heroic to burn off the tattoos. Nothing would change in him. No one would pardon him. He thought of the war, the samurai officer at the train window. He sat on the soiled sheets of his bed and wondered if it was possible to be a hero in the cause of evil.

By late August the soy-bean pods were splitting open on their stems. He cooked a harvest feast of beef grilled on hot stones, raw salmon and tuna-belly, and soy-beans boiled with rice and rice wine. He opened a can of beer and sat listening to the drip-drop of rain. When it stopped he opened up the deck-chair and sat outside, drinking. It was cold and he wrapped a blanket round him, like an old man. The dog wanted bones. He fed it the last of the meat instead. The sky cleared and he could see the stars. He didn't know their names, he tried to remember if he ever had. He recalled the Star Festivals. Somewhere up there were Vega and Altair, the lovers. He tried to recall if he'd ever been in love. Then he drowsed, the beer in his hands, thinking about what the skin-digger had said. He felt how much he wanted to live. It was a hunger. Hunger was a part of it.

When it became too cold he went inside, lay back on the bed. He dreamed of the tattoos. They were growing, covering his neck and face. The stems of tattoo flowers wrapped around his arms and legs. On his back, the skin around Fudo the guardian began to sear and furl.

He woke. His body was drenched with sweat, the tattoos shining. He felt the moisture between his fingers. The moon was already past its apex. Still half-asleep, he walked into the mini-kitchen, switched on the striplight. From the icebox he took a bottle of fortified rice wine and a box. He opened the wine and poured some into a chipped blue mug. He set the mug and the bottle between his feet and opened the box. He took out the first flask. It was half-full.

He took off his shirt. His right arm was scarred where he had cut himself with the pruning-saw. He laid it across the draining board. The skin seared away from the damp mouth of the flask. He held the arm steady. The smell made his nostrils flare and tighten. The pain helped him concentrate. He moved the flask up from the dragon's belly to its jewelled head and it disappeared. Slowly, he moved on to the other designs. A scroll of cloud. Blue sky. The velvet-black wings of a butterfly. He began to feel giddy and he paused, heart banging against his ribs. He took a long drink from the blue mug. The rice wine was cold inside him. He damped the blood off his arm with a dishcloth. Hauled himself around to face the door. Put his left arm up on the board and picked up the flask.

Outside, the yellow dog began to bark. The headlights of a car scoured the walls of the trailer through the small windows. The man felt Fudo the guardian on his back, gripping him. Always out of reach. He heard the dog's rope snicker, a car door closing.

The dog stopped barking abruptly. The man could still hear it panting, somewhere outside.

'Tom.' A foot chuffed the top step. 'Tom-chan. Tomoyasu, are you there?' The door opened. The man was taller than

Tomoyasu, and broad. 'It's me. Kozo. Do you remember? You shouldn't have done this.' He ducked his head to enter, looking left and right as if crossing a road. Cautious. There was something in his hand, almost hidden in the calloused fist. Tomoyasu could only see the black lacquered tip of a muzzle. He sat in the chair, waiting.

'I didn't know you used guns.'

'We. That was always the problem with you. You were never really one of us. You never followed our way of thinking. And god knows, I never knew what you were thinking. Anyway, times change. Guns? Shooting's an art. Elegant, like swordfighting. And they're a commodity. What's so bad about that? Better than cleavers.'

His eyes were alert, intelligent. Not unkind. Tomoyasu could see the carcass of the dog in the light from the open door.

'You must've known we'd find you, eh? Why did you run? We were pleased with the way you kept quiet in court. Why didn't you come to see me, your friend? Explain to –'

He saw the flask and registered the pickled-pork smell at the same time. He raised the gun like a club. 'What are you doing?' He recoiled, terrified. The trailer vibrated as if a lorry were passing on the expressway. Tomoyasu gazed back at him. 'I am making myself naked again.' He tried to remember the face of Kozo the boy. They had swapped shoes, and no one had noticed. But the face was gone. This Kozo had tightly permed hair and a linen jacket. The man backed into the door. He raised the gun sharply. 'You fucking animal!' He kicked the door closed. Swung back.

'You were always a stupid bastard. That skin was the best part of you and you're nothing to us without it, nothing –' The floor vibrated again. It bucked sideways and up as he shot. The powder-flash singed Tomoyasu's face. It smelt of mustard. Kozo had lost his footing. The earth shook twice and the trailer lurched up off its blocks, fell back. Dishes smashed against the wall and Kozo twisted upright athletically. Tomoyasu sat watching him. He wanted Kozo to go away. He stood up to push the man back.

49

His hands thumped into Kozo's chest. There was a crash as something fell over in the next room. The taller man staggered backwards and the trailer jolted to meet him. The iron hemisphere of the wok smacked against the back of his head as he shot again. He collapsed, clutching his head. He didn't scream. Breath escaped between his teeth in a hiss.

Tomoyasu looked down. The gas canister from the cooker and two bottles of acid had fallen together, cracking the acid-ware. The floor steamed and roiled. The box lay on the ground in a corner. He knelt down. Drew out the last two containers. The white ceramic was slippery in his hands. He walked over to the fallen man. Opened the bottles. Listened to the man scream. It went on for some time.

When it was done he took the gun, went outside, got into the car. The waterlands shuddered as if a typhoon was passing. He remembered the first picture, the photograph's monotone. The spy, the boy's light hair. Brightness and darkness. He sighed and turned the ignition.

8: Missing Persons

'Excuse me, please.' They looked down at him. Carefully, he unfolded the printout picture. 'Have you seen this man?' One of the men removed his construction helmet, took the photo, nodded. He handed it back.

'Fu Manchu, ain't it? Haaaa. He's in Madame Tussaud's, most probably, isn't he, Ev? Oy, Everton.' The second man put down his sandwich. Yasuhiro noticed how sweat emphasised the blackness of his skin, the angularity of his cheeks. Everton swallowed the last of his sandwich while he studied the picture. He took a breath. 'Nah, seriously man, listen. You are never gonna find this guy. Never!' Both the builders laughed. 'I mean! I mean look!'

He swung his arm out at the crowds outside Tower Records. Pigeons and tourists competed for space around the aluminium-grey statue of Eros in the centre of Piccadilly

Circus. The builder spoke slowly, his eyes wide and sympathetic. 'London is crowded with many of you nice Japanese people. Innit, Tel? You are not going to find this man.' He stood straight, turned away to unwrap another sandwich. 'Like looking for the prawn in fucking prawn chow mein, yeah?'

The first builder stretched. 'Now excuse us. Everton, get that sarnie down you, will you? Time's money.' Yasuhiro apologised but they were already moving on.

The pavement was full. He had to walk half in the gutter and listen out for bike couriers. London exhausted him. It was worse than Tokyo, more unpredictable, like a natural force. An earthquake. On the Underground he had sat and watched while a young boy tugged a poster out of its frame, rolled it up and stuffed it in his puffa-jacket. The poster had advertised plastic surgery. Yasuhiro wondered if the Yakuza had money to buy facial treatment. The thought depressed him. In Oxford Street a woman had followed him through the crowd and pushed a piece of paper at his face. He had tried to read it but the writing was a diagonal scrawl of broken English. At the bottom there had been a pound sign. He hadn't given her money, because he didn't have money left to give. There seemed to be as many people living in the streets as in houses. He stayed at the YMCA and ate supermarket canned tuna in his room. His room-mates were from Inverness and they were both called Ian. They had nicknamed him Fish. Apart from that, he couldn't understand them. He had been in London for eighteen days.

The sun set early between the high buildings. He walked up Air Street. Grey arches of old stone cut out most of the daylight and he stumbled against a pile of rubbish sacks. He came out into Brewer Street. The pavements were lined with fashionable Japanese restaurants, elegantly designed. Yasuhiro went into each one. Two of them had posters in the windows from his previous visits; the man's face, reward information and the YMCA telephone number. Most of the restaurants had refused to put up the posters. They didn't want to be linked with the Yakuza. It was bad for business. No one had called him.

In the second restaurant the owner asked if he could take down the poster. Some of his customers had complained. He apologised to Yasuhiro and made him a bowl of red-bean soup. He drank the soup greedily. It was hot and sweet and for a moment he felt his old confidence return. He took down the poster and left, promising to come back whenever he had time. Depression settled back on him as he walked. He tore up the poster and threw it down on the pavement among the burger wrappers and Coke cans.

He came out into Wardour Street. Already it was getting dark and the pubs were filling up. Across the busy road was a narrow alleyway. There was illumination at the far end, emphasising its length and the height of the buildings on each side. He craned his head, trying to see the far end. As he did so there was a sizzle of radio static to his left. He looked up. There was a police car parked outside the Dog House club. A woman sat at the wheel, watching Yasuhiro, while her partner spoke into the two-way. Yasuhiro had been to Tottenham Court Road police station on his second day. He had worn his only suit and good shoes. He had explained about the Yakuza and the killing in north Japan. They had held him overnight while they checked his visa. There had been three other men in the small cell, two of them passed out on the bunks and stinking of vomit. Yasuhiro had crouched in a corner, back against the cold wall. The other man had sat opposite him, breathing through a harmonica. The wheezing discordance had gone on all night. Yasuhiro still dreamed of it sometimes. There had been two metal buckets instead of a toilet. By morning they had been slopping over. Yasuhiro's good shoes had been soaked and he'd thrown them away.

Avoiding the police car, he crossed the road between grid-locked traffic. The alleyway was filled with soapy water from an overflow pipe. His sneakers slapped and echoed on the concrete. Metal dustbins higher than his head blocked the way. He wheeled them to one side, squeezed through.

Behind the blank backs of inner-city buildings was a court-yard. The ground had been concreted over and whitewashed. There was nothing to see except bulging bin-liners and a British Telecom stand in the far corner. Yasuhiro walked over and picked up the receiver. It felt clean, as if newly installed. He realised he couldn't remember Keiko's number. He fumbled in his jacket for his Filofax, found the number. He dialled without allowing himself to think if it was what he had planned.

Her mother answered. 'Ah, Yasuhiro! Is that you? Oh, I'm so glad to hear you're all right. That's the most important thing, eh? Yes.' Suddenly he felt like crying. He pinched his eyelids shut, hunched under the cold shelter of the telephone stand. He didn't register the silence until she spoke again. 'Keiko's asleep, it's a little early here. I'll go and wake her, all right? Just a moment.' He panicked, trying to remember what he wanted to say. He imagined Keiko's mother, slow in her house-slippers. Then the phone clicked as Keiko picked it up. Her voice was furry with sleep but clearing fast. 'Hello, Yasuhiro?' He had frozen, unable to speak. 'Yasuhiro. Are you there?'

'Keiko. It's me. I'm in London.' He heard her sigh. It sound-ed like relief but it could've been anger. He felt the panic melt back. 'I've been here for a long time, it feels like. Looking for him. How are you?'

'OK.' He didn't want the conversation to stop. He tried to think of something else to say. 'Is Murasaki looking for me?'

'No. At first you were a missing person. Then you sent the postcard. I told them where you were. So then you weren't a missing person.' Her voice was neutral, almost monotone. Yasuhiro shifted his back against the courtyard wall. 'Have you solved it yet? Whatever you're trying to solve. Yasuhiro?'

He closed his eyes again. 'I've lost him, Keiko.' She didn't say anything. He listened to the empty line. He wondered if the sound he could hear was outer space or the bottom of the sea. 'It's too big. I don't even know if I want to catch him. If he should be killed for what he did. I used to know all that. How are you, Keiko? Are you well?'

'I'm fine.'

Her voice was sharper. His card ran out and he struggled to insert a new one before the line was cut. The receiver swung on its cord. He grabbed it again. 'Hello, Keiko?'

'I'm still here. How are you, Yasuhiro? Are you well?'

Her tone was formal. He stood for a moment, desolate. 'Keiko. I've lost him. And I've lost myself.' There was a rat in the rubbish sacks. Its tail had been eaten away. 'I don't know what to do, Keiko. I don't know, I don't. Tell me what to do.' He was whispering. 'I love you.'

'I don't believe you!' The line went dead. Her voice had been harsh. Brittle, as if she had been trying not to cry. Yasuhiro slid down the wall until he was crouched, a small figure in the corner of the empty courtyard. He cried gently, smiling. He wiped his face and pulled himself up. Then he dialled the operator and asked for Heathrow.

She is on the tube every Tuesday, Wednesday and Thursday. On the eighth Thursday she smiles at him. She's beautiful. Her hair is strawberry-blonde. Not like the phrase, he decides, strawberry like strawberries. A pale copper, red in the Underground light. English words are often like that for him. They eel through his thoughts or stick, harsh and inaccurate. For years, before, he barely spoke his own language, but now he misses it. In his language there is no word for 'Miss'. He yearns for that absence.

He washes dishes every night in the Mayflower Sichuan restaurant in Edgware. They don't pay him much, but they let him sleep in a room on the third floor. None of them ask him where he comes from. The room has a freezer-cabinet against one wall and it smells of fish. Every day he rides the Northern line from end to end. He never tries another line. He sits in the soft, dirty seats, miming sleep, large white hands folded in his lap. He considers it the perfect way to learn English. People speak carefully on the Underground, deafened by speed as he is deafened by distance. They leave silences between words, in which he can think. He isn't stupid, he finds, but his mind is slow and methodical. Sometimes the silences grow until he's sure that the carriage is empty. He opens his eyes and finds the seats and aisles full. Then he mimes sleep again, listening to their confinement.

She always gets on at Hendon. She always reads the same book, too. The cover shows an old oil painting of lovers in a forest. The title is *French Romantic Poets*. She rarely gets beyond the first chapter and when she reads, she starts by picking her teeth and ends up sucking her thumb. On the eighth Thursday the carriage is full of sunlight. Two young men get on after her. He moves slightly in his seat, so he can see her properly. Her eyes are several colours at once, grey and green and tawny. It puzzles him. Then she looks up quickly from her book and smiles at him.

He looks down and tries to concentrate on his English. He holds the ticket in his hands, hands on his thighs. Listens. 'Man, I can't wait for summer. Know what I'm going to do? I'm going to chill out in the park *every day*, yeah. Watch the people, you know? Maybe some football. On the sweet hot green grass. But mostly I'll watch. Just lie back and watch the people.' He watches the foreign country outside the windows. Streets of pebble-dash houses approach the railway and come to dead-ends against the high fencing. He sees a woman in a sweatshirt cleaning a jeep. Then the woman is gone. He sits back. The train descends into darkness.

At Tufnell Park the doors are open before she stands up. She has to run to block them before they close. He watches the doors reopen and she gets out. He sees her book, two seats away. He moves quickly for a man of his age. His jacket pulls back along his arm as he reaches for the door. It reveals the puckered, rippled skin of a major burn victim. The flesh is a uniform grey, anonymous. He pulls the sleeve back down as he jumps out.

The platform lighting is a faint blue flicker. The train pulls out before he realises that there is no one else but them, they are alone together. He feels embarrassed and he stops for a moment before walking to catch her. Their footsteps are very loud, his faster and longer than hers. Before he reaches her she turns round, her face drawn harsh with fear. He stops. The echoes fall away into silence. He looks down at the book. He wants to throw it away. He holds it up because he can't think what else to do. Her face breaks into a smile of relief. He waves it and she laughs. They walk towards each other. The muscles of his arms relax under their sheaths of skin.

A Honeymoon in Los Angeles

Honeymoon diary, first day. The taxi-driver wore two wedding rings. This is what he said:

'Hotel Angeline, of America's wonderful Second City. Now get the hell out of my cab, you fucking Nips.'

The airplane was so beautiful. The food came with the sashimi in one package and the vegetables in another, everything clean. The clouds look like a world without any waste. I wanted to stop the plane and step out and rub cloud on my hands and face. It must be cold and smell of iron, like snow. Los Angeles smells only of cars.

The taxi-driver's shoulders were freckled like the skin of a salmon and red hair grew on his upper arms. When he insulted our country, he didn't even turn his head. I think he was shamed by his own anger. I have never heard such an insult. Not even on TV.

I was crying when Shinzo helped me out of the car. He said nothing to the driver. A garbage truck, black and yellow like banana meat, was parked in front of the Hotel Angeline. In the tourist brochure there was no garbage truck and there were baby palms in European pots. Shinzo had to carry our luggage from the taxi himself. He said nothing, not then and not later. We went and stood by the Pacific Coast Highway. Over the lanes of traffic we watched the ocean dance in its skin of sequins. After a short time Shinzo pointed to where Japan must be. We sat on the dirty rocks which are not like Malibu Lagoon and we waved until the hotel manager found us. He was wearing a silver suit and he looked unhappy. He took us into the Hotel Angeline, up to the honeymoon suite. The air-conditioner has baby angels painted on it.

I think perhaps Shinzo is a weak man.

*

Honeymoon diary, second day. The honeymoon suite is pretty and clean. I have been sitting by the balcony window for twenty minutes, practising my English. From the window I can see this:

Ocean. Palm trees with swan-necks of white paint. An empty space where young black men are playing basketball. They are graceful as dancers. Two tall girls are watching them from a high window. A stall, selling sunglasses for $3.99 and juice for a dollar. Bougainvillea flowers in front of a pizza delivery and a thin dog chained in the back. Green hills in the middle-distance. Mountains up above them. There will be coyotes out there. Roads like snakes of cars. Some have fins, some are the colour of champagne. Some are green as the chartreuse my mother drinks on Thursdays when she plays mah-jong. A dark haze in the low air which is the same colour as barley dust at harvest: the exhaustion of a great city. Is Los Angeles bigger than Tokyo?

Shinzo sleeps like a dead man. His hollow cheeks are painted with sweat. My husband, my father's heir. My father says he is a good businessman. They sell umbrellas all day from the factory, and at night they drink together in the kind of bars where the owner is called 'Mother' and only salarymen go. Now he has me, he should not go to those places. Not until I have a child. That is the custom.

Last night we made love. My husband has the hands of a rice-field frog, cold and moist. Under the soft skin, his desire is clumsy and cruel. Like something kept too long in a narrow cage. He hurts me. I have been his wife for three days and he was not my choice.

Soon I will order an American breakfast. Then I will wake Shinzo and he will miss the smell of miso soup which I cook well. Then we will make love again, although I am still sore. Then the choices will be mine. We can go to Hollywood and Universal Studios, and then to Sunset Boulevard where I will spend my husband's money. He will be quite bored but he will say nothing, because he is a coward. It is my honeymoon and I will buy American clothes in the city of the angels.

*

58

Honeymoon diary, third day. My mother said that Los Angeles was not a good place for a honeymoon. She said to visit Europe. She said there is no love in America now, only hate. It is a dying country, she told me. But I needed to make a choice very much.

When I was six I already knew about my insult. I don't remember who told me first but I remember my mother told me again that year, and I already knew. She told me at breakfast, without listening to her own words. The steam from the miso soup covering her face. It was her shame as well, that she had given the family no boy. I was hers. But I was the shame.

This is what I saw today: Universal Studios and a young actress in a car with green wings. A movie in an American movie-theatre. Beverly Hills where the streets are red with flowers and the houses are too large for real people – only temples should be so big. A Mexican skirt in Olvera Street. It has purple thongs and I bought it. Shinzo was not bored at all. He likes watching me, he watches the way I move.

After shopping he took me to see a movie by Walt Disney. There were seats in the theatre – at home in Tosa there are no seats in the movie theatre – and outside was the actress and the beautiful car. In the movie theatre Shinzo stroked my hair, very gently. He is trying very hard.

No one walks in Los Angeles, only the street people. There are more types of car than people and the air is sweet and grainy with their smoke. There are cars from all over the world and the sound of them is everywhere, like the noise of oil cicadas at home in the summertime.

When we came back to the Hotel Angeline I wanted to show my Mexican skirt to the hotel manager, but he was talking to a woman on the telephone. He was angry, and so his face was full of blood. He didn't greet us.

Now Shinzo is in the shower. He is singing an American song. He knows all the American songs from his salaryman karaoke evenings. Sometimes he teaches me the words, which are strange and not English at all but American. He is kind and he has a good heart. But he is weak.

My father is a brave man. The Aomori family is old and respected on our island of Shikoku. When my father was young all the families in the prefecture wanted to marry him in. But when he was seventeen, he volunteered to fly a cherry-blossom plane in the war against America. He was the only son. The family would die to save the country.

And then the war ended so suddenly, so that they didn't want kamikaze pilots anymore, only businessmen. Now my father is an old man, but his voice is still filled with strength. I love him very much. I would not let him be hurt. It was not planned that he should die so young; and it was planned that I should be born alone. An only girl-child. A shaming of my ancestors and the death of a name. My father deserved a son.

But now my father and mother have found Shinzo, who loves my body and who has taken my name. My death will not be shameful now. My father will die happy, and so I must be happy. I must try to be happy for everyone.

Now Shinzo is watching the TV news. His body is fish-white and thin but quite fine. On the TV a reporter is showing how police kick black people in slow motion. Do Japanese police-men kick people? I think my mother is wrong. America is full of death, but there must be love too. I will make love.

Honeymoon diary, fourth day. I must have a boy-child soon. I want my father to see it before he dies. I wish Shinzo was a stronger man. I am not sure I want him to be the father of my children. It is wrong to think this on our honeymoon.

Today the hotel manager gave us a surprise present – a free car for two days. The speed is measured in miles and the colour is pink. The hotel manager says this is because it is the honeymoon-suite car. Shinzo says it is primer paint. I think it's pretty. The hotel manager says we should go out to the desert for a few days, to Disneyland or further. But I want to see Los Angeles. It excites me. The buildings are made of mirrors and sun-glass and they are sharp as knives in the sun.

After the car, I telephoned my mother in Tosa. Her voice sounded dusty and tired. My own voice echoed like a stone in a well. She asked what Americans are like when they are in America. I told her they are more emotional than Koreans. She asked me if I was being a good wife but I didn't smile at that. I am not a good wife. I just carry a name, like a baby that never breathes or smiles.

For lunch I had ice-cream at Denny's Diner. Shinzo had eggs and sausage, and there was a fight between two women. I didn't feel scared because women fight on TV all the time. The colours were bright, like a Hollywood movie.

My ice-cream sundae had syrup and maraschino cherries on top. Then there was English Breakfast ice-cream, coffee wafers and lemon sorbet, and underneath it all there was Coke. I was almost to the lemon sorbet when a woman started screaming behind me. A small man with a beard on the end of his chin jumped up next to Shinzo. He hit the table with the heels of his hands.

'Cat-fight, by god!' he shouted. Then everyone was clapping and whistling. I turned round and there were two waitresses. One had straight yellow hair like corn silk and she was kneeling on the floor and coughing. The other waitress had very dark skin and she was thin, but also strong, because she was holding the bigger woman up by the hair. The black woman was shouting. 'Tell me again, you fucking white trash, was they just doing their job?' Then, 'You going to call them? Hey, I'm going to kill them. You going to call them, trash? Why not? They're your stinking pigs.' Her forehead was bleeding and she kicked at the woman on the floor. Then she let go of the blonde hair and stood staring at nothing. Her mouth was sad, as if she was about to cry. Quickly the blonde woman got up. There was a tall glass of fudge syrup on the bar with a silver spout on top. The blonde woman picked it up and hit the other waitress in the mouth with it. All her teeth broke. When she bent over blood and syrup came out together, brown and red. Then we left.

Shinzo is quiet now. He thinks about the women's fight in a

61

different way from me. I watch it like TV. For him it is more real. That is why he is so weak.

It's hot today. There is a man juggling outside the Universal News Agency and his sweat has made his clothes into a second skin, black and red and blue. No one gives him money today. None of the cars stop. America is full of hatred, but we are Japanese. This afternoon we will drive the honeymoon-suite car and see the whole of Los Angeles.

Honeymoon diary, fourth or fifth day. We are going home now. A man from the Japanese consulate found us airplane seats. It is midnight or later. From the window I can see stars and the wing, which is only an absence of stars. I can see the whole city below, drawn in light. Around it are the big darknesses of the desert and the ocean.

There is a string of fire in the west, where the factories are, and one north of Sunset Boulevard. But most of the fire is in downtown. There are no noises up here, no smell of burning, so it looks quite pretty. When we were lost the noise was terrible. A city coming apart. Maybe whole families have been killed, fathers and children.

Shinzo is asleep now. I have put a blanket over him. He is my husband and I must care for him.

First of all there were two explosions, but Shinzo said that they were car tyres melting in the heat. We were trying to find Olvera Street again but then we came out onto Colorado Avenue. Next to Tower Records was a pet store with the alarmbells ringing. Shinzo stopped the car.

The store was called Anything Except Aardvarks and there was a rabbit with long ears sitting in the doorway. The shop window was smashed, and a boy was standing in it. He was black and there were patterns shaved in his hair like dog-teeth. He was watching us and saying something. Then another boy came out by the door. He had black hair and tanned skin. He had a macaw parrot in his arms, cradled like a baby. He kicked the rabbit out of his way and both boys ran down the street.

The rabbit sat in the gutter. I wanted to get out but Shinzo wouldn't let me. A woman stopped and tried to catch it, but it ran down the street, like the boys. Someone said they would call the police, and so we left. We drove away, and soon there were trunks of black smoke quite near, to the south and east. People were running in packs, like dogs. There was a giant painting on a wall of Presley and Monroe. Then Shinzo got lost.

Now he is sleeping and I wish he would stay asleep, like a dead man. In the departure lounge I slept on the floor and dreamed of our families. They were alive, like trees, and their skins were cold, like Shinzo's. Then I woke up, crowded on the floor with hundreds of other people. I watched Shinzo sleeping. He is the carrier of my name. He repulses me.

There was a beautiful car on fire on Colorado Avenue. It was a black Jaguar, very old, and someone had poured red paint on the roof and set fire to the paint. There was a Korean, too. He was standing in front of his grocery store and asking people not to steal from him. His English was not very good and some girls were laughing at him, but nobody had broken into his store yet.

I was excited and not so scared then, because nobody noticed us. It still felt like TV. I lit a cigarette with the honeymoon-suite car lighter and asked Shinzo where we were going.

'We are going to the hotel. Then we will leave this terrible country,' he said. His hands kept slipping around the steering wheel because he was sweating too much. He turned south and bumped against a fire hydrant. Water burst into the air and came down on the car with a slap. Shinzo whined quietly, like a child who does not want to be heard. He turned around and drove down a side-street. When I told him we were going the wrong way, he commanded me to be quiet in very masculine Japanese. I sat back and let the cigarette curl into ash.

The side-street was full of cheap motels and small movie-theatres showing films about naked women. Outside them three girls were playing dodgeball in the road. There was nobody else.

'Wait here. I'll ask them the way,' said Shinzo. He pressed the car horn softly and started to get out, but the girls ran away. Then Shinzo got angry and hit the horn again, harder. It echoed between the buildings with their mirrored glass and sharp edges.

'A mad country!' he shouted. 'Foreigners are animals who kill for food. Shit, why did we come here? We should have gone to Hawaii.'

I stubbed out the cigarette. I told him Los Angeles had been my choice. He looked at me and began to get scared again. Then we heard shouting. The girl-children had returned with lots of other people.

'Chinks! Hey, rich Nips!' they were shouting. There were many young black people, like the ones who were playing basketball days ago. Now they had shopping-trolleys full of food. One boy picked up a pineapple and threw it at the honeymoon-suite car. It hit the roof with a bang, then rolled down the windscreen. There was a dent in the metal above my head.

Shinzo sighed – not tired, but terrified. He tried to start the car and it stalled. Everyone laughed and now there were more people. They kept throwing food, but most of it missed. An egg hit my window and I screamed. I told Shinzo to start the car, but it was dead. A fish hit the windscreen and left a trail of white slime. Then all the people were chanting and throwing eggs and fruit. It went on for a long time. Shinzo tried to put his head between his knees, but his seatbelt held him up. He covered his face with his hands instead and wept.

Something in me died, then. He was disgusting. I knew I wouldn't have his child. Then a can of food hit the windscreen and it broke into a thousand diamonds.

I was leaning over Shinzo and trying to start the engine. Then there was the whoop of police cars and a megaphone. The crowd shouted louder and threw more cans. I had to hide under the seat. There was red juice or blood on my hands. I shut my eyes and sang children's songs, and when I looked again, most of the people had gone. The police cars were in front and behind us. A policewoman was knocking on Shinzo's door. She looked very worried. I think she had been there for a long time.

I wonder what it is in me that has died. Not my family, that passes away so easily. What do I have left? After my father dies, I will divorce Shinzo. Can I do that? Then there will need to be work, maybe in a school, or kindergarten. I will play with the children and pretend they are mine. It is the children in me that have died. I am not so young, and I will be divorced. No one will marry me again. I have been married for five days.

The paramedics gave Shinzo sleeping medicine. I asked them to take us to the hotel first, to pick up our luggage. The manager was gone and the door had been kicked in. It was evening. I went and stood over the traffic of the Pacific Coast Highway while they searched for our possessions. From the bridge, the ocean was on fire all the way to Japan.

Losing Track

Past the last billboard is where the desert starts. Off the black-top, onto the dirt. The sidewalks just tail away. No one comes out here.

'No one hears the trees.'

'What?'

I don't say anything.

'There are no trees, Calvin. Keep walking.'

'Okay.'

I look up to read the board as we go under. Harry Connick Jnr is playing the Excalibur. I hear a dog bark, way back. There's so little noise out here. No one hears the trees fall. I keep walking. I'm trying to write in my head.

'Good boy. Just walk. You make me happy when you walk. I'm happy, you're happy. Happy campers.'

I'm trying to remember the skyline behind me. It has no buildings or mountains or trees. Just neon. I miss it. I'm measuring off the yards away from it. I don't know when to stop. Walk (*scrub grass, packed earth*). Listen (*chuff and trudge of dirt*). Feel. I can smell ginger.

One time, I was getting dinner in Circle-K, it was after the midnight shift and nothing left except BeenFeest burgers and a Yahoo. Socrates the shop boy, he's telling some guy they got no cappucino Häagen-Dazs. One minute they're arguing and the next he was shot.

I read in a book that a bullet travels faster than sound; you don't hear it till it hits. First the feeling, a kick in the guts, then the sound. Like a joke. Bugs Bunny with his face all burned black, and then a little flag coming out of the gun, BANG! Socrates laying on the freezer-cabinets, saying I'm sorry, I'm sorry, in his Latino voice. Blood icing up pink on the cold glass.

I want to hear it first, is what I want to say. If I get shot ever. People get shot all the time in Vegas.

'Okay Calvin, you got the job. Congratulations. I tell you what they tell me. Which is: you dress nice, you never screw the customers, and you never, ever, screw the company. Oh, and take the wrist-watch off. You don't want to wear that in the Palace.'

That's Sebastian. He's Management. There's marlins stitched into his silk necktie. Knuckles raw. When he talks his hands curl up and the knuckles go white. He likes the way I deal.

'Now here's a tip from your new boss just for free, son.'

His breath smells of hot-dogs. Meaty sour-sweet. We're in the Eiffel Lounge, seventeenth floor. Croupier interviews. Croupier means dealer. This is back in April.

'People lose two things in Vegas, three if you count cherries, but mostly our customers have only two things left to lose and they're both the same thing. Take their time, you take their money. Take their money, you take their time.'

He leans across the table. 'But you take care of your time, Calvin, and you shit green presidents. Like me. Let them lose track, yes? And never lose track yourself. This is the Palace. There's always money to be made. You like money, right?'

The Palace of Versailles. I like it here. I work on Plaza Five. There are no clocks, but I got used to that. I got used to the noise too, the slots and crowds and big-win bells. There are clock radios in the four-poster bedrooms, alongside the check-out times, and from the stained-glass arcade on the first floor you can see the giant digital over the Midnight Hour wedding chapel on Las Vegas Boulevard. That's all.

There's this poem called 'The Lotos-Eaters' by an English Poet Laureate, where people eat fruit and the world goes plain out of their minds. That's what the Palace is. Lotos fruits, all different kinds. Lemons, cherries, plums and bars. It's from the Greek. When I get off work I always read a poem. It's a sign of

67

worth. Then I sleep. I got a place with a view near the Golden Nugget. Mostly I just work, though.

I got a black Casio I keep zippered in my waistcoat pocket. Fifty metres water-resist. I won it on the Trawler-Crawlers in basement three. I check the time whenever I go to the men's room. I keep track.

I do cards, triple-shifts. My eyes are twenty-twenty for long periods. I got potential.

Sebastian is from Culiacán, that's Mexico. He doesn't talk about that much. Him being a foreigner, he doesn't talk about that. One time he told me. We were drinking. He probably forgot now. Back then he used to take me out drinking uptown. He drank silver tequila chasers. He said, *Money in the desert. This is where we live, Calvin. Only we don't get it. The money. We get green baize and burger bars. If I could turn it all back. Make it liquid. Liquid money. You like money, Calvin? Sure you do.*

Once I'm walking home, late night. The stoplights outside my place, someone's stolen the colour filters off of them. It goes green, white, white. It makes me think of Sebastian. Making it liquid. I stay away from him.

Then it's four months later and there's this woman.

Midnight Hour is two elevators away and she isn't wearing a wrist-watch. I've been checking on her between deals. I'm on blackjack, table E14, E is the row, fourteen's the aisle. Today I was on baccarat shift but I changed with Sevvy, I always do because Sev says baccarat muff has got class. That's what he says.

I checked the time too. On the Casio, just now in the locker room. This woman, she's been losing a lot of time but not much money. That's smart. No big wins, just give and take. I guess I didn't start counting until she took off her hat and I saw her hair. For definite, she's been playing that same slot for seven hours and just gone ten minutes.

The hat's a panama. Not real panama. The kind of thing they give away with Chicken à la Colon at the Dunes. Her raincoat's army surplus. That's how I know she's from out of town. Wearing a raincoat.

She comes out from the elevators and stops when the noise hits her. Wheels and dice and the three thousand slot-machines. She looks at it like she was only going to the mall and took a wrong turn someplace. Wrinkles her nose at the smell. The tang of static and electric motors, like pennies and oysters. A carnival ground with no sky is what she sees. The inside of Las Vegas. In the first alley of slots she stops again.

She touches one of the machines. A Desert Bandit, hubcap chrome painted with red and green diamonds. An accumulator, that's when the money goes up and up the longer it waits. Tokens come crashing down somewhere, over on the Cashcades. Her hands snap shut.

Two young girls trail away from the third slot on the left. She walks up to it and takes off her hat. She runs her fingers across the arm and doesn't jump at the little tug of static. Just smiles. I smile too.

I lived in trailer parks with my Ma when I was young, and that's why I have good vision. Looking at the world through moving windows. It was practice. I see everything mostly. Gas station faces, WELCOME TO, rain coming beyond porch windows. Faces turning a winning card, private Fourth-of-Julys, lips moving when they need to pray.

This is all wrong. This isn't what I want to say. I'm walking up a desert ridge away from Las Vegas. The man behind me shouts *Keep going Calvin, good boy.* This is the place where no one hears. There's not enough time. What I want to say is

Before the hair, I see the way she stands. Ankles touching, like a woman waiting on a cold street. Lipstick too. Gloss. She looks like the street-people, one of the young ones who hang out down by the dog station. The Greyhounds I mean. The ones who call up for pizza and steal it from right out of the trashcans when nobody collects it.

That's what she looks like. Hungry. She looks up at the chrome ball of a security camera and smiles. Then she takes off her hat and I see her hair.

It's ginger. Not ginger like the word. Ginger like ginger: the lion-fur of the root when you cut against its grain. I can't take my eyes off of her. Sometimes I feel this way with women I can never meet. At a window. In a photo. On a subway train. She's very beautiful.

I'm not a dozen feet from her. Her coat pockets are full of silver dollars, she's running one hand through them while she plays. So I guess she didn't walk in by accident after all. She plays well, too. I keep watching while the blackjack players burn and bust. I can tell the time just from their drinks. GTs and Marys in the afternoon, rocks and straights as evening comes in. After an hour she changes arms, starts pulling with her left. Milking the slot while she flexes blood back into her right hand.

Then Hutch the floorman is behind me with his hand on my shoulder. Just too tight.

'Everything all right here, Mister Halliday?'

That's me. Calvin Halliday. 'Yes, sir!'

I don't say nothing else and Hutch's hand loosens up, so nothing else was the right thing to say. Hutch is like Sebastian's Rottweiler. They drink uptown a lot, I guess. Hutch is built like a wall but if his head wasn't tucked into the neck of his tuxedo, he'd lose it and not even worry. Like them lizards with their tails.

'Make sure you give our customers your undivided service and attention. Make their stay a happy one.'

'Yes, sir.' I don't talk too much as a rule anyway. I don't do patter like some dealers. I ridge the cards, cut them, deal. There's only two players but I couldn't tell you their faces. I win a hand. Take bets. Look up.

Hutch is with her. Not standing too close, not close enough to scare her. Touching her when he can. Her arm to guide her to the slot, her hand to the lever. The light shines off his dress shirt and his teeth and for a moment it looks like they're dancing.

Then she moves back from him, stands with her arms wrapped across her belly while he grins. He spins the slots for her. He gives her his personal demonstration. Now he's telling her his joke about jerking off the slots.

She waits for him to go. Just standing, head down. She looks tired, her arms must be hurting by now. She just lets them hang.

He goes. She never smiled, not even when Hutch was telling his jerk joke. I watch her for hours as the Palace fills and empties. Lipstick and light all the colours of carnival-glass. I see her mouth move when she prays and loses, hear the bells when she wins a hundred.

Once she looks over at the mirrored glass that's Management. Sebastian is there, leaning against the glass. Watching her with his arms folded sharp against his tux. She looks away then. There's some kind of feeling in her face. Just a twist of muscles, it could mean anything strong. I see that. I keep track. My eyes are good.

A truck goes crashing past on the 115. It's a long way back now. It just makes the desert seem quieter. A place emptied out of life. I can hear the man breathing as he climbs. Soon it'll be time to stop walking.

Not yet. Not yet. Wait.

She's very beautiful.

One time I saw Madonna in the Flamingo Café and this woman, she's beautiful like Madonna. The way people watch her. They want to be with her, a part of her. Like the waitress at that café will tell her grandchildren how she met Madonna, and when she gets Alzheimer's, she'll tell them nothing else all day, how Madonna took extra sugar and cream and how she licked her spoon. A part of her.

I wish I could be with her. Someone this beautiful, the world must be different for her. I try and imagine it. Maybe she gets used to it. She looks cold.

Seven hours, ten minutes. There's shadows under her eyes the colour of new bruises. When she pulls the bandit's arm she grins. It's not a smile. It's her teeth coming together with pain.

A working day she's been here. All that time on the same slot. Never coming over to the five-dollar tables, not even trying a different bandit. She's fed a lot of silver into that one machine, and milked some of it back out. Third Desert Bandit on the left. Maybe she saw it in a dream.

The eye-shadows make her look like that boy in the Charlie Chaplin movie. *The Kid*. She's so young. I want to know where she ought to be, a whole working day and all that cash gone by.

I have to keep track of the table. There are cards in my hand and I don't know what they are. This is what I'm good at, but I'm not doing it good. I don't like that.

There's an old guy in blue jeans with four cards, he's got numbers written all over the backs of his hands. Another man standing behind, drinking Long Islands, sometimes sitting to play and sometimes not. A couple with East Coast haircuts, Jesus, I'm not even watching them. The wife clicks another red disc down and drinks her sweet martini. Lipstick on her teeth and glass.

Couples you got to watch because they slip up together for a kiss and then maybe slip cards. I lose the hand too. The East Coast lady kisses her man on his bald spot. The Marlboro Man swears, crosses out the numbers on his knuckles with a ten-dollar Palace fountain-pen.

I keep watching her, though. The woman. She could be gone each time, and that's why I have to keep looking; I might never see her again. She doesn't take her eyes off the machine. Chews the insides of her mouth. I do that, when I'm thinking. I want to know what she's thinking. One time when I look up I can see Sebastian in the floor-to-ceiling cut mirrors. He could be watching me, or just looking through me. It's hard to tell from his eyes. He looks bored.

I deal. Cut. Play the cards. Head down. There's a rhythm to it. If I get the rhythm right, I can keep track without ever looking at the Casio.

'Any more bets?'

I try not to watch her. I try hard to keep my eyes on the baize.

72

Red chips stacked up in their black rings. Small-time gambling, five dollars a hand. The systems man works with one-dollar silver discs, clicking them together in his hands. All nerves and addiction. The green table is everything.

I stop hearing the noise of the gambling halls. For a while I stop thinking of the beautiful girl who dreams of one slot-machine. There's just me and the players now. I go for unsafe hands; five card tricks or splitting fives. If I win I don't smile. My face don't show nothing at all. I bust a six-card hand and deal again. The haze of smoke hurts my eyes and I blink. Once, twice.

'Deuce and nine is eleven showing, ladies and gentlemen. House shows one queen and holds. Standard bet is five, House wins draws. Does anyone wish to raise the bet?'

'Can I play?'

She's standing right next to me. I never heard her come up. I can smell something on her, perfume or her hair. Her voice is hard and nervous, teenaged. Nevada accent, and mostly Nevada means Vegas. I keep getting her wrong.

Her nails are bitten short. No paint, no gloss. They don't go with her lipstick. She's wearing no socks. Just sneakers. The rubber peeling off of them. She's talking again. I have to talk back.

'You're welcome to play, ma'am, soon as the next game starts.'

'Oh, sure. I'm sorry.'

She watches while the House wins and the man with systems on his hands gets up and swears and walks away. She smiles at the East Coasters as she takes the empty seat. The husband won't look at her. He sort of nods at the space around her. I can understand that.

'Just a couple of hands. Then I have to take five.'

'Yes, ma'am. Good luck.'

I'm not supposed to say that. I say it quiet, so maybe she won't hear with the casino background noise. But she smiles at me. There's gaps between her teeth. I'm surprised because it doesn't make her less beautiful. Only less perfect.

73

'Thanks. But this is no big deal. Just a chaser.'

She sits back. She talks fast, her voice going up a little at the end of every sentence. It's her accent. It makes everything a question I want to answer. I deal the cards. Ace showing, eight down.

'To go with the slots.' I don't plan to say that. It just comes out. I look up.

She's not smiling. Her pupils have gone small in their green irises. When she smiles again the pupils stay small.

'Excuse me?'

'A chaser, you said. To go with the slots.'

She starts to look behind her at the Desert Bandits, then stops. 'You were watching me?'

The way she says it, it's something bad. Like she was naked. I try to smile but it's hard, I want her to stay, I know it shows now. 'It's my job.'

'To watch me playing slots?'

'Well, just to watch all the players. Ma'am.'

'Hey. Speaking of jobs.' It's the East Coast wife, tapping a red disc on the baize.

I start to apologise again. Then Sev is behind me, down from the baccarat gallery, whispering garlic breath in my ear. It's the end of my shift and I didn't even know.

'Chow time, Cal.' He clucks his tongue against his teeth like the ranchers out in Clark County. Lowers his voice. 'Hutch says go get changed, you look like a 'coon in heat, you're disturbing the customers.'

I follow his eye and she's watching me. I want to say something. Just so she remembers me. But there's no time. I pick up the cards. When I talk I'm looking at her.

'Excuse me, ladies and gentlemen, I hope you've enjoyed your time with me, and I'll be handing you over now to another of our highly trained croupiers, Sevvy. I hope you have a good evening.'

And then I just stand there, looking at her. I can't stop myself. Hutch the floorman comes up, he's saying something, laughing, pulling me out of the way. I want to tell him he's

74

hurting me, but it sounds so weak. I don't want to sound weak with her there. I catch my footing and don't fall.

When I look up she's still sitting there, watching me. She shakes her head. Then she puts down her cards and goes. She just goes. She doesn't look back.

'That's it, Calvin. You can stop now. Turn around so I can see you.'

I lost my breath a little, coming up the ridge. The desert is out ahead of me, I know that. But in the dark there's nothing. Only wind coming with the smell of rock dust and cactus pears. I could be on the edge of the Grand Canyon, it's that dark.

'Turn around, Calvin.'

I could do that. Look back at Las Vegas. The Strip laid out in neon from the Tropicana on in. I'd like that. But I want to be sure. If I hear it first, or if I feel it. If I look, I'll never be sure.

I keep walking.

I lied. That bit about what I do, work and sleep. I write too. That's what I do, like what I want to do is what I mean. Like this, writing in my head. It's instead of talking.

I do poetry. You can probably tell from my style. I'm not so good, I don't really know why. My Ma taught me. We used to do poems when she was driving.

> When the moonlight's deep,
> banked up against walls,
> you can skate on it
> or pack moonballs.

That's what I wrote last night. Lying on the worn-down bed in my rented room, thinking of her. I've never seen snow, only sand which might be the same sometimes. On TV I have. Seen snow.

I lie in my room, thinking of her. I've never seen someone so beautiful. Not up close. She's like snow. I think of her hands, running through pockets of silver. That's how I'd touch her. If I could ever.

I think of it all night, half-dreaming. Sebastian in the mirrors, the third slot on the left, silver dollars streaming out like liquid. Making it liquid. I think of the way he watched her. Bored. Intent. There's light on the ceiling coming in off the Golden Nugget and game arcades. Red and gold. Like her hair when she walks under the striplights and chrome.

Then it's today. I'm still waiting to sleep. I can tell when it starts to get light without moving. The neon fades against the ceiling, thinned with sun. I go down to the public phone outside and ring Lakeisha at the Palace to change my hours.

It should be Sebastian I call. I don't want to talk to him now. I get Lakeisha to put me on blackjack again. Table E14. She doesn't ask why. One time she called Sebastian a pimped-up bumfuck hick. Only once, though. She told me since then she's never been alone with him, not anywhere. She makes sure. I like her.

I eat a hamburger breakfast and walk to the Palace. The stoplights are mended now, but it's early, there isn't much traffic. The lights click through patterns by themselves. Red–amber, green, amber. I try and think what I'm going to do. I can't think. Like I'm hiding it from myself.

I knew she'd still be there. I'm not talking smart. I think slow, I need time. But I thought all last night and I see mostly everything. At the Palace I check the jackpot updates outside Plaza Five. The Desert Bandits are up to three million three hundred twenty seven thousand dollars seventy-seven cents. The Cashcades and the Louis XV are higher, nearer four.

Lakeisha lets me check her file copy and it says the same. But there's a note on the Bandits, faded-out with photocopying: URGENT AUG. SEE % slot ref. 212. Percentages are odds. Lakeisha doesn't have odds records. That's different from jackpots, only top management sees those. Sebastian could get them, I guess. If he wanted them bad.

There are no windows in the gambling hall, no line of sight out to the sun. You can tell it's daytime, though. There's a different crowd, not so many couples. This time of day lots of the tourists are out in the Mojave, looking at orange poppies or Joshua Trees. What's left are the addicts, the systems-people, the last-chance players.

There's less laughter, more time. My table goes quiet around late afternoon and I look up. She's been there the whole time. Third slot on the left. Not losing too much. Moving only a little as she plays. Saving herself.

One thing about millionaires and poor folks: they think about the same thing, money, all the time. One way or the other, money is what makes them what they are and they have a hunger for it. Once you got it, that hunger, you never get rid of it.

That's what she's like. It's in the way she treats her silver dollars. Loading them slowly, not wanting to let them go, warming them with her hands, talking. She'll never have enough of it. She loves it, like Sebastian. *You like money, Calvin? Sure you do.* It's in the way her eyes sparkle when she's watching the machine. Wet.

I put the cards down and look up. I know what I'm going to do. The cameras will see me, because they see everything. I could lose my job just for leaving the table.

It doesn't matter now. I walk up to her. She has her back turned, so she doesn't see me till I'm right there. I didn't plan what to say and I don't want to say the wrong thing, but there's no time. She turns and I start to talk before she recognises me.

'I know what you're doing. With the slot and Sebastian.'

A cheer goes up from the crap-table crowd. I have to shout a little. 'I don't mind. All I want you to do is talk to me. And let me talk to you. And then I won't tell no one.'

'Just talk?'

She doesn't even stop to think. Maybe she was expecting me after yesterday, I can't tell. Her eyes are punched-out with exhaustion. 'Where? Somewhere private?'

She's laughing at me a little. I nod and she looks away.

'I'll have to ask Sebastian. No. You'll have to ask Sebastian

77

for me. Somewhere where the cameras won't see you. Tell him we'll be an hour. Go.'

I walk away between the knuckle-crack of roulette tables. I try not to think about what I'm doing. My chest hurts, it's the excitement. Sebastian's office is behind the security room, but I don't need to go back there. There's just him and Hutch on cameras for Plaza Five. They've been watching everything I done.

He looks up at me, Sebastian. Just looking without expression, then back at the screen. 'You're off your table. I should fire you.'

I go over. On the close-circuit is the woman. She's waiting by the Desert Bandit. Not looking up. I guess she knows we're watching anyway. She doesn't look beautiful like this. It's gone like figures in landscapes from a car: a woman sleeping, a face. The car moves on and the angle is gone, there's just mesas and dunes. I can't get it back.

It's not important. What matters is I'm not here to watch people play. I'm part of this now. I don't understand it all yet but I'm trying to learn. It feels good. Sebastian sighs and stands back. He looks at me like he's expecting me to say something. So I do.

'You're keeping track, right?'

'Right, Calvin.'

'Right. I saw that. But there's always money to be made. You said that too.'

'Yeah.' He sounds real tired.

'Are you making money now?'

Hutch swears and looks away. 'Calvin. Please,' Sebastian says. His hands are fists, blood draining back from the joints and bones. 'She could win any second. Any second now. Just say how much you want.'

I look back at the screen. 'What's her name?'

They wait. It's quiet in here, soundproofed. I talk into the quiet. 'I want to be with her. Just for an hour. Just talking. She says it's OK and to tell you, she'll be an hour. That's all I want. You can have the money.'

Hutch starts laughing. He does it real quiet, but when I look at him later there's tears running down his face and it's hard to tell if he's laughing or crying. Sebastian just goes on looking at me a long time. He lights a cigarette, even though smoking's not allowed inside the security rooms. All the time he looks at me until he lets out the first mouthful of smoke.

'So go.' He shrugs. 'What are you waiting for?'

'What's her name?'

He grins. His teeth are like hers. 'Whatever you want, Calvin. Right now you call her what you like.'

'Goodbye, Calvin.' He says that as I'm going. A cheer goes up as I step outside. Someone winning big over on the crap tables. I walk between the watchers and players, the floormen and waitresses. I can feel the cameras following me. A pressure on the back of my neck. I don't look up at them.

She sees me coming across the hall and leaves ahead of me. In the televator we don't say nothing, it's just the two of us. The TV screens playing *Happy Days* with the sound down. Muzak Sinatra. Not looking at each other at all.

We get out at the Atrium and walk outside and it's already dark, the moon round like an oven-dial, hot against our faces as we walk. She's fast, I have to run a little to keep up. She's taller than me, I didn't see that before. I guess I don't see everything. I try and concentrate on her face.

She talks without slowing down. A little breathless. 'Stop watching me. Stop it. What do you think I am, MTV?'

'I'm sorry.'

She sits down on a concrete bench. I didn't know she'd do that, I have to go back to her. She pulls out a packet of cigarettes and lights up. I sit down. There's nothing else to do.

She's blowing smoke, shaking her head. 'I don't believe it.' Then she looks at me, not talking, just shaking her head like yesterday. I try and think of something to say.

'Don't believe what?'

Her eyes keep moving, like she's trying to see inside my head. She's frowning. Not angry now. She looks amazed. 'You know they'll kill you. They can't just shut that slot down.

79

Someone could be hitting that jackpot right now. If that happens, they'll kill you. They'll just walk you out into the desert and shoot you.'

'I only want to talk.'

She leans forward with her elbows on her knees and puts her head down. 'What do you want to talk about?' Grinds the heel of a hand into her tired eyes.

It's not going right. I stand up. This wasn't how it was supposed to happen. 'I want to go somewhere else. I mean us. I want us to go somewhere. If you want to. Are you hungry? We could have dinner together.'

She stands up and smiles. A kind of grin which don't have much to do with feeling. It's just the bone showing through. 'It's your time. What's your name?'

'Calvin. Halliday.'

She doesn't give me her name. We shake hands. Cars go by on the Strip. Faces looking and looking away. 'Actually I'm not hungry, Calvin. Can we just get a drink somewhere?'

'Oh sure.' I look around for somewhere. But you can drink anywhere in Vegas, anytime. 'How about Union Plaza? Is that OK?'

She takes my arm. I feel it like static. 'That's fine, Calvin. We can walk.'

And we do. Down towards Fremont together, the sound of a siren somewhere behind us and the warmth of her, the warmth of her arm, closer than I ever imagined it could be. After a little while her breathing changes, slows. I feel her relax against me.

'What are you doing here, Calvin?'

I shrug. 'I just ended up here.' We walk through automatic doors. The elevator closes around us. I want to tell her. To explain. 'I'm just road trash. You know, Vegas has been a place for road trash and white trash ever since the Mormons bought it off the Paiute for eighteen bucks.' We find a table. She orders drinks. Turns back to me and nods and smiles.

'I like it here, is why. It always feels – If it ever got out of season, the Strip would be the biggest ghost town on earth. But it never is.'

'Never is what?'

'Out of season. I like it that way.' There's a tall glass of alcohol the colour of apricots. I pick it up and drink. It burns. 'The neon meadows. Like coming on water in the desert. That's why I'm here.'

She's nodding, looking past me. I don't turn round to see if there's a clock there. I don't want to see that. 'How about you?'

Her eyes focus in. 'You know what I'm doing here.'

'I mean why?'

She doesn't answer. Just frowns at me for a while, then looks down. 'You're a very strange person, Calvin.' She sits forward. 'I'm here for the money. That's what I want. That's all I want. I don't care if I die with no friends, no fuck, no family. As long as I'm rich. Do you understand that?'

'Sure.'

She smiles. A real smile, the first time. 'No you don't. What do you love, Calvin?'

I could say her. I don't say that. 'Poetry. Really. It's what I try and do. It's hard.'

'Tell me some poetry.'

'I can't.' It's true. I can't even look at her now. Her voice is different. Quiet. 'I'm no good at it.'

'So tell me what you want to write about.' She sits back and drinks. Her glass is almost empty. I take a breath and talk without looking at her.

'Well. The rain, maybe. Mostly it never rains but sometimes it does. Saved-up and coming down hard. Like an accumulator. Raining millions. Have you seen that?'

She nods, sure.

'So when that happens I go walking by myself, the Strip and Downtown. The boulevards and backstreets are full of reflections. Neon and laser-spots and glitterballs and spangleboards.

'I walk nearly all night, some years. There's the smell of food from air-vents and the light all around, it keeps me warm. Up to the Trop, down around Glitter Gulch. It's like walking in the sky. Then next morning it's gone. Dried away into the desert. So fast. It's frightening. That thirst.'

I stop talking. She hasn't looked back at the clock. Her eyes are trying to find a way round mine again. My hands are sweating. I wrap them round the cold of my glass.

'I want another drink. You want another?' I nod and she orders. I close my eyes while she's looking away. In the dark I lose my balance. I haven't slept for a while now. We wait for the drinks to come.

'You know, when I said what are you doing here, I meant here. With me. I meant why did you do this.'

'Would you have come with me if I hadn't?'

'No, but –'

'I've never talked to someone like you. Nothing ever happens to me. I'm the dealer, it's not supposed to. But I just wanted to talk to you. You're so beautiful.'

'Thank you.'

'It's my pleasure.'

She doesn't touch me. She just smiles, her face softening into it. She looks beautiful again. Maybe it's enough. Then Hutch is there, I see him coming across the room, multiplied in the smoked-glass mirrors.

'Calvin.' His dress-shirt has come out. He still looks like he's been crying. He has one hand in his jacket pocket, the fingers curled tight. 'I've been looking for you everywhere.'

She doesn't look at me any more. She stands up, her eyes going wild. 'It happened didn't it? Hutch? It's gone, isn't it? Oh shit.'

'Get up, Calvin.'

They look down at me. Together they're similar people, I can see it. It's a trait, like green eyes or a love of meat. 'Calvin the poet. Calvin who thinks he's God's gift to fucking oxygen. Get up.' Quiet voice. It could be her speaking. I can't tell. I stand up and she looks away.

'I feel like you're polluting the air in here. I'm going to have to ask you to leave the building with me. You're fired, by the way. Now let's go.'

I want to tell him they could try again. Or that I'll keep quiet, I can. I could do that.

Instead I think of her, her hair. I wish I could have touched it. At the street I look back for her, but she's gone. I start to write it down, in my head.

The Strip is long and quiet, Hutch ten steps behind. I listen to his steps as we walk. We come to where the city stops and the desert begins and he tells me to keep going.

No trees, no one to hear them fall. Once I look round quickly and he's standing under the last billboard, hands in his pockets. Shadows from the sodium lights fall down over his eyes. Then he starts up again and we go on. A long-haul truck passes on the empty road. Then the road is gone. I'm on the ridge. There's nothing but the smell of dust and stone.

'That's it, Calvin. You can stop now. Turn around.'

I keep walking. I just want to hear it first. Before the pain. I want that fact. Behind me the man with the gun is shouting my name. In my pocket the Casio alarm goes off, and as I pull it out I hear the sound of the jackpot and I smell the colour of her hair.

Hammerhead

'No! –'

He sits up in the narrow bed, hugging his chest. The knife is already warming to his body-heat. He can feel the point of it inside, obstructing his heartbeat. His hands slip, feeling for the wound. But it's like picking meat out from teeth, he can't find the intrusion. He uses both hands.

'Oh no no –'

He starts to cry. 'Not yet.' The part of him which is still dreaming sees how he bleeds. The warmth is going out of him along the cheap black plastic of a knife handle. He tries to hold the blood in. In his panic he has smeared moisture across chest, ribs, abdomen. The place around him has gone small and dark and he recognises nothing.

He puts his hands against the senses of his face, hiding himself from himself. When he moves, the blood is cool on his skin. Like sweat.

Then he is awake, calming. His wrist-watch ticks in the small room. Perspiration has collected in his sparse white hair, his beard and the loose folds of his belly. Sweat stings his eyes. He looks for the sheet to wipe himself dry. It is tangled around his feet and he tugs it away. The motion of cleaning brings him back to himself.

There is pain in his chest where the nerves are still waiting to die. He throws the sheet onto the floor. Lies back.

It is an effort to think of other things. The dark in the room is blue against white concrete. He tries to remember which language it is in which 'darkness' and 'blue' are one word. The specific information is old and distant. He worries at it for the sake of worrying. After some time he lets it go.

The room comes back to him as a slow accumulation of data. One cicada chirrs in the mango trees outside. There is the fetid smell of mangoes, the hush of high tide. A fan rotates towards him, cools him and turns away. He gulps like a fish in the hot air. Pulls the sheet over his chest, holding it there. He lies back, eyes open.

After some time he makes a sound, *Ah*, smiling at himself. An airplane goes over, heading south across the Amazon to Brazil. He can hear it for a long time. Then there is only the sea, the fan, the watch-tick. He closes his eyes again and sleeps.

'Felicia. Come here. Felicia.'

She wakes. The sun is up, she can smell the gutters outside, fallen fruit and skins rotting in the heat.

She has overslept and there is no money, nothing except her credit with the butchers and fishermen, her persuasion in the bank manager's air-conditioned Puerto La Cruz office, and 2,000 bolívars in the hotel deposit-box, the notes folded and refolded by so many hands over so many years they have taken on the consistency of an old woman's skin.

It comes back to her, the fear which has been waiting while she sleeps. There was money in her dreams; the Interior, tree-frogs with golden eyes. She killed them for the gold and their blood was white. She frowns, trying to remember.

There is a hand across her, rough against her breasts. Hector. No. Ricard. Hector was before. Almost a year ago. Last year was better.

She opens her eyes. There is light against the foot of the wall. Five-thirty, six o'clock. A half-empty bottle of sugar-cane alcohol on the bedside table. A used condom congealing against the foot of the bottle. *Like scar-tissue*, she thinks. Her throat is dry and she needs to urinate.

'You like this?'

'Get off me.'

'You like this, eh?' The hand moves down to her crotch, greedy and painful.

She sits up. 'You make me sick.' She pulls on a T-shirt and cut-off jeans, goes into the bathroom. There is a cockroach

85

sitting on her toothbrush. She knocks it off, washes the bristles under the cold tap, does her teeth and hair. Next door she can hear Ricard finishing the bottle of spirit. Screwtop scraping on glass.

'So. Are you going into town today?' His voice is languid, angry but too lazy to do anything about it. 'Felicia? Because you need some more stuff. Things. Unless you want babies. You want my babies, Felicia?'

She doesn't answer him. She can hear the chug of fishing boats coming back in. A radio talk-show in one of the adjacent rooms. The chatter is distorted through the wall. It sounds like frogs at night. A rhythm of noise, without words. 'You going to tell the old man today, Felicia?'

Noah. She had forgotten. A pang of guilt.

'Eh? He has no money to pay, you kick him out. You want me to kick him out for you?'

'It's none of your business, Ricard.' She looks at herself in the mirror; her mouth is downturned. It looks strong, but she has not been strong. She leans her forehead against the glass. When the man in the next room has fallen asleep again she walks back through, out into the yard, the sun hitting her square in the face.

'Hola, Felicia.'

'Felicia.'

'Felicia, look at this, you want some?'

It is one of the older fishermen, from the edge of town. He holds up a tuna in one scrawny hand. A beautiful fish, the colour of steel-wool, gills still working. It is too heavy for him and his arm is shaking a little, his brown grin gritted. Felicia wants to tell him to put it down, but she can't. 'Good eating. You want it, Felicia? Five hundred a kilo. Good eating.'

'Hola, Felicia.' It is the Brazilian. She tries to remember if he owes her money for his room. Then she is guilty at the thought. She nods. 'Euclides, good morning. What do you have?'

He opens a cast-net between his spread hands. All Felicia

can see is the flexing and folding of oversized fins, flesh mottled red and blue. She leans closer, trying to see.

The older fisherman tuts. 'Flying fish. Stew-meat. They don't concentrate, Brazilians. He was thinking he saw sharks all morning, this one. As if we don't know when there are sharks in our country. Too much drink, eh? Too much ganja. How much were you going to ask the señorita for those?'

'Four days' rent.'

There are dogs scavenging under the mango trees, digging for ghost-crabs. Felicia hisses at them and they run away sideways, stilt-legged, barking. She turns back. 'Two days'.'

He nods, hands her the net. The old Venezuelan lowers the tuna into his arms, cradles it, walks away without speaking.

'Thank you.' He smiles. His teeth are already a little rotted by sugar-cane. She smiles back.

'I hope they make good stew.' She wonders what he is doing here. In the middle of nowhere, in a foreign country; and why she sounds strong in her own ears. Taking his fish, leaving him his money.

It makes her think of Noah. She looks round.

He is up already, sitting under the concrete awning in his wickerwork chair. Not frowning but staring out inland towards the oil fields. He is wearing shrunken blue swimming-trunks and a torn cotton beach-shirt. There is something held on the table in front of him and Felicia shades her eyes to see. A pen and paper. She wonders how long he has been sitting there.

He doesn't look up until she is beside him. Hesitant, looking down. His writing is angular, leant back on itself. She frowns, translating the French. 'I had a terrible dream.'

He looks up. For a moment his eyes are wild and out of focus and she is scared.

He smiles. 'Felicia. What do I owe you, sex or money?'

Money, Noah. You know that. She doesn't say it. He is an old man. He deserves respect. She leans against his chair. 'Good morning, Noah. How long since you ate flying fish?'

*

87

Santa Fé, 16 May 1996

I had a terrible dream.

Ascension Day. There are no newspapers. The boats still go out. Euclides the Brazilian catches flying fish. Felicia cooks them in the hotel kitchen. The meat is good, sweet.

He writes slowly, pausing between sentences. Looking away. Inland is the see-saw of derricks over the hotel roofs. Felicia has hung her pans on a cashew tree by the kitchen window. They bang together in the sun and wind.

His eyes are tired. It is easier to look down at the paper, to write. The ink dries quickly in the hot shade.

They sleep in the holes of the reef, where the nets are no good. So Euclides is proud today. A handsome, honest, proud young man. I would like to see him old. Or to see him lie, I would like that. He holds up two flying fish for the tourists to see. Mister Eels from Room Five takes photographs. Children unfold the wings. Ribbed, like wet umbrellas.

I hate him because I am jealous of him. I am jealous because he has never fought a war. Imagine that, to have never fought a war. All his life, he has only had to fight for what he loves.

This is the dream. I am in Paris. The Île de la Cité and the cathedral over water and trees. I am young and clean-shaven. It is summer, 1946. I know this because there is no war in my dream. War came before and then later.

It is summer in Paris, and I am walking along the promenade with my only jacket over one shoulder. I am twenty-three years old, a soldier for four of those years, and I believe I am done with war. On the promenade there is the sound of women talking. Laughter catching in their throats, high and low. Like the voices of boys when they are about to break.

The wind smells of last year's burning and the Seine. It tugs at my jacket. I look back and there are men following, sixteen or seventeen years old, already they look like boys to me. It was not the wind I felt against me.

I feel for my wallet, the brown leather fold with my identity card, discharge papers, American dollars with their smell of cordite. It is still in the jacket. I can see the boy now, apart from the rest. Frowning eyebrows and the oily down of a first moustache. Still following. He is not much of a pickpocket.

I wait for them. I watch them come up to me. What can they do? I am not an old man, this is not Cassino prison camp or the siege of Dien Bien Phu. This is peacetime, my peacetime. I smile and stare at them. I am waiting for them to look away and go on under the trees and over the bridges.

'How much for three nights? In dollars?'

'In dollars? Twelve. For you both.'

He puts down the pen again, looks across the yard. Felicia is unlocking Room Seven for a tourist couple. Blond hair, checked shirts, matching purple backpacks. Seven is a good room, he thinks. Felicia must like them, they should take it. He doesn't call out to them. His mind is somewhere else. He picks up the pen.

They do not go. The pickpocket starts to shout. He is offended. I have embarrassed him here, on the Boulevard Saint-Michel, in front of the women with their new dresses and laughter. Is he hurt enough to fight? He never stops moving, shifting from foot to foot. Certainly he is angry and scared (what is he scared of?). He waves his arms and swears at me in Breton.

This is how people die. Angry and scared. It is the way their stories end. Sometimes it is also the way people kill. The boy wants to hurt me and I wonder why, and if he can. It seems trivial. My flat is not far. I apologise. I walk away from the boy with his aggression and wretched face.

At my door they catch up with me. What is the boy shouting? Why doesn't he leave me alone? I smile and apologise again. I put my hand out to his shoulder. To touch him, to show him how alike we are.

The other young men kick my legs away and hold me down. Together they are ridiculously strong. One of them hits the thief and he falls down. Why do they do this? Is it to make my killing look like self-defence? But this is only a dream. They are pressing something into the boy's hands. It makes sense only as a dream.

I call out again. He sits up and throws the knife. I feel the coldness of it in my chest, smooth between ribs. I am still alive. I stand up and reach for the black plastic knife handle. Now I will kill them if I can.

But they are running away, the young men, whispering. They hide my killer in their crowd. The sky goes red but it is only my eyes. I sit down on the hard pavement. I am starting to die and I cannot stop. I sit up in my old man's bed, alone in Venezuela, with the sweat cold in my hair and on my skin.

All morning this has stayed with me. Not because of the death. Because they wanted to kill me and I do not know why. I wanted clear reasons and to die knowing them. But there was no reason. I did nothing.

'Nothing. I want to deserve to die.'

'Noah?'

He turns, disoriented. 'What do you want?'

It's Felicia. He searches for something else to say, some civil word. But it's all right. He can see the white of her teeth.

'I want to know why you are out here talking to yourself.' She comes over, walking easily across the hot sand, not hurrying. 'What are you writing?'

He turns the pages over, weighs them down with his hand. 'Nothing. History.' He sighs, coming back to himself. 'A history. Of French cheese.'

'Really?'

'Maybe not. Maybe a history of French wars.'

'Really. You lying to me?'

He puts an arm round her waist. It is warm and solid against the skin and bones of his hand. He leans on her a little. 'Yes. I'm lying.' He tries to stand but his legs have seized up, he has been sitting too long. 'I'm thirsty.'

'What would you like? Beer?'

He waves her away. 'God, no. Rum, I want rum. With ice.' He watches her walk towards the beach bar. 'Golden rum,' he shouts after her. 'Not that white trash from the islands. On my tab, eh? Felicia?'

He sits back, distancing himself from the description of last night. The pen is still gripped in his hand. He looks at the tension in his fingers. The back-slanted writing on cheap lined paper. The pen.

It is from Hanoi, lacquer worn down to metal where his third finger habitually rests. He remembers picking it up on a house-search there. Indochina, the third year or the fourth, a war they still believed would be won. He laughs to himself, quietly, in the shade of a concrete canopy. He remembers with his eyes open.

The house of Mister Nguyen. French windows, Laotian incense-urns, a verandah with bell-beetles in a cage. He recalls walking through the echoing mahogany rooms with his uniform and American gun. Pen and ink laid out on a writing-desk. Just picking up the pen and walking on. Mister Nguyen sitting in the courtyard while they searched. Thin hands in his lap, reading Maupassant. The pages catching light as they turned.

He wonders what happened to him, after the war was lost. Today it seems important. There are Chinese characters etched into the steel. He has never been able to read them. He lets the pen go.

There is a tall glass on the formica table. Ice clinks in the yellow alcohol. Noah looks up, dazed. Felicia is talking to him.

'– do you think?'

'Delicious. Good.'

'Noah, listen. We have to talk about it. Can we? Tonight?'

'Sure.' He smiles up at her and then away. He's said the wrong thing. Has he said the wrong thing? He doesn't want to see her eyes. Her hand is on his shoulder and he reaches up and holds it. Against her skin his own is dark with veins and liver-spots. He doesn't want to see that either.

He looks out across the hotel's dirt courtyard to the beach. Euclides and Mister Eels are playing dominoes on a little table in the shade of a coconut palm. Beyond them the sea is blue under a blue sky.

He wants to tell her about the dream. About what he deserves. But he can't. He thinks of something else to say.

'Damn beautiful day. Good for a swim. Every day here is a good day to swim.' He drinks, closing his eyes at the cold sweetness of it. The alcohol reaches him almost immediately. A slow, uneasy excitement.

'Not today.' Felicia picks up a carton of cockroach poison and a broom. Noah watches her walk towards the guest rooms, unhooking the keys from her sand-paled jeans. *She looks tired,* he thinks. *Last year she looked better.*

'Why, you think I'm too drunk? Too old? Come with me. We'll swim to Puerto La Cruz,' he yells after her. 'Bring back the newspapers.' But Felicia is already gone. He sits back, alone with himself. The wicker creaks under him.

'Don't swim today, Mister.'

He turns at the voice. Screws up his eyes to see. Euclides is standing under the palms, a bottle of beer in his hand. *Listening,* thinks Noah. *Standing behind me, waiting. Like a pickpocket.* He smiles with anger.

'I saw a shark this morning. When I was out. Near by the reefs.' Mister Eels is squatting beside the young man, arranging dominoes in their box.

Noah pushes himself up. He looks round to see that Felicia is gone. Then he walks quickly across the hot clean square of sunlight, towards the shelter of the palms. His open shirt flaps against the tanned bars of his ribs. 'A rogue shark? Close in?'

Euclides nods. 'A hammerhead.' Noah leans back against the palm tree and the ridges dig into his skin. Painful and undeniable. It feels good. He smiles again.

'Well. It must be fifteen years since a hammerhead came in. All sharks are scared of hammerheads, did you know that? Why do you think that is?'

Euclides shrugs. Avoiding the old man's eyes. Noah leans forward. 'You know how long I've been in Venezuela, Euclides? Thirty-two years. I killed the last hammerhead here. Four shots in the neck. How about you? You've been here what – ten months now, double figures, eh?'

'The sea is the same where I come from.'

The Brazilian's eyes are strong. Not aggressive. Embarrassed of their strength. Of Noah's weakness. His hand is cold and he looks down. He is still holding the glass of rum. He knocks the drink back.

'Did it kill someone? Attack a boat? When you were catching flying fish like little birds?'

'I saw it. Hiding in the reef holes.'

'In the reef holes? Oh, it sounds big. Christ, it sounds dangerous. We have to kill it, yes? All the boats. A rogue shark hunt. It's been years. I'll get my gun. When are we going out?'

The young man looks away. 'Tomorrow.'

'For a hammerhead? A real man-eater? But – I see. The other fishermen, they don't believe you, is that it? Señor Flying Fisherman?'

He is shouting again. Euclides is walking away towards the shack of the beach bar, draining his beer, the bottle swinging in his hand like a weapon. He doesn't look back. Noah grins. The rum feels feels good in his gut.

'Are you going to swim?'

He turns round. Mister Eels is still standing, the domino box in both hands. He is wearing discoloured yellow swimming-trunks and a T-shirt printed with a faded slogan in Portuguese, BRAHMA BEER – TASTE OF CARNIVAL! He is frowning, the way he frowns when he plays dominoes, unable to work out the mechanics of prediction. A simple man, thinks Noah, and he feels another tightening of jealousy. The vigour of argument begins to ebb away from him and he looks out at the flat light of the sea.

'It's a good day to swim.'

'The fisherman says it's dangerous.'

'*Fisherman*.' He tries to be angry again but his voice is quiet, the force gone out of it. 'You make him sound like St Peter. He's a boy. He thinks there's a shark, he should ask me. He shouldn't tell me. It's too cold for rogue sharks.' It's not true. He sighs. 'The others don't believe him, do they?'

'He's Brazilian. They are Venezuelan. They don't trust him.'

Noah looks back. The tourist's burnt skin is still white around the eyes, where sunglasses have protected the pigment.

Pallid blue irises. Angry or wincing against the sun. Waiting for something.

Noah pulls a crumpled packet of cigarettes from his trunks, looking down from the other man's face. The lighter is jammed with sand and he has to shake it clean.

'You know when I had my first smoke? My seventieth birthday. I thought, what the hell? I am old now. I need all the vices I can get. In Vietnam they tried to teach me. But I was young. Like you. I was in Vietnam, did you know that? They are lovely people, the Vietnamese. Beautiful. They can sell anything. But I was proud of my body. Young and stupid.' When he finally lights the cigarette it tastes harsh and hot. He inhales, coughs, throws it away.

'Will you swim?'

He shrugs. A caricature Frenchman, scrawny arms lifted, thin shoulders hunched. 'Of course. I had a shit life. So now I swim. Every day. OK? Is that OK with you?'

He walks away, not wanting an answer. The sand hurts his feet and he is glad to reach the hotel. Pelicans watch him from the wooden pier as he stops to open the lobby door. It grates in the dust and he has to lean against it and push. The air-conditioning is a pleasure against his face.

'Buenos, Ricard.'

Felicia's man is behind the counter, watching a soap opera. He waves a hand without looking away from the screen.

'Noah. You well?'

'I'm always well.' He stands for a moment, watching the TV. Catching his breath. On the screen an old woman with dyed-blonde hair and a baby pram is standing by a blue swimming-pool. Noah can see the shadow of a cameraman on the water.

'It's a beautiful day. You should get outside.'

When he turns his head, Ricard's teeth show. A smile or jeer. 'Fuck off. In here it's always a beautiful day. I only go outside to piss.' His eyes are staring. Territorial. Noah is flattered by their aggression. If he could mention Felicia, he would. Just to feel the adrenaline.

Ricard looks back at the television. The pink tiles of the lobby are cool against Noah's bare feet. 'But it's a good day for a swim. Can I use your snorkel?'

'Two hundred bolívars.'

'You owe me a thousand.'

Ricard hisses irritation, 'Che! Do you want to talk about debts, old man? Are you here to pay your hotel bill?'

'We have a deal.' He means with Felicia. They both know that.

'Do you fuck her for money?'

'No.'

'*Deal*. You have no deal, Noah. You think we pay you to drink?'

He shakes his head, tries to smile. Something bangs against the formica counter and he flinches away.

'Take it. There are no real guests to rent it anyway. Only backpackers who are so poor they steal each others' clothes-pegs. When you come back, we talk about the money. Maybe we kick you out, eh?'

Ricard sits back laboriously, shirt pulling up over his belly. Noah picks up the snorkel and diving mask. He imagines this man with Felicia, the thick weight of him on her. The rubber smells bitter and chemical. He turns and walks away. He wants to feel the sea's weightlessness. The false vitality of his arms moving through water.

'Kill the hammerhead, you can stay another week.'

He pulls at the door, not looking back. The set lines of his face make his emotion look artificial, like a painted mask. He has to stop again outside, an old man crouched over in the heat. Someone is calling him from the beach bar. He looks up.

'Noah!' Felicia is standing by the wooden tables, waving something. At this distance it looks like a white flag. 'Your writing! I keep it for you.'

'No, no.' He swears in French. Raises one arm and brings it down, pushing her away. 'I don't want it. Get it away from me.'

She can't hear him. He turns and starts to walk down the

beach, away from the hotel and the sound of people. Felicia is still calling him. He ignores her, concentrating on his footsteps in the hot sand. Frowning up at the harsh scrub of the headland. The goggles bang against his leg as he walks.

He thinks of the hammerhead. Ten, eleven years ago. First the pelicans and dogfish, washed up on the beach in haloes of their own blood. Then the first man-eating. A girl-child from Santa Fé, Alia or Alicia, was it? He remembers the shark better. Skin like dead skin, long as two boats, its eye-stalked head seamed in the middle like an arsehole. Obscenely ugly. He had never killed a shark before. Only people.

When they were hunting he listened to the fishermen's talk. They kept him awake in the sway of the boat. Voices, stories. How no shark swims with a hammerhead, not even the great white. How the hammerhead can swim backwards, its head a tail. Not the biggest shark or the fiercest, but the one who never gives up. Smelling old blood in its long head, waiting and remembering.

They knew the stories. But it was he who shot it. Not talking over the chug of the engines. Watching. So that when the white bulk passed under them, Noah leaned over and fired the shotgun four times into the neck and dorsal fin. A year's rent, that had been worth. Paid for by the Rural Constituency of Santa Fé. He tries to remember how much he owes now. More than a year, less than two. But he has no money left. Felicia will take care of him.

The hiss of surf reaches his feet and he looks down. Without intending to he has walked diagonally down the beach's slope, to the sea's edge. Here the sand is cold and hard with water. Noah pulls off his shirt, struggling with it in the shore breeze.

He throws the shirt above the tidemark. It falls short and he has to go back for it. He carries it up the beach and leaves it bundled against a burnt-out oil drum, sheltered from the wind. Walking back he almost falls on the wet sand. He sits down in the shallows, pulls the mask over his head, bites on the snorkel's rubber mouthpiece. Then he just sits. Listening to the way his breathing hisses in the plastic pipe.

'Hi.'

He looks up. Above him is a tall young man with pale two-day stubble and a checked shirt. Coming up behind him is the second backpacker, wind catching in her hair. 'Hi,' she calls, and waves. Through the salt-stained glass they look faded, Noah can't make out their expressions. He pulls the snorkel and mask off, rubber tugging painfully at his white hair.

'Hello. You are Americans?'

'Yeah.'

'Americans.' He tries to think of something else to say, something better. 'Don't worry. I understand. It's all right. Later we'll have a drink, eh?'

They stand together, looking down at him. The girl turns away abruptly, shields her eyes. A formation of birds goes over, high up over the headland. 'Wow. Patterns in nature.' She shakes her head, grinning back at them.

The boy bends down, hands on knees. Embarrassed by his height. 'So. What do you do here?'

Noah shrugs. 'Nothing. I am old.' He looks away.

'You been here long?'

'Thirty-two years.' He takes out his cigarettes but they are already damp from the sand. He turns them in his hand, half-smiling. Enjoying the attention.

'That's incredible! Really? Why?'

'This is where I ended up. I don't know why. You don't like it?'

'Sure, but –'

'I ran away from war, and this is where I came.' He looks away from their surprise. He is surprised at the sound of his own voice.

'Which war –'

'Any fucking war. All of them.' He cuts the boy off and is surprised at himself again. 'Oh, Second World, Indochina. That's Vietnam. Cold War. All of it. Six years, eight years, eight more years. They liked me, they kept asking me back. I looked better then. I didn't smoke. My life was shit. So now I smoke.'

'You fought in Vietnam?' The girl is kneeling down now. Concerned, as if he might be rambling. He wonders whether he is rambling. He frowns.

'Not your Vietnam. Ours, France.' He presses his hand against his chest to signify possession, and the dream comes back to him. The knife a cold obstruction in him, where his hand is now. He stands up shakily, feeling his chest, the young people moving back from him.

'I like it here. I deserve it, you understand?' He thinks he is shouting. He puts the mask back on. They are saying something, he can't hear words, only their worry. 'And I am going to swim. Because every day is a good day to swim in paradise.' He bites on the snorkel and walks away from them. The water rises against him. He keeps walking out into the sea until he goes under.

He is surrounded by fish the colour of air bubbles. The water is warm against him in the shallows. Out to the left is the dark line of the reefs along the headland. He turns his head slowly to the right, where the sea-floor drops away, the Atlantic deepening to a solid blue. There is no sound except the tick and skitter of sand against sand.

Coral trees rise up towards him. He moves with the strength of his hands, drifting out along the line of the headland. There are flying fish between the corals, asleep on the sand, just as Euclides said. *Exocets*, Noah thinks, and the French name makes him think of war again. Ice freezing in his nostrils and tear ducts. The far north of Canada, Echo Bay Base. Alaska, where they could see Soviet troop-carriers across miles of ice. He kicks away.

The headland goes on down underwater. The reef slants away from him. He pauses, buoyant with air. The corals are larger here, brain-stems and cypresses growing massive in their salt gravity. Leopard eels slide through the passages and branches. A shoal of mackerel comes out of the blue and splits around Noah, glittering and round-eyed. The muscles in his shoulders begin to relax. His beard floats up in front of his face and he pushes it away. He grins, salt water trickling into his mouth.

This is where I came to be, he thinks. *Nothing is relative here. I am not old or poor. I have what I deserve. I don't deserve to die.* The point of the headland is up ahead, light flickering in the deeper blue beyond the bay. Noah waits in the crosscurrents, looking down between the rocks for shipwreck timbers or shells. *This is my sleep without dreams.*

There is a shell caught in a bank of seaweed, some ten or fifteen feet down. Noah can't make out its shape, only the dazzle of mother-of-pearl where the light reaches it. Something large and heavy. A conch or nautilus, the current moving it only a little.

He treads water, gauging the depth. A conch would be good to take back. Something to show Euclides and the tourists. A kind of proof. Something to give Felicia instead of money. She would like that, Noah thinks, and he owes her. Light winks between the movement of kelp fronds.

He exhales, sinking towards the rocks. The pain begins almost immediately, pressure aching in his ears. The water around him becomes cold as he falls, the headland looming up above him.

Better than money, Noah thinks. He looks down as he gets near. Lodged in the rocks is the white-and-tan disc of a nautilus. Broader than two cupped hands, the mouth empty and bright. But he can't turn and swim face-down, his body is too weak. The slowness of his descent is comic, it makes him smile. His lungs begin to spasm and he shuts his eyes to concentrate.

He reaches out for the curve of the shell and holds it. When he opens his eyes again the shark is there. Ten feet away, watching him.

He thrashes upwards. The mask pulls down across his face, choking him. He can't see the shark's movement, only the thick whiteness of its chagrin. The last air goes out of him in a muffled shriek as he breaks the surface.

99

'Help me!' The voice is old, garbled with water. Noah can barely hear himself. Something tugs at his shoulder. He lurches away from it, towards the headland. But his arms are exhausted, all the muscle has left them. He coughs at the acrid taste of sea-salt in his nose and the back of his throat.

He reaches the rocks and lets go of the shell, reaching out. He has to scrabble in the dirt, fingers catching in the sharp hill-scrub. He pulls himself up against their roots.

Then he is out. The snorkel is caught round his neck and he pulls it away. There is no sound on the headland except wind. He can hear the way he whines with fear. He looks around, staring, so that for a moment he recognises nothing. When he looks down, his legs are matted with blood.

He bends down to find the wound. There are black sea-urchin spines in his calves and the fronts of his thighs. The blood is already lessening, pinked by sea water. He looks out at the sea.

The shark hasn't moved. Noah can see mottled patterns across its back. The nose shaped like a missile, the ventilation-slits of its gills. 'Sand shark.' He whispers it to himself. Without the magnification of the diving-mask, the shark is less than three feet long. Its pectorals move gently in the current. Its eyes are quite still, fixed on nothing. As if it never noticed he was there.

He begins to cry, cursing himself in French. *Crétin*, *idiot*. The sobs are like laughter, then no longer like laughter. The old man's face is screwed up, tears running into his beard. He tries to wipe them away but his face is already wet with sea water. He tries anyway. He sits on the rocks until the blood and water have dried on him and he is shivering in the wind.

The nautilus shell is at the water's edge where it fell. He picks it up. The sun has dried the mother-of-pearl, the lustre is gone. The colours of the shell are dull with dust and erosion. He tries to wipe it clean. Then he stops.

He stands up. It's a long way back to the hotel and the people waiting there for him. He starts to walk, the shell cradled in both hands, so that it will not break.

The Memory Man
for George Szirtes

She is dressed as a waitress. She is running the fingers of her left hand over the knuckles of her right hand. Feeling her own movement through her skin.

'Anything to go with that?'

I look away. Next to me is an older woman with a pad and pencil, waiting. Long crimped hair, the same nylon uniform. I shake my head because I can think of nothing to say. She brings me my tea and leaves me alone. I sit and watch Mercedes as she serves the late-night customers. She speaks English with an accent like mine. I try not to stay too long or to attract attention.

This is not what I expected or where I expected it to happen. I have been looking for this woman for twenty years. And now I have found her I don't know what to do. She is still very beautiful. A lone pensioner comes in. He leans towards her as he speaks.

'Do you have our three Scotch eggs, love? For our tea.'

She looks up. Black skin, blonde hair, blonde eyes, a scar between the eyebrows like a frown. She points at the plastic menu on the wall. The old man cranes round. He has a fading cardboard name tag on his jacket: CAMDEN LIBRARIES HELP GROUP: ELDON EVANS.

'I can't be doing with that, do you not have our Scotch eggs?'

She shakes her head. He calls her a bleached hoor and leaves. It is three minutes and eleven seconds to midnight and the display glass is oily with steam and perspiration. I am the last customer. She doesn't recognise me. She leans against the end table, taking the weight off her legs. Her hair is not bleached.

I sit at my own Formica table with my hands closed around my cup of tea. I have already been here too long, watching her.

There is nothing left to do except talk to her. But I don't know what to say and I don't want to scare her. I sit and watch her living in this place we have both come to.

The Alba Fish Bar. I came in to get out of the rain. It smells of potato bleach and the cigarettes of stallholders from Chapel Market. The neon lighting is the exact blue of a pregnancy test. There is a fishtank in the display window, empty and scummed with dry algae. Where my hands have touched the table they smell of bleach.

Cod costs £1.95, rock salmon £1.50. The junior fryer microwaves factory peas in polystyrene dishes. At closing time Mercedes eats scratchings with vinegar, crouched avidly over the plate. I can see her teeth through the curtain of her hair.

She looks like a killer; it shows in a disfigurement of expression, a lack of warmth. No one seems to notice. The fryers stand at the chrome counter in their plastic straw hats and argue in low voices.

'Come on, Ev. Let me clean up now.'

'Wait.'

'Come on, Ev. There's just one more geezer.'

'Five minutes. Tuck your shirt in.'

The fryers call her Di, not Mercedes. I had almost forgotten that searching for her would lead to this. But I have never forgotten her. She is the only woman I have ever hated. I mean this not-forgetting in a special way. After all, I have never forgotten anything.

I must go gently. At five minutes past twelve I leave without talking to her. I spend the night in the King's Cross Scala Cinema, watching a cheap triple bill of science fiction films. The seats are warm and smell of hot-dog mustard and stage dust. I try not to think of her. My eyes are dry with concentration.

The next day I come back at noon and she isn't there. I order a piece of fish. It tastes of oil and refrigeration and I have trouble finishing it. A notice has been lodged inside the window above the fishtank: VACANCY FRYER. A number and address in White City.

I walk to Angel Underground and ring the number from a telephone shelter. A man with an island Greek accent answers. He is busy; he asks me to come tomorrow with my passport and papers. I have an interview.

I stay in a hotel behind Tottenham Court Road and sleep for several hours. In the morning it is hot again and my thin hair sticks when I comb it across my scalp. I walk to the business address. Twice I make wrong turnings. Around me London is grey as its name. When I arrive I am more tired than I should be, dizzy and sweating. The man who opens the door doesn't shake my hand.

He has the sour mouth of someone who worries about no-claims bonuses. His sweat smells of raw onions. 'Bloody diabolical ozone weather. Hot as Cyprus. Have you been to Cyprus, Rafael?'

'Not recently.' In the corner of the office, an electric fan revolves its head to face me. The man puts down my curriculum vitae and slicks back his hair.

'I have to tell you, my friend, I have never seen a résumé like this. You get around, don't you? You've got everything here except relevant experience.' He presses his soft palms against the desktop and stares at his hands. As if they are holding something back.

'Let me ask you a question.' There is a pepper mill next to his hands, orange plastic. 'Where d'you see yourself in ten years' time?' The pepper mill rests on a pile of dusty menus for the Alba Fish Bar. The office feels like a shut-down restaurant. Traffic hoots in the gridlock outside.

In ten years I will most certainly be dead. I think of something more appropriate.

'In your seat.'

The man smiles. His name is Tony Dumitriu. He owns the Alba Fish Bar. He is going to give me a job. The sun does dental work on his gold teeth.

'I like it,' he says. 'Eh? I like my fryers with a bit of life in them.' He's nodding and shaking his head, as if I've made a good joke. 'You're right, though. Chips is where I started out. Now I got my own place. First chips, then up to chicken, then fish, with the skill and responsibility of that kind of position –'

The fan turns towards me again. I close my eyes to preserve their moisture. I visualise my memory as a bare bulb in a room without windows. It clicks on. Perfect illumination.

In my head is an image of the office, more accurate than a photograph in its depth of sensuality. An eidetic picture. The diffuse window-light smells of turpentine. This is a side-effect of my condition; odours of light and shades of sound. A pastiche of senses.

My eyes swivel behind their physical lids. Total recall. Worked in wax, Tony Dumitriu sweats behind his desk. The menus are in front of him. There is an eleven-digit telephone number on the menu covers. I don't need to read it now; I have it like a photograph. Above the number is a picture of the Alba Fish Bar. Five fryers and waitresses lined up in front of an oversized stainless-steel extractor fan.

The late-shift waitress is the only one not smiling. Black skin, blonde eyes, blonde hair, a scar between her eyebrows like a frown. Her name is Mercedes Dolores Delaura Oe. Her skin tastes like sea salt.

I open my eyes. Only Tony Dumitriu and the rotating fan have moved.

'You don't mind me smoking,' he says. It's not a question. I watch him wet the cigarette with his damp fingers. He exhales. The fan drives swathes through the smoke. He looks at me properly for the first time.

'Rafael Tanigawa. I've never heard a name like that.'

'My parents came to Brazil from Japan after the war. Refugees. It was not unusual.'

'OK.' He stubs out the new cigarette and licks his lips. 'I want to give you the job, Rafael. But I have some queries. Forty-seven's a little old to be starting at the chip-frying level. You could be using some of this other – he waves at the paper – experience. Croupier, sign-painter, accountancy, yes? I won't pay you extra just because you're good with numbers. So let me ask you one last question: what do you want out of the Alba Fish Bar?'

I fold my hands in my lap. Not because I want to move them, but because my lack of motion is making the man uncomfortable. I put my head to one side, like a waiter, and smile. 'To be honest, Mister Dumitriu, I need the money now, I saw the advert now. I hope I can be honest.'

His face relaxes back into a smile. 'I'm glad you want to be. Makes me feel good. Well, I think we can arrange that. Any questions?'

'Do you know of a room to rent near the restaurant?'

Of course he does. He deducts the deposit from my first month's wages. I find my own way out.

The first thing I remember is not my birth but the dull sweet smell of rice and black beans, my mother counting out cruzeiro bills under a 'Pictures of Jesus' calendar. I am four years old. Since then I have forgotten nothing. Ten years later my voice broke. I understand very little about either of these changes. But they seem natural to me. I accept photographic memory in the same way I accept my voice.

I cannot face the walk back across London, so I wait by the side of the road for a taxi. It takes a long time. I have to lean against a fence topped with razor wire. I think about this, my first memory, until a black cab arrives. It is an effort to raise my arm.

I have a clear image of my memories. There is a small room with white walls, no windows, only a bulb hanging on its flex. When I click on the bulb, I can see the memories. Everything I recall is in this room, but the room itself I remember from no time. It may be like a dream. I have never had a dream.

It makes me more human, the not-forgetting. I have complex emotions. I am not sure if I have had a happy life. I have always been alone, except for Mercedes. With Mercedes I was part of something. Since then I have been a witness. My eyes are camcorders. My head is a cenotaph.

*

The room is two floors above the fish bar. The light is a fused gunpowder-blue through the blinds. I put down my suitcase. The bed has metal springs and a thin mattress. I sit on the bed and look around.

There are pictures taped to the ceiling, pages torn from fashion magazines by a previous occupant of the room. Most of them show women in underwear, Sellotape yellowing across their heads and feet. In the half-light, one of the women looks like Mercedes. She is wearing a velvet beret, pinned to her mane of hair. The photograph is turning green with exposure.

I pull the picture down. There is a topaz hat-pin in the beret. The topaz is shaped like a thistle-flower. I smell the photo. The hat-pin carries the odour of encrusted silver-polish.

When I close my eyes to blink, my memory unlids itself: *1982, an auction room, page seven of the catalogue. The hat-pin is made by the Englishman Charles Horner. It is more than a century old, one in a batch of fifteen. The catalogue page is stained with shadow and a sheen of light from high windows. Outside a starling sings like a traffic-light.*

All in the blink of an eye. It means nothing to me, this memory. I lie back with my eyes open, unblinking. This way the recollections are less exhausting. After a few minutes my eyes begin to water.

I lie still and wait for the night shift.

'Like dough.' I am talking to myself in the bare, empty room. Often I do this, to keep myself company. Few people have the capacity to talk with me as equals.

There is a freezer cabinet against the far wall. The heat of the long afternoon makes it hum, and there is a smell of half-defrosted fish like wet, sweet dough. I close my eyes and breathe in the smell, feel it. After some time I begin to sleep.

Memory interests me. My father worked half his life at the docks in Salvador, loading up oranges, unloading telephones. After a while he couldn't remember what he had begun to put on the ships or take off. It was Alzheimer's disease. By the end he could not remember how to eat an orange. I watched him try. His body still went on moving like my father. Fixed in its ruts. I watched him to see what was left, with memory gone. I stayed with him until I was quite certain.

There are only so many ways a foot or head can be deformed. There are limits. Memory is different. Deformity is normal. After my father died I kept case-notes in my head. In Buenos Aires there was a woman who could not remember tastes. In Russia there was a documented case of mnemonism, like my own. Close to Salvador, near where we lived, there was a girl who was born without memory. My mother told me that. I didn't think it was possible.

The daughter of a respectable whorehouse manager, she said. *He treats her like she might shit gold*. I didn't believe her until I met Mercedes in her father's kitchens, seven years later.

We ran away together, like lovers. Then in Rio we became lovers. It didn't matter that she was deformed, only that she couldn't admit it. I tried to help her, but she ran away. I have missed her so much.

'Mister Tanigawa? You in there? Er. Rafael Tanigawa?'

I open my eyes. The light is lower and cooler, it no longer smells of gunpowder. I have slept for some time. A woman is knocking at the door, light taps. I remember her voice. Her name is Terri and she is head waitress in the Alba Fish Bar. She has a slight northern accent. As I screw my eyes shut to massage the sleep out of them, I remember her from further back. This often happens. The world is smaller for me.

In my head there is a London hospital computer, eighteen months ago. I saw the console screen for several seconds as the GP scrolled through names. Terri registered HIV positive in a confidential test on blood donations. Like me. I wonder if she knows yet.

'Yes.' I unlock the door. I look at her in the way I would examine a dog, to see if it is in pain. She doesn't know.

'Oh, hello. You all right in there? Not knocked out by the smell or nothing? Better get used to that.'

107

She's wearing different earrings today. Green glass fish. When she shakes my hand the fish wobble like water tension.

'Getting ahead of myself as usual. My name's Terri, I've been waitressing here for donkeys' years, I was born in Hull and I'm a blinding pool player. Now you know my life story. I just came up to check if you were ready for your first shift. Five minutes, OK?'

'Of course.'

'Any questions you got, you just ask me, all right? About the Alba, I mean. OK?'

You have nothing to tell me, I want to say. Let me tell you about the Alba. It is never full or quite empty, there is just a slow drift of people in corners and people against walls. No one eats with other people at the hard Formica tables. The radio is half tuned in. The pensioners won't sit near the door. When they eat, they do it with their overcoats and anoraks still on. Nothing gets finished here, not food or talk or newspapers. The tiled walls are dirty-clean and no one touches them. It is a place for people to remember things with their eyes open. It is a place for people to forget when they step out into the street.

I don't say this. I think of something more appropriate.

'Is it Alba like Albatross?'

She shrieks with laughter. 'Buggered if I know, love. I'll ask Tony for you, all right? See you in five minutes.'

The restaurant is cool and empty. Neville the junior fryer is washing down the pavement outside. The doors and windows are all open and there is a slight breeze. Everton the senior fryer is sitting on a wooden customer's chair, stirring batter in a large tin bucket.

'This is Neville,' says Terri, pointing him out with her hand on my shoulder. 'Watch him, he's a right wide boy, aren't you Neville?'

'Yemun.'

'And that's Everton, he'll show you what to do. The other

waitresses'll be in when we open at seven. All right, Raff?' She lets me go.

The work is fast and loud, stainless steel clattering on white tiles. Everton is a large, shy man, uncomfortable in the role of teacher. He guts the great slab of a halibut, scissors off the gristly fins and dips the steaks from batter to vat in a smooth, stroking motion. He sweats only along the line of his lip. He keeps his mouth shut.

When I try to copy him the gutting knife slips, the flat running cold against the heel of my hand, and the fins fold away under the pressure of my scissors. It is important not to bleed here, I do not want to infect anyone. The chips in their three boiling vats are harder work, but easier. When the timing bells ring I haul out the straining nets and shovel fresh chips onto the hotplates, where they soften and hiss. By nine-thirty my forearms are liver-spotted with oil burns.

'They want trout.'

I look up, sweating and confused. Mercedes is waiting by the counter, order-pad in her hands. There is a symmetry in the way she stands, like the statues of saints in Salvador, which are really effigies of the Voodoo spirits.

Her voice sounds different in English. Her face is very still, mask-like, the leonine irises full around the retracted pupils.

'Who wants it?'

She looks furtively at her pad, back up. 'Table six.'

'Your English is very good,' I say. 'How do you remember it?'

Her face hardens, the hundreds of muscles drawing back against the bones. Then a familiar smile creeps back; malicious, charming. I feel love expanding inside me like indrawn breath and I narrow my eyes to hold it in. 'I remember my name too. Mercedes,' she whispers.

'I know. Your hair is like that of the slaves in Ouro Prêto, Mercedes, do you remember that story? From Brazil?'

Her face is rapt. 'Yes. They had to work in the gold-mines. The women hid gold-dust in their hair. The chapel crosses in Ouro Prêto are dusted thick with their gold. Do you know that story, too?'

I lean across to her. 'I taught you that story, Mercedes. Do you remember me? Do you remember what I promised you?'

She shrugs and smiles. 'Memories are sick. A sickness. They make you slow and stupid. Like fever. I make up whatever I want.'

'Yes. You have Korsakoff's syndrome, do you remember that? I took you to the doctors, Doctor Berman and Doctor Beller in Rio, to make you better. And you ran away from me. Do you remember this, Mercedes?'

The smile freezes slowly, while the light goes out of her eyes again. She frowns and looks down. The pad is in her hand. She reads it and looks up.

'They want trout. Table six.'

I reach closer, so we are almost touching. I can smell her breath; sweet and warm, like that of a wild animal. More than anything I feel love for her. And I am outraged that she is still alive. My opposite who sneers at memory, whose mind is in sags and tatters while mine is so close to perfection. I walk through crowds as powerful and invisible as an angel. But Mercedes is living proof that I am not.

'Do you remember your father, Mercedes?' I whisper.

Then Everton is beside me. Such a quiet man. I don't know how long he has been there.

'Tell them we got no trout tonight, Di,' he says to her. She purses her lips, squints round at the tables for a moment, then walks away. Everton takes the chip basket from my hands and gives them a slow shake in the boiling oil. He speaks without looking at me. 'You met her before or something?'

I shake my head, no. 'But she sounds Brazilian. Like me.' Everton sighs and massages his temple.

'Yeah, maybe. Sometimes she says Brazil, sometimes America. We call her Di. Like the princess, but she's got enough names for herself for all the days of the week. Just make sure she's got her notepad and she does fine. Are you married, Rafael?'

I shake my head again and he sets the strainer down and wipes his hands on his apron as he talks.

'She's got something missing. Not just memories, but other

things that go with remembering. Like sympathy. And a conscience.' He sighs. 'She's out of order. Do you know what that means? Like a, a machine or something, but also like she's wrong, different –'

'Solving the problems of the world, are we?' It's Terri. Her lips are pursed in a thin red line of disapproval. 'Only we got two trout and chips, two rock salmon and salads and a chicken and chips waiting for you to finish.'

'No bloody trout,' mutters Everton. He ducks back into the kitchen. Terri winks at me and eats a chip. Then the timing bells go on two chip-vats at once and I have no more time to spare until closing-time. I try and watch for Mercedes but I miss it when she leaves. I just look up and she's gone. It feels like homesickness.

'She remembers me.'

I'm talking to myself again. I've slept for three hours. From now until morning I will lie here and remember. The bedroom is half-dark. Outside the window a streetlight has come on. Sharp slats of white light wince through the blinds. They taste like sugar-cane alcohol.

My suitcase is flat on the floor next to the bed. A fillet of cold fried fish and a polystyrene carton of chips with a wooden fork sit on its top. But I don't want to eat now. I say her name softly until it stops making sense. Mercedes. I close my eyes.

My memory is a bare bulb swinging in a small dark room. It clicks on. I remember.

Kitchens. Air dusted with flour. The thud of dough against a wooden board. Beams of sunlight heavy and flat.

'In French we call those things shavings.'

I look up. The speaker is dressed in a cook's apron. She is a head taller than me, but I am not a tall man even at twenty-two. Flour ghosts her dark skin.

'For the evening light. The way it shaves the earth, eh?' She looks up, grinning, hands still working at the dough. 'But we have more words in French.' She shrugs, slams the dough against the board with finality, slaps her hands clean with satisfaction.

'So. Can you cook? Make bread? Do you drink, boy?'

Her name is Nestor. She is cook at the Pan-Americano restaurant in the Nazaré-side shanty town of Salvador, Brazil. She was born in 1899 in New Orleans. Her father died in the war between America and Spain. She has a bracelet round her left wrist made of tanned chicken-skin. It keeps ghosts out of her dreams.

She means nothing to me. She is a feature in one picture in the perfect zoetrope of my memory. This is part of what it means to be a mnemonist. I cannot forget Nestor, in the same way I cannot forget the weight of the sunlight, the yard door hanging on one hinge, the rustle of her chicken-bone charm.

It is 1970. I have come to the Pan-Americano to apply for a job. The owner of the restaurant is a Japanese Brazilian, a distant acquaintance of my parents. His name is Noboru Oe. In just under two minutes he will come through the door to the dining room yelling 'Bloody little shanty thief,' and haul me out through the yard door.

In less than a day he is dead, electrocuted in the metal-walled toilet cubicle of his own restaurant. I push that memory away: *Nestor the cook. Raw red coffee-beans in a cracked white basin.*

Noboru is not here yet. I turn away from Nestor, already bored.

There is a girl in the open doorway, watching me. The sunlight catches in the yellow tangles of her hair and silhouettes her nearly-black skin. When she steps in out of the backlight I see her eyes, which are almost the colour of her hair. In her left hand she is holding an old machete with a green plastic handle and a shining wet blade.

'Mercedes!' Nestor puts her hands akimbo. 'What have you done now? Oh my sweet Christ . . .'

Mercedes looks down. In her right hand is a headless chicken, blood drooling into its matted plumage. She holds it up, astonished. She talks in a child's gabble.

'I found it swimming in the river. I caught it like a river trout in my hands, tickling its belly. Do you want it, Nestor?' The cook is already walking towards her.

Sixty seconds have passed. For a moment I think, Time is running out. But of course it can't, not any more.

'What are you thinking of, girl?' She's bellowing into Mercedes'

face, bullying, scared of the younger woman and jealous of her beauty. 'Did I tell you kill a chicken, eh? Well did I? No. I'll tell your father, and this time he'll punish you. One of these days he'll give you a hiding. Jesus, the thing isn't even plucked. Give it to me.'

'I killed it for you.' She's looking at me again. Her face opens out into a lopsided smile. A beautiful expression of malice. It hurts me in a way I don't quite understand.

'I won't remember you. Do you believe me? Remembering is for fools.' I believe her. I feel an inkling of fear, instinctive.

'I remember everything. I can remember for you if you like. I promise. Only if you like.'

The smile fades, then comes back. Now it is an expression of happiness, not just a showing of teeth. Nestor swears in English at both of us. She pushes past Mercedes to the yard, throwing the first fistful of feathers out into the warm evening air.

'I can do anything,' says Mercedes Dolores Delaura Oe, 'because I am like a mad dog. People say so.' She growls in her throat and grins. 'Mad dogs don't remember. They do what they like.'

She is young, fifteen, but in the shanties this is older than in some places. As she comes into the kitchen she takes small quick steps like a capoeira dancer, the machete still in one hand. The other hand is smeared with chicken-blood.

'If you forgot like me, you could do anything you wanted, too.'

She kisses me. The shock of what she has said holds me still, but her hands are spreading out like wings. She doesn't close her eyes. I can taste her skin and the rhythm of her breath. Then she pulls back and licks her lips clean, rubs them together. She smiles.

'Remember for me?' and as I nod yes she backs away, dropping the machete, blinking the memory out of her eyes like sleep. By the time Noboru Oe opens the door behind me, she is looking away, down, entranced by the drift of chicken feathers that move in across the cracked and tiled floor.

I wake coughing. There is no blood, but my head hurts at the back, near the spine, and my arms are sore. I pull off my shirt. There are dark sarcoma bruises under my arms. I go out to the bathroom for a drink of water and then sit by my window, staring out so as not to blink, thinking.

Until I saw Mercedes I thought forgetfulness must be a kind of dying. When I saw her, how strong she was, I realised I could be wrong. To Mercedes, forgetting is a gift, sweet and kind. A freedom to act.

I don't believe this. I am the mnemonist. Humanity is nothing without memory. I am nothing if not superior.

And when I go down into the hot kitchens tonight, Mercedes will be there again, Mercedes who can dream anything, who has no nightmares. Who is like mad dogs, which grin and sweat with freedom.

I refuse to die believing this. She is one of the broken and the botched, one of the many. A danger even to those she thinks she loves. A cripple. And I will prove it to her. I have come here to do a simple thing; to remember for her what she has done and forgotten. Just as I promised.

'How could I forget?'

I sit up against the wall and eat the cold fish from the carton on my suitcase. It is light by the time I have finished eating. Fifteen hours until Mercedes arrives. I wash my face and shave and read Amado and Márquez and Neruda in the pages of my head.

It gets dark before evening, flat grey cloud building up over the brick walls and rooftops. Mercedes arrives late, just as the rain starts. The pavements outside hiss with it. Thunder falls like rubble.

There is only one customer in the restaurant, a plump female skinhead who sits with her back to the window, steadily eating four orders of chips. Everton restacks fish in the freezer-room. Terri and Neville argue about nothing until the rain begins. Mercedes stands by the end table for an hour, watching me as I wipe down the counters and cooking surfaces.

I wait for her to come to me.

She drifts over. 'I remember you. Rafael. Is that your name?'

I put down the cloth. 'Yes. We spoke yesterday.'

She shrugs. 'Maybe.' She reaches back, over her shoulders,

tying up tendrils of her hair as she talks. 'I remember you from a long time ago. We were lovers, no?'

I nod. She laughs, eyes bright half-moons. 'I knew it. I knew we were.' She leans towards me. 'We were married. In the cathedral in Rio. The stained glass made my white dress green and blue and yellow.'

'No. We were never married.'

'We were. You can't change it if that's what I think.'

I take her hands. My forearms are trembling. I am exhausted already. I am so sick. And she is so full of life.

'Listen to me. We went to Rio because of what you did in Salvador, to your father. We had to leave. And in Rio I took you to the doctors, to cure you. Do you remember that? You are not well, Mercedes.'

She is looking out of the window. Rain patters against the glass, catching light as it runs down.

She touches her forehead. 'They hurt me.'

'Yes. They gave you electric shock treatment. For a while you remembered everything. But you relapsed. I came back to the hotel and you were gone. I have been looking for you since then.'

She twists round towards me, fierce. Out of order. 'I can do anything I want. They were wrong, I don't want memory. I can dream anything.' She sneers, challenging. 'What do you dream?'

'I have never dreamed, Mercedes. I don't need to. My sleep is peaceful because I have nothing to learn. I know about your father. More than you know. Shall I tell you?'

Our voices echo in the tiled room. Terri looks over. 'Oy, what are you two jabbering on about?'

Without realising, we have been talking in Portuguese. I feel pain and look down. Mercedes is gripping my arms with her nails.

'I know better than you,' she says. 'My father is a New Yorker. He sells sports cars. Diablos and Jaguars. They cost too much for people like you.' I shake my head as she talks.

'Your father was a pimp and your mother was a whore.' She

punches my face hard. Neville laughs and slaps his thigh. The skinhead goes on eating, head down.

'Every night your father's restaurant was full of his whores. He was greedy and stupid, like my own parents. Then one day you killed a chicken, just for kicks. He was angry when he found out and he beat you, for the first time. It's all true, Mercedes.'

She is shaking her head, narrow-eyed, as if I am trying to sell her something rotten. I keep talking.

'So you did what you wanted to do. You followed him into the restaurant toilet and cut the wire on the electric fan in there and left it against the metal wall of his cubicle. The fire that started with his body burned down the whole restaurant. They say his ashes stank of shit.'

She slaps me again. I don't feel it. I'm smiling. 'You killed your father like you killed the chicken, Mercedes.'

She smiles brightly. 'But I don't remember.'

'That's why I am here. To remember for you. I promised I would. We are like two halves, Mercedes. I am your conscience, and I have come back to be with you forever.'

I find I have nothing more to say. At the periphery of my vision I can see Neville standing, Terri with her arms folded, the skinhead eating. I can smell the fumes of the chip vats, oil vaporising at boiling-point. Mercedes has the handle of the strainer in her right hand. The knuckles are white. She is crouched slightly against its laden weight, ready to throw. Her face is snarled around the nose and teeth.

'No. Oh no.' Tears shine in the wrinkles of her skin. 'Oh no.' Her tears soak together with her sweat. I touch her arm and it falls to her side.

'I'm sorry, my love. I am only here to help. Come here. Come.' I hold her. She hangs broken in my arms. It's a long time before she stops crying. The rain has eased off. Over her shoulder I watch a wasp drone in with its yellow cargo of vindication.

Brolly

'Why can't they play indoors?' says Rebecca. 'Why don't they just play on the damn computer till they drop? Isn't that what they're supposed to do now? There's satanists and god knows what in the woods, even when it's light. Foxes nailed up and hedgehog skins where the tinkers eat them. Ripped-up porno mags.'

'And no one gets raped in virtual reality, do they? Anyway, you know what they'll be doing in there. Safe as houses.'

'What'll they be doing?' Pam looks up at her husband, handsome in his casual holiday clothes. Who would've thought it, she thinks. Me and him. Let his kiddies get lost. All the more of Kent for me.

'Oh.' Kent waves his hands like a conductor, fetching up words. 'One of them has the brolly and a blindfold and has to get home. Tappity-tap, crashing into bushes. The others stop the poor bugger from falling down manholes.' He taps a knife against the dishes on the garden table. It chimes delicately on the translucent willow-pattern of the cups.

'We used to play a similar game when I was young,' says Lily. 'There was an uncle on the Dublin side of the family who was killed by a toothbrush. He bit the head off and it lodged in his windpipe. I suppose he must have been tipsy, don't you think? And the object of the game was to find an object that couldn't kill.' She smiles with her overbright dentures. 'Awfully difficult.'

'That's completely different, mummy. That's a theoretical game,' says Rebecca. 'And they do not all help, Kent. One of them spends the entire afternoon scaring the others sick.' She clicks open chrome-tinted sunglasses, puts them on. They effectively conceal the extent of her anger. She shakes her head and lights a cigar. The smoke is warm against her skin in the cold autumn sunlight. 'They should be indoors. Why are they so bloody violent?'

'I suppose they just make do with what they have until they find the words,' says Kent. 'Isn't that what we did? Heavens, there's nothing wrong with Brolly. Fine game, family tradition. Morally sound, too. Help thy neighbours and all that. You used to love it, Becky, before you got all those dear little responsibilities.' He looks down at the five children sprawled in the long grass. Rebecca's three, his two. Talking.

'You should patent it, love,' says Pam.

Kent grins. 'Absolutely. Make a mint.' He leans back in his wicker chair with a creak. 'There's something about cousins, don't you think? Family but not family. They might end up getting married and having monstrous children. Very interesting power politics. Mother, will you pass those sandwiches? The ones with the fishes in.'

'"Fish", and they're anchovies, Kent. Don't pretend to be ignorant. Here. I don't know what you mean about the children. What strange ideas you have recently,' says Lily. She moves with great care, since her bones are as fragile as the chipped and mended teacups on the table. It lends her grace. Her daughter and daughter-in-law watch her with benign envy. Little cows, thinks Lily.

'All the better to see you with, ma,' leers Kent, and Pam scoffs a laugh, cake crumbs tumbling across her chin.

'Pam,' says Kent, 'if you're going to laugh then do it properly, for Christ's sake.'

He turns away from his wife, from all the women, shielding his eyes against the sun. The children have finished their own picnic. Now they lie talking in a circle. Roman emperors, thinks Kent. Between them, the black spear of Kent's City brolly leans from the turf. Lily's red silk headscarf trails from the curved handle. Like a pennant. 'What are they waiting for?' Kent asks.

'Not noon yet, stupid,' says Rebecca. Her younger brother winces in his broker's shirtsleeves. 'Brolly game starts at noon. Don't you remember anything?'

Kent squints up at the sun, high above Lily's rambling limestone house. He hopes that Jeremy is Dog.

Pam peers down at the children. 'What are they up to now?' she says.

'Talking,' says Kent. 'Just talking.' Bargaining, he thinks. Raising the stakes. He feels a rush of adrenaline. Jealousy working outwards like a hormone from some small and twisted gland. Rebecca sighs, missing London, its isolation. The tea cools as they wait.

They lie in the sun and bargain to be Dog.

'Rachel just wants to help whoever's Mixie,' says Matthew, rolling down his shirtsleeves. 'That means it's between us four.' Pulls the shirtsleeves over his hands and begins to tear nettle leaves from their waspy stalks.

'Everyone can be Dog or Mixie. That's how it works,' says Jeremy. He rolls a cigarette from a horse-chestnut leaf. Its sap feels cold and sticky on his fingertips. He looks across at Karen, flat on her back in the sun. Black hair fanned and tangled in the thistles. 'No one changes Brolly rules.' Unrolls the flat green knife of the leaf. Rolls it again. 'We've got fifteen minutes till noon. And everyone gets a spliff if I'm Dog. I'll roll them up on the way and we can smoke them by the bird-bridge. Best Brolly ever.'

Matthew isn't listening, has wandered away. 'I'll be Dog,' he calls. 'A hundred nettle leaves.'

Red-cheeked, like a bloody cub-scout, thinks Jeremy.

'Fuck off, Matt,' says Karen. She turns her head towards the rape fields below the woods. Sick name for flowers, she thinks. 'Nettles are for kids. Last year was the cat-in-the-box. This time has to be worse than that. And weed's boring. Leonard's too young, anyway. He'll get stoned out of his skull and puke up.'

'But it'd be nice, in the woods,' says Rachel. She sits beside Leonard with her dress yanked down over her knees. If I help him, Jeremy won't make me be Mixie, she thinks.

Karen sits up. Graceful, like her grandmother. She pulls tares and thistledown from her hair. 'It won't be nice. Leonard'll fall down a rabbit-hole and we won't get to play until next year.'

Leonard watches his sister with bruised-looking eyes, washed-out face. I'm too big to fall down rabbit-holes, he thinks. He takes something out of his parka pocket and holds it in his lap.

'Let me be Dog,' he says softly, making it a question. He has been waiting to say it for three days. He holds the object in both hands, as if it is precious and delicate.

Like Dad's hand was in the hospital, thinks Karen, and looks uphill at her mother. She has put on her sunglasses, which means she is sad or angry. Karen hopes that she is sad.

'Whoever eats this can be Dog,' says Leonard. 'I'll eat it.' He is holding a Sesame Street pencil-case, floppy imitation leather. Big Bird and the Cookie Monster are eating the moon.

Jeremy swears and laughs. 'What's in it, fucking Smarties? Shut up, Lenny. I'll be Dog and we can all have a nice smoke down in the hollow, OK?' He stands up, brushes off his black jeans.

'I think Jeremy should be Dog,' says Rachel.

Smart little sister, thinks Jeremy, and: Look at me, Dad. I'm the king of the castle.

'What you got in there, little Len?' Matthew squats down by his brother. 'Sweeties?' He takes the pencil-case, feels its weight. Soft and dense, like a bag of frogspawn. He drops it at the thought, picks it up quickly. Unzips it carefully and wrinkles his face. Savagely, an animal's snarl.

'Bloody Jesus, Leonard, what is this shit?' Jeremy leans over to see. The case is brimful with an ivory foam, flecked with tiny threads of emerald. The threads twist slowly in the murk. Dying, thinks Jeremy.

'It's spit and greenies,' says Rachel shrilly, and bursts into giggles.

'No it ain't,' says Leonard angrily.

Karen comes over, bored. ' "Isn't", Leonard. Talk properly if you're going to talk. It's cuckoo-spit.' She sounds surprised.

The green larvae twist in their protective wombs of white froth. 'Loads of them. Where did you get them, Matt?' Her brothers both look at her guiltily.

'Me?' says Matthew. 'I've never seen this before. Never seen so much cuckoo-spit in my life.'

Leonard stands up. His grey hair brushes the bottom of Jeremy's bomber jacket. 'It's mine. I found it,' he says. 'I got it in the fields yesterday and the day before and I'll eat it. That's better than spliffs.' He darts a look at Jeremy, a tiny current of electricity. A threat.

Jeremy hoists the umbrella out of the ground, across his shoulders. Drapes his hands on it. 'There's no way you're going to be Dog. Who's going to be scared of you? What are you going to do, howl? You'll sound like a fucking poodle.' Matthew and Rachel laugh in their thin church-choir voices. 'No one can eat that crap. It's poisonous, otherwise the sparrows'd eat it. I'm the Dog. Now let's go to the bird-bridge and choose the Mixie.'

Leonard stares down at the pencil-case held to his chest. 'I'll eat it,' he whispers. 'If I eat it, I'll be Dog.'

Rachel puts her arm over his skinny shoulders. 'You can't eat it, Lenny. It's poison. You'll die. You'll go green like the little worms and then you'll die.'

Leonard throws her arm off. He watches the others with his sleepless owl-eyes. 'If I eat it, I'm the Dog,' he says.

'Jesus,' says Jeremy, too loud.

'Don't swear, Jeremy,' Lily calls from the hill.

They all look up at the people, high up at a white table and dark against the sky. Then Jeremy throws the brolly down and rakes a hand across the stubble on his cheeks. He remembers last year. The cat-in-the-box. They had caught it and hidden it by the bird-bridge, starved it for two days. Karen had almost put her hand in but the animal had hissed like an adder in the scratching and darkness. Jeremy had done it, so he had been Dog. It didn't hurt because the day before he'd closed the cat's mouth with chicken-wire, round and round. Afterwards he'd shot it in the rape fields. It took seventeen shots with the air-rifle. Red blood in the yellow field. Got to be the maddest, he thinks.

He looks down at the thin little boy with the Sesame Street pencil-case. 'I think it's poison, Lenny,' he says softly, 'but go on and do it. You might go blind like the rabbits with myxomatosis, with the moony eyes. The Mixies. But if you're alive, you can be Dog.'

Leonard kneels down, like in church. Matthew crowds in behind him. He looks down at the pencil-case. The Cookie Monster leers at him with a crazy grin as he pulls debris from a blue cookie-moon. Leonard brings it to his lips and thinks, Is it poison? He closes his eyes. It doesn't seem important. If the poison is slow, he can be Dog first. He begins to drink the warm, bitter fluid in swift, deep gulps. Smells its decay, three days old.

'Oh my God,' whispers Karen. She gazes down at her little brother with a smile on her lips. Rachel sneers with disgust. It is over in a few seconds. Leonard leans back against Matthew's thighs.

'Are you OK?' says Matthew. 'Lenny? What was it like?'

Like poison, thinks Leonard. He tries not to cry. A sourness like grass-blood stings his guts. He draws a breath and feels it shudder in and out, the body's reluctance to accept it. There is a rushing in his ears like a strong wind in the heavy trees of summer.

The cuckoo is a monster, he thinks. It kills its cousins and hoots with laughter. Its heart is rotten with green worms and it spits them in the fields. Birds fall dead from the sky when they eat the cuckoo's spit.

'Don't fucking die on us, Leonard,' says Jeremy, high above.

Leonard's belly contracts, his eyes fly open. He rolls forward onto all fours and vomits into the long grass. Hears Rachel laughing, laughing.

Karen pulls a tiny lace handkerchief out of her denim jacket. She wipes her brother's mouth with it. 'How are you feeling, soldier?' she asks.

Leonard staggers up. 'I'm Dog, ain't I?' His voice is clogged and nasal. He gives a sickly grin.

'You puked it up, Lenny,' says Jeremy. He shrugs. 'Maybe if you'd kept some down, but you spilled your guts. There's nothing in you, so you didn't eat it. Sorry, mate.' He stands up and stretches, the brolly in his upraised hand.

Karen walks up to him, too close. The soiled lace is balled in one fist. 'You don't bloody well decide, Jeremy. We all do.' She looked better last year, thinks Jeremy. When she was Mixie. He smiles brightly. Fox-teeth, like his father's.

'Well then, we'll have to vote on it, won't we?' He points the umbrella at Leonard. 'How many for this sick little prick?'

Rachel watches, braiding her hair, uninvolved. Matthew raises his hand until he sees that Karen has turned away. He lowers it, wipes his nose self-consciously. Karen kicks at a bank of cow-parsley and feels the anger build inside her. She wants to leap on Jeremy, scratch out his eyes and she may, in the woods. She knows Leonard is too weak to be Dog. She looks away from him, towards the bracken and the gloom of the pines.

'That's that, then,' says Jeremy to Leonard. They have been left facing each other. The older boy looks briefly up the hill, then takes out a packet of ten Benson & Hedges. Lights up, blue smoke drifting up towards the sun's apex. 'Next year, yeah? Benny Hedgehog?'

Leonard takes one miserably. His hand shakes a little and he tries to hide it. The heavy tar numbs his throat, burns away the cold poison. 'Yeah. Next year. Thanks.' He tries to smile but his inarticulate white face only grimaces.

Jeremy looks at his watch to hide his distaste. 'One minute to noon!' he shouts.

Matthew jumps up, shocked, and grins. 'Race the lot of you,' he calls. 'To the bird-bridge!'

Rachel screams and runs after him. Jeremy puts out his cigarette on his heel and smiles at Leonard. 'Come on then, you nutter.'

He jogs towards the bracken. Leonard stands, the excitement

rising inside him. Brolly, the only game that never changes. He sways a little.

Karen grabs him from behind. 'Come on, Leonard. Race you!' and he does. Into the echoing cave of elders and beeches. The world is fragmented with tears but he blinks and it comes together again. He smiles. Over the woods their shouts and calls reverberate and vanish.

No One Comes Back from the Sea

December

' "Sing me one of your songs, commanded the Captain as they drove off together, with Bumpy at the back, licking Noddy's ear every now and again. So Noddy sang.

> Here we go,
> The Captain and I,
> Riding on land
> That is nice and dry!
> The sea is wet,
> And terribly salt,
> Though I know of course
> That it's not its fault.
> The waves are enormous,
> And when they break –" '

Laughter outside. The slam of a car door. When I try to stand up my legs have gone to sleep. I shift on the bed and the blood prickles back into its vessels. It's too dark to read but I know this story by heart, it's always been the twins' favourite. I can't see a thing except their hair, white on the pillows like sand on a beach at night. The screen saver too, a moving light on the corner desk. Fish eating fish. There's worse places to be than this. But I've lost my place. Anywhere will do.

' "WUFF, WUFF, WUFF! Bumpy rushed to the front gate – and there was little Tessie Bear with Big-Ears! They had heard Noddy was back. How they hugged him, and how his head nodded making his bell jingle loudly!" '

More laughter outside. A man's voice, then a woman's voice, high but throaty, familiar as salt. I stop and listen for a while.

'No. No! *No*. Really not. Ring me, though, will you? Page me, e-mail me, fax me. Fax! Goodbye. Bye.' She's whispering now. The kiss rasps like a match. A front door clicks open and shut.

It's ours. 'Dan, are you home?'

I put my hand in my jacket pocket, feel the letters. Six of them. Final demands. Tomorrow or the next day, the whole house will stop like a worn-out battery. I can't tell her. I could do with a drink.

'Dan. DANNY!' Plastered, listen to her. Standing at the foot of the stairs, bawling. I've got some catching up to do. The bed creaks. 'Daddy, you didn't do the necklace bit.' Ah, bollocks.

'We're almost there, love. Right. "Oh! A pearl necklace! Oh, Noddy, NODDY! For me! Goodness, I never in my life thought anyone would give me such a lovely necklace. I'll put it on."'

The bedroom door opens in a flood of light. She leans there, a cup of water in her hand, hair like glass fibre. Her face is dark, though. I can't see what she's thinking. Then she leans her head to move hair off her face and I see the slackness of her eyes and mouth.

'Have they been OK?' She doesn't whisper. June opens her eyes, yawns.

'They were sleeping like babes until you came in.' She folds her arms, balances the cup against her breasts.

'Gee, thanks. Am I supposed to feel guilty?' She's not looking at me. Her eyes are on the screen saver. The little fish swim faster than the big fish. The big fish have orange teeth. I sit back against the headboard.

'I can't tell you what you're supposed to feel.'

She snaps back fast, 'Don't be smart, Dan. I just asked if they were OK.'

'They're fine, Julia. Tickety-boo.' She sighs.

'Fine. Say goodnight to them for me, eh?' She shuts the door behind her, but carelessly. It swings ajar.

One of them shifts under the duvet, whispers. 'Beautiful shells, Daddy.'

'Shells, yeah. Sorry, pet. Almost there. "She looked sweet in it, and Noddy was very pleased. Then he gave Big-Ears the sack of beautiful shells. For your garden and mine, he said. And some for Mr Plod too – to put round the edges of the flower-beds.

' "Wonderful! said Big-Ears, astonished. But what was it like, Noddy, at sea? And where's your ticket back, Noddy? Can you tell me that? Because no one comes back from the sea." '

'May, are you awake? Eh?' Page-hiss, white falling across white. A simple movement doing complicated things. '"Hurrah! Hurrah! Hurrah! Three cheers for Noddy! Two cheers for Tubby! One cheer for Bumpy! Hurrah! Hurrah for the Captain! Hurrah for everybody! The End." G'night May, night June.' Whispering now. 'Love you to death.'

'Night, daddy.'

'Goodnight, daddy. Goodnight.'

November

I open my eyes and the air smells of classrooms. I've had this dream more times than I care to count in the last six months. A going-back-in-time dream, trying to make things better. Always a little different, always the same stars: me, Julia, the computer, the twins, the train. They'll all be in here somewhere. A small pantheon of death gods. I close my eyes and wait for someone to say something.

' "Time takes a cigarette"?'

'What?'

'Like in the song. You know, Bowie? Oh, Dan-*ny*.' I concentrate on her skin, how her neck glows between the furl of her school shirt. She's so beautiful. Was. Is. And I'm the Four-Eyed Paddy Git again. My trousers are too short. I get nervous when she's around. I get nervous quite a bit. My hands smell of her hair and Star Wars bubble-gum cards. I try and keep that for when I wake up.

'So? Have you got one?'

'What?'

'A fag, Dan! Jesus.' I know I look shocked.

'But we don't smoke.'

'How would you know? Anyway.' She looks off towards the science buildings, folds her legs. Hiss of cloth against her thighs. She turns back to me, frowns and smiles. It makes my stomach lurch. I must be dreaming teenage hormones. 'What do you want to be today?'

This was one of our games. Something we had in common then. 'A computer games programmer. Ace, that'd be.' When I grin it makes my glasses slip and I have to stop grinning and push them back up.

'*Ace.*' She tuts. 'I'll be a photographer and a magician.'

'You can't be two things.'

She kisses me. So fast, a quick little sigh of a kiss. While she's up close, she says, 'I can be anything.' Then she stretches and sits back. 'What do you think is the most important thing in the world, Daniel?'

It's a catch-out question. She's going to show me up again. I don't mind, though. I shrug up scrawny shoulders inside my worn jumper. 'Computers. They're cool. One day they'll do everything. Drive cars and have babies even, I mean' – Christ, I'm blushing in my sleep – 'deliver the babies. Like doctors.'

'Brr-brr.' Julia makes a game-show buzzing sound with her lips. 'Wrong. It's miracles because they can happen anywhere and do anything.'

'Then there must be miracles in computers, too.'

'Yeah, like what? Passing maths CSE?'

'I don't know, but you said –'

'You're so stupid, Danny! I was joking, all right? There's no such thing as miracles. Ha!' She jumps off the wall, dusts herself down. She's won again. Losing scares her too much to lose. I feel a shiver of anger.

'This is just a dream, Julia. I know what's going to happen. The twins catch a grasshopper on the yellow platform line. I'm buying you a paper from the stand. Are you listening to me, eh?' I'm shouting it. 'The grasshopper jumps and the train door opens before the train stops. It takes no time at all. It's all done with, now.'

She straightens, looks at me, begins to cry. She's taller now, heavy-hipped, standing with one hand supporting the pregnant swell of her belly. Twins. Behind the wall a train rumbles closer. Click-clack click-CLACK. I can't turn my head. Julia wipes her eyes and starts to walk away. I stand up on the wall.

'I'm sorry. Stay, Julia! The twins are coming back soon, I promise, you'll see. The computer will bring them back, because there are miracles in computers too. Don't leave me with the twins, Julia. Please stay.'

She doesn't turn round. I sit down again. The bell goes for third period. The train sounds its klaxon, a long low hysteria. No one can hear me now.

'The twins are coming back. Please stay.'

October

'Daddy, will you play Beanz with May?'

'Not right now, love. Give me five minutes, eh?'

I always loved the smoothness of the computer screen. Different from a TV, because of the possibilities. I can make such wild things happen behind this thick water-grey glass. The keyboard, too, the sound of it. Rhythms helped after the twins were killed. Anything mindless – cooking, walking, typing. They helped me think not to think. I run my fingers across the solid plaques of letters and numbers. Shift and Enter click like dice.

It always smelt of children in here. Even while the twins were gone. Especially then, actually. Milky sweet. On the floor below the window, May and June are doing a jigsaw puzzle called Beanz. It's of baked beans and it has a thousand pieces. The twins seem to love it. They never get bored. They never even ask if they can leave the room. As if they just know they never can.

This is what I do. If I ever went out now, and people asked me 'What do you do?', this is what I'd have to say. I sit in the bedroom of my dead children while they play games beside me. I surf the Net on a computer that has its power switch welded permanently on. I watch my children fade literally while my wife and I fade virtually and I wonder what to do about that. And I wait for my wife to come home.

I look up at the window; not dusk yet. She'll be gone for hours yet. I think she might be seeing someone else. We survived our children dying but we can't get through their coming back. I sit, one hand loose at my side, the other clamped to the mouse. I start to surf the Net.

The first Window I enter is a 'chat room'. Someone called Pharmer Gyles (www@worm.farm.co.cymru) claims he's found an anti-ageing gene on worm farms. He's trying to sell the copyright to three other Names. I sit back and watch for a while, then Exit and roam.

When I was a kid I dreamed of this. It's magic, the way I make Windows transpose and overlap. I can control all of it. Chat rooms, texts, graphics. Julia hated it until I showed her how to do it, back in the summer. Then she was mad about the freedom and chaos of it. All the New Age mystic stuff. For a while.

There's a tinny electronic trumpet call and a window appears on the top of the stack. A private room, a one-to-one talk. I could make it go away. My hand waits spidered over the mouse.

WEBSTER? YOU THERE?

YES.

GREAT! DID YOU GET MY MESSAGES?

I DON'T KNOW. I DON'T KNOW WHO YOU ARE.

MUCHOS APOLOGIES. AMY NAKAJIMA FROM ANCHOR-AGE UNIVERSITY? www@anchor.ouija.com. FROM THE INTERNET OUIJA, REMEMBER?

WEBSTER?

'Daddy? May's thirsty again.' It's June, tugging my left hand. She pulls the fingers apart, tries to braid them. 'Hold on, June,' I whisper, 'Daddy's busy.' I don't take my eyes off the screen. I type.

YES.

IT'S JUST YOU LEFT YOUR ADDRESS AND STUFF ON THE ENTRY FORM, AND THE NET OUIJA WAS MY DISSERTATION

PROJECT. 'PAGANISM AND SOCIOLOGY'. DEADLINE'S IN TWO WEEKS, (ARGHH!!)<: I REALLY NEED TO FIND IF ANYTHING HAPPENED. SO MANY PEOPLE TOOK PART, BUT

HOW MANY?

CLOSE ON A MILLION. ALL OVER. GLOBAL OUIJABOARD, WEBSTER! AND I'M GETTING SOME PRETTY AWESOME QUOTES ABOUT RESULTS. THINGS YOU WOULD NOT BELIEVE. ACTUALLY, I DON'T EITHER. THAT'S WHY I MAILED YOU. THE NET'S SO FULL OF ODDBALLS. I NEED AN UPRIGHT CITIZEN. LIKE YOU. A GENUINE PROGRAMMER! IS WEBSTER YOUR REAL NAME?

NO.

WELL CAN I HAVE IT?

NO.

OK, NO PROBLEMO. I'VE GOT YOUR WORK DETAILS. HERE'S THE KEY QUESTION, WEBSTER: DID YOU EXPERIENCE ANY RESULTS FROM TAKING PART IN THE FIRST INTERNET OUIJA?

'Dada-*da*ddy, I'm thirsty.' She's jumping up and down on my foot. I Exit from the private room, Exit the Net. A screen saver comes on; flying toasters bumping into fluffy clouds. My heart's still going too fast. I haul the twins into my lap as I spin the chair round.

'Aha! A thirsty girl! And what would you be thirsting for? Would it be bird's-nest soup?' Their bodies are cold as refrigerated meat.

'No.'

'Would it be borscht?'

'No.'

'Could it be orange juice with ice in?'

'Yes. Daddy, what's borscht?'

I go down to the kitchen and crack three ice-cubes into each glass. May's glass has elephants on it, June's has giraffes. It's so good to have them back. My chest aches with it, so that for a minute or two I have to stop. Arms pressed against the counter, head down.

September

Julia took this one four years ago, back when she was into Incan mysticism. Our Neo-Hippy Trail days. It's of a mountain town, one cobbled street with train tracks narrowing to vanishing point in the right-hand corner. Two women in black walking into that distance, already small.

The houses look like Spain but in the foreground is a postbox-red train carriage, rusting up on the tracks, and painted in gold lettering it says FERROCARRILES ECUATORIA (SEGUNDA CLASE). The twins are standing in front of the carriage, arms at their sides, smiling, shy. Their heads don't reach the top of the carriage wheels. This is the last photo we have of them before the crash. The train carriage looming behind them.

It was in June's My Little Pony travel-bag, I don't know how it got there. Julia found it when we began, month by month, clearing out the twins' bedroom. At the time it seemed like a message of some kind. That seemed logical. There were signs of death everywhere back then, echoes of the twins. Ghosts and auguries. Nights when I couldn't sleep I used to just sit with this photo, the PC and the Anglepoise, looking for information. Writing it all down. Saving it.

For example, why aren't I in the picture? I remember seeing Julia standing in the doorway of the town bank, under a cast-iron awning, camera blotting out her face. So what was my perspective, could I see the twins at all? One of them, June I think, is looking off to the left instead of at the camera. What does she see up there? Is that where I was? Was I looking back at her or was I thinking of machine code and new software designs?

Then there's the fifth figure. Under the chassis of the train carriage, crouched between the iron girdering of suspension and the black radius of a wheel. White trainers, dark hair, small as the twins, with something cradled in its arms. How many times was it before I noticed this hidden fact, the shadows resolved into a face? Many times. Did I see it on the day? And what is it holding so carefully? What does it feel, caught there on film in that secret place? I can see the whites of its eyes. So close. It looks terrified. It terrifies me.

It's just a snapshot. A coincidence. There are no miracles. June is not looking up the rusted tracks. Nothing is coming that she could have seen.

August

'Do you think they're OK?'

I'm down on my knees in front of the PC, injecting Super-glue into the gaps around the power switch, when Julia comes in. She watches the twins as if they were patients on a leukaemia ward. My hands are spongy with sweat. Autumn never used to be like this.

'I don't know. Why don't you ask them?'

'They're . . . pale.'

I stop and look. May is standing in a path of thin sunlight, singing a TV theme tune, lost in her own world. The TV's on behind her with the sound turned down. I can see it through her chest, a movement of pink light. Like a bare bulb held against fingertips. I turn back to the computer.

'*Pale*. Is that what it is?' I'm on the edge of laughter. I take a deep breath. 'They've been like that since last month. Haven't you noticed, love?'

She doesn't say anything, just lights a fag. Bad for the computer. She should worry about that. 'Dan?'

'What.'

'What if there's a powercut?'

'For fuck's sakes.' I stop myself, sigh. 'Then the PC would shut down. For hours, not seconds like last time. All right?' Now the switch is welded to the main casing, permanently powered. With the screen saver on all the time it should be fine. I move over to the wall socket and squat down, start on that.

Julia sits down on June's bed while the girls get dressed. She doesn't help them and they get stuck with their new shoes. She doesn't come in here much anymore and they can't leave the room, so she doesn't see them a whole lot. I don't see her a whole lot either. She goes out most nights. Gets away.

May goes over and stands in front of her, solemn and almost albino-blonde.

'It stings, Mummy.'

'What stings?' Harsh voice. Waiting for the punchline.

'The sting. It stings.'

'I don't understand.'

I put down the tools and look at them. May leaning forward, Julia flinching back.

'I don't know what you're talking about, June –'

'May!' I tread on the glue as I stand up. It instantly hardens yellow against the bedroom carpet. 'It's May. Jesus, do you not even know your own child now?' She's up and running, pushing me back against the wall. Hissing.

'No, I don't, Danny. I do not know my own child. I don't understand what's happening.' There's a little quiet while we breathe. I shake her off, stare her down.

'A wasp got in this morning. It's the first time she's been stung. That's what happened. That's what she's trying to tell you.' Hair hangs down around her face. It looks like she's grinning when she cries.

'That's not what I meant, Danny.' Whispering tears. 'You know that's not what I meant.'

'A miracle, my love. That's what's happened. A computer miracle. Our children came back. Aren't you happy?' When she starts to shiver I go forward and gather her in. Hold on to her tight. Behind her, June has just learnt to tie a bow.

July

'Night, Mummy.'

'Goodnight. Will you give your dad a kiss too?' Their skin is warm and smells faintly of milk. Just like always. May has a

99p price sticker hidden in her hand and they press it against my hair, giggling, the three of them, Julia's flank warm against mine. After a bit she sighs and I let them go and stand up and yawn.

'Fancy a bite to eat?' Julia says. I nod, grin. She comes up, kisses me. 'Then I'll get a bit of what you fancy.' She quietly opens the bedroom door.

I stand in the half-dark, full of happiness like an open bottle. I can hear them settling down and I want to hold them again. Then the PC screen saver catches the corner of my eye. It's been on for ages, I think. Weeks. Ever since the miracle. I've been so wrapped up in the twins coming back, I didn't even notice. I walk over, switch it to shutdown and click it off. Its light narrows to a median line and winks out.

I turn round and start walking towards the bedside light before I see they're gone. The bedclothes are flat, rumpled slightly by the vacant impressions of their bodies. I start screaming. Beyond the weird high pitch of my voice I can hear the sound of Julia belting up the stairs. So fast it sounds like she's falling. The door slams open and I'm scrabbling at the computer, still screaming.

'What? Oh what – Dan, please tell me what –'

I can't tell her. I don't know. The PC powers up. I'm whining now. The main menu comes on in a flare of light, multicoloured icons in a blue field. Nothing but work folders and the twins' games. Julia's arms on my shoulders, shaking me off balance. She's shouting but I throw her off. I drag the mouse across its table-mat until the arrow is on the games file. Double click to open.

'Dan! What have you done?' She's bellowing in my ear. More pain. The games come up, icons strewn untidily around the window. A box of children's toys. Rubix Conundrum, Street-Fighter II, Desktop Invaders. I start to cry. 'They shut down. I didn't think. They just shut down –'

'No. That's not fair.' Her voice has gone dead. Her hands against my back. 'Oh God, Daniel –'

Face pressed there. Wetness. I jab the arrow up to Exit. Back on the main screen I start double clicking randomly on work files, Freelance A, Freelance B, Internet.

Internet opens up. In the middle of the box is a ringbinder icon, WEBSTER. I pull the arrow across to it. My hands are shaking so that the mouse quivers on its mat but I line it up eventually. Open the icon.

'There!' Julia stubs her finger against the screen. There's an envelope-shaped icon, one of many in the window. This one says INTERNET OUIJA. 'There's nothing in there,' I say, but I'm moving the mouse already. It clicks open.

A small box-menu comes up. There are two icons, little clock faces, counting down to zero. I don't know how they got here. I double-click on the one marked MAY and the bed creaks. I feel Julia push herself up and round. She sobs. Somebody starts to cry.

June

'What's this? An index?'

'That's right. All you have to do is double-click where you want to go. Any preference?'

'Um.' Greenish light spills across her face. There are a lot of lines there that weren't around four years ago. She still seems young, though. Something about the way she holds herself. And I shouldn't be thinking about the twins, tonight of all nights. Twelfth of June. Deathday.

'What's Lovebytes Anonymous, then?'

'Well, my guess is that it's some kind of on-line trainspotters' house party. But I could be wrong.'

'We'll give that a miss. Am I squashing you?'

'No, no. I'm quite comfortable, thanks for asking.' Comfortable is what we're like these days. Four years ago tonight I felt like I'd died twice. But the days kept coming. We've kept each other going. Julia was talking about starting work again today. Updating her portfolio. 'Are you putting on weight?'

'Mind your own business. Internet Ouija! What's that?'

'I don't know,' I say. I kiss the back of her neck. 'Why don't you try it and see?' The keyboard rattles. Only her second lesson and she can type with two fingers. She sits back against me.

'Oh, this is interesting. Look. First ever Internet Ouija. We just turn up at midnight GMT and use the mouse. What time is it now?'

'Almost that.' I read over her shoulder, DO YOU BELIEVE IN COMPUTER MIRACLES? 'Would you like a drink while you're ouijing?'

'Wine. Please.' She gets up and I go downstairs while she types in a questionnaire. I can hear her talking to herself from the kitchen. Then it stops. I look up; three past, but the kitchen clock's a little fast. Julia yells from upstairs.

'Dan! Quick, it's working, hurry!' I jog back up the stairs with a half-corked bottle to the children's room. The spare room. The mouse revolves slowly under her hand, leaving a groove in the mat.

'Don't push so hard, will you?'

'I'm not! It's the mouse –' Words and binary code flicker across the screen. The keyboard starts to ripple like a pianola and a complete sentence forms in the centre of the console. I walk forward, lean towards the words.

MAY'S THIRSTY AGAIN. WE CAN COME BACK NOW.

'Oh ho ho.' The screen goes dead. Julia swivels round. In the light of the console, her pupils look like pinheads. 'I don't understand.'

My left hand is heavy; I look down and see the wine. Lift it up. She laughs and leans against my thigh. I kiss her hair and she raises her face. No one remembers to turn the computer off.

I wake up to the sound of crying. Someone is in the spare bedroom, knocking very gently at the handle. Like a child coming back from a nightmare. I get out of bed and open the doors and pull them up together into my arms before I know what I'm doing.

'But where were they? Do they know?'

'No. If you ask them they just sulk. Lick?' She takes the ice cream, bites off a chunk. We're walking along the Southend pier, under the bright shapes and grey voices of gulls. The sun catches Julia's hair and pulls it out into white braids and streams.

This is where we came after the train crash, while I was still convalescing. I remember crossing the yellow platform line to pick up the laughing twins, the InterCity coming in past us, the thick weight of a door swinging open. There was an arm opening the door, pinstripe-suited. No watch. Have I said this before? I think of it all the time.

Four years ago now. I haven't seen Julia joyful in all that while. Only happy. Happiness is a solid; joy is a liquid. I read that once, somewhere on the Net. Now I can feel it. Joy. It's hard to control.

'You look good,' I say. She laughs.

'I look good? Daniel –' She stops, puts her hands on my arms. The boardwalk smells of tar and burning. 'When they learn to leave the room we'll bring them here, OK? And we should buy them souvenirs! Lots of them. Are there any sticks of rock round here?'

'It depends what you had in mind.' We kiss. After a while someone claps and takes a photograph. We find a shop that sells rock and sea-shells and Apocalypse by Chocolate Cake. We buy four slices. Further out there's a bench in the sun between two abandoned shopfronts. We sit and watch the sea whet the bright edge of the beach until it's time to go.

The World Feast

She walks into a bar in Prague and there he is, drinking absinthe at noon. He's hunkered forward, eyes and lips screwed tight with concentration as he turns a sugar-cube over the flame of a paper match. He holds it expertly over the small glass of lighter-fuel-green alcohol. Then she says his name, Angus, and the hot sugar burns his fingers.

He drops the match and spills the glass, swearing as the table is sheeted with blue flame. She helps him put it out with her hands. His teeth are brown with aniseed.

'Alia!' he says and leers. 'From the World Feasts, yes? Do you still eat, my dear? I mean, really, eat? I've never forgotten. Do you remember anything?'

She remembers everything. She remembers the delight of the first supper, live lobsters opened up like secret mechanisms. Their flesh already filleted inside the livid exoskeletons. It tasted exquisitely sweet and Alia felt faint with the sense of power. She remembers mammoth, hacked from Icelandic permafrost, as a hot weight in her belly. But most of all she remembers Angus, the red wetness of his lips, talking through mouthfuls at his favourite students. Letting them wait for the secrets. Letting them do nothing except breathe. Like wines.

Now he is back, smiling and smelling of fast food grease. She almost feels sorry for him. She wants to bare her teeth at him because she has never stopped thinking of him. Of his talk, from the last meal to the first time he picked up the telephone and said

'Today is raw meat cultures, can you ring back?'

'Oh. But I'm –' Alia is standing bent over the Arts B phone, frowning at the number she has dialled. The note on the

Accommodation Board reads WANTED: ONE FIRST-YEAR. NO SMOKERS NO VEGETARIANS. RING ALAN ON 01273-090166. She thinks about putting down the phone and going back to her warm B-&-B in Hove. But it's the second week of term; there are only a handful of notes left on the greasy fake-cork noticeboard. She tries again.

'It's about the room. Are you – is it still available? My name's Alia. Are you Alan?'

'How lovely. Are you black?'

'What did you say?'

A student with greasy blond dreadlocks is waiting to use the phone. He has a turquoise lamé mountain bike. He bounces it against the corridor wall as he waits, grinning. Alia turns her back on him and tries not to shout.

'Did you just –'

'Ah. I'm sorry, here he is. Goodbye, Alia.' The phone clicks against something, a hall table, then there is nothing. Alia feels her anger begin to bubble up into a giggle. She closes her eyes and imagines a hallway, a telephone table, the tick of a clock. If she concentrates, she can hear a clatter of pots and knives. It is the noise her aunties used to make in their Birmingham kitchens, as they fried spices the colours of rust and dry earth in hot ghee. The phone clicks.

'Hello.'

Alia jolts back, knocking the mountain bike behind her. Someone sighs at the end of the line. A smiling, patient, male voice.

'Hello. I'm ringing about the room.'

'Yes.'

'Do you still need someone?'

'Oh yes.' Behind Alia, the bike-rider gives up and rides away down the corridor. Doors slam in the distance. Suddenly the hall is quiet. Alia wipes her forehead. She is sweating.

'Well can I – can I come and see it?'

'Of course. Come tonight. All right?' The phone clicks dead and purrs into her ear until she hangs up. She takes a deep breath and smiles. Then she realises she doesn't have the address and she starts to panic again.

She rings back twice but the line is engaged. She can imagine the receiver lying on the hall table. She doesn't want to leave it there; she's put in too much time already. She pulls the note off the wall and goes to the Admin Office, where the kind, paste-lipped school secretary sits with her. Together they find a name, Alan Gould, and an address: 40 Southover Street. She stays for a cup of tea.

The road is steep and narrow and badly lit. Before Alia reaches the house she is already hot and out of breath despite the cold. The flour-sweet smells of bar food steam from pub doorways and extractor fans further down the hill. There is music coming out of the small terrace houses where students are already settled in; REM, The Stranglers, The Cure. Tie-dye sheets hung across windows. The smell of Pop Tarts, fish fingers and marijuana.

The house is opposite a small row of shut-up shops – an organic butcher, a Happy Shopper grocery, an ironmonger's. There is a lamp-post outside and the bright light shines oddly on the empty windows, hollowing them out like fishtanks in an aquarium.

She rings the doorbell of number 40 and waits, trying not to look at the shops. There is a faint light in the front window of the house and a movement of shadows that might be people. She rings the bell again, leaning on it. The shadows go on moving against the pale linen curtains. There is a rattle of rollers from the first-floor window.

'Angus! You came. What are you wearing? Let me see.'

The voice is teenage, high and seductive. Alia steps back from the door and looks up. At the bedroom window a girl with white-lit blonde hair is craning out. Her face is beautiful but much too thin, the features drawn back against the skull. It makes Alia feel cold again and she pulls her baggy coat around her. She tries to smile. The girl at the window doesn't smile back.

'Who are you?'

'My name's Alia. I've come about the room.' The girl shakes her head. As if she doesn't understand or Alia has made a terrible mistake. 'I telephoned, before. Earlier, at lunchtime.' The girl's face clears.

'The room.' There is disappointment in her voice. 'Hold on, then.' The window clatters shut. After some time Alia hears footsteps in the hall and then the door opens. The girl is dressed in ankle socks, plaid skirt, American varsity sweater. Sophisticated, nothing cheap.

'I'm Lorna.' She waits for Alia to step in, then shuts the door behind her. They stand in the unlit hallway, not moving.

'Well,' says Lorna, 'you'd better meet us.' It's Sylvia Plath, thinks Alia, the way she's dressed. Lorna has opened a side door. Light spills out across her face. 'Boys? This is Alia,' she says into the light. Her voice is hushed. 'About the room.'

There is a creak of furniture. 'Well, bring her in, Lorna, will you? She must be freezing.' Lorna turns quickly to Alia, takes her hand, and pulls her in.

There is a log fire in the grate and Alia feels something inside her relax as she sees it, feels it against her thighs. Lorna moves past her and sits down in a sagging armchair. There is a second armchair, and lying across it is a young man in a Japanese dressing-gown. He examines Alia without moving. The gown is too short and Alia tries not to stare at his legs or the ruddy tangles of his chest hair.

She looks away. There is another man in a hard chair by the window. His hair is straight and black, and his eyes behind their too-small wire-rimmed glasses are narrowed with epicanthal folds. He nods at Alia and the corners of his mouth pull up.

'That's Kozo,' says Lorna, 'he's from Japan, and the slouch is Alan. He owns the house.'

He puts down a newspaper and sighs. The same patient, resigned sound he made on the telephone. He forces a smile at Alia. No one in her family owns a house. She tries to smile back.

142

'Hello. I'm glad you found us. Sit down.'

They wait. She looks around, but there are no more chairs. Her knees go weak with embarrassment and she feels herself begin to blush. She has to make herself walk forward, sit down on the elegant hearthrug, stare into the fire as it cracks and pops. The heat blankets her face.

She counts to ten, feeling their eyes on her. The room smells of expensive fabrics and white skin. When she is ready for them she looks up.

Alan has gone back to his newspaper and Kozo is hunched forward over a library book. Only Lorna is watching her, sitting up with thin hands clasped in her lap.

'Where are you from, Alia?'

'Dudley. In Birmingham.' Lorna nods, her eyes wandering as she searches for something to say.

'I noticed the accent. It's nice.'

Alia turns her face away from the heat. 'How about you?'

Lorna looks back, amused. 'Oh, from all over really. My dad's Army. So. And I'm doing International Studies. The boys are Sociologists. We have the same personal tutor. Professor Hayter.'

She looks across at Alan and smiles. He looks up at her, jinks his newspaper flat like punctuation, and starts to read again. There is no sound except for the fire and a clock ticking on the mantelpiece. Alia tries to steal a look at it.

'Here is a fascinating passage,' says Kozo.

'I expect you're going to read it to us then, aren't you,' says Alan. He goes on reading while Kozo talks.

' "The feast for the enthronement of Archbishop Nevill at York in 1465, at which were eaten one thousand sheep, two thousand pigs, twelve porpoises and seals, four thousand rabbits –" '

'Don't you have any luggage, Alia?' says Lorna. Alia stands up, looking between the three of them.

'It's at the hotel, but –' She can't think what to say. Alan stands up.

'Well, yes. Do you smoke? No? Do you like the room? It's forty pounds a week, I'm afraid.'

She laughs. 'I don't care. Really, I just need somewhere to live. If it's anything like down here, it's fine.' Don't sound so bloody desperate, she thinks. But she can't help it. She looks round at Lorna. 'My stuff's all in a B-&-B down by the sea front,' she apologises.

Alan raises his eyebrows, looks around. 'Any votes against?' No one moves. 'There. We'll get your things later, shall we? How about a drink to celebrate?' He stands very close to her, smiling. She can smell spice on his skin. Ginger, or crushed cardamom.

The telephone rings from somewhere in the folds of the armchair. He sits back down and hauls an old dial machine into his lap.

'Hello?'

A smile spreads across Alan's face, making him boyish. 'Angus. Yes, very well.' Lorna goes and sits on the chair arm next to him, whispers in his ear. 'Lorna asks what time we are expecting you?' He listens, eyes moving to Kozo.

'Yes, he's been preparing it all day. Enough to feed an army. Hang on. Kozo? Would nine o'clock be too late?'

The Japanese boy stands up, holding the book tightly. 'No. Of course. Of course not. Nine o'clock is fine.' His English is stilted, but fluent. Alia notices how well he moves despite his weight. His face is slightly puffy with fat, bow-lipped, like a Noh mask. When she looks back at Alan he is watching her curiously.

'Ah. Angus? One thing. The girl who telephoned this afternoon. Alia, yes.' He listens. 'Yes, she is. Oh, pleasant, smart. Sexy.' He winks at Alia, then turns slightly away from her, voice lowered.

'No, she says she's from Birmingham. I haven't asked. By all means.'

He holds the receiver out to Alia. 'It's Professor Hayter. He sometimes does our tutorials here, and he's coming round tonight. I think he just wants a word with you.' Alia takes the phone.

'Alia! "Close to heaven", is that right? We spoke briefly, didn't we?'

'Yes.' His voice reminds her of TV chefs. Smooth and rich, wined and dined. Hard as a butcher.

'What a good name. But we have a problem, my dear. I'm teaching my personal students tonight and I don't allow people to sit in, yes?'

'Oh.'

'What are we to do, Alia? Do you like food? Do you cook?'

They are all watching her now. Lorna twists lint between her fists. 'Yes, of course.'

'But do you eat? Do you really eat?'

She stares at Alan. He nods. 'Yes. I like to eat,' she says.

'Good. Well. It is a good name, isn't it? You'll have to change personal tutors. Tomorrow, will you? Mm. Say I recommended you for my International Studies special module, can you? And tell Kozo we'll be five for supper, I'm sure he'll be so pleased. Goodbye.'

She puts the phone down. After a moment Lorna comes and sits beside her, drapes a slender arm around her. 'Well, what did he say?'

She shakes her head. 'He said I could stay for supper.' She looks at the others.

'I knew he would. How nice. A new student,' says Lorna. Alan nods cautiously, still watching Alia.

'I thought he might. Well, I'm sure he's right. Kozo is cooking Japan tonight. I hope you like fish.'

Kozo stands in front of her, squinting down. He picks up her hand and shakes it gently.

'I will be happy to eat with you. We cook extensively. Because we are foodies. We are food-crazy. We explore world cultures and break down taboos. I hope you will enjoy tonight.' He smiles. Alia sees gold fillings glint behind the white dog-teeth. She stands up, unzips her coat. Smiles back.

He is massive in all senses, in the bone, with close-shaved hair that makes Alia think of skinheads in bus-stations and dark streets. The chopsticks are enveloped in his hands. He flexes them like fingers made too small to grab whole mouthfuls. She feels hungry just watching him.

'Food and religion are always linked. Why is that, do you think? I think it must be a question of purity and poison. Christ is poisoned with vinegar but purifies with his blood and flesh. Cultures that have traditions of eating raw meat, or bleeding their meat, often have exaggerated religious concerns with purity. Shintoism in Japan, where the white snake, salt and rice are holy. Or poisons in Judaism, even better – blood and mud. Alia, are you Muslim, would you say?'

'No.' She feels thick-headed, as if his role as eloquent teacher has boxed her into a sympathetic dullness. She sits back on the hard chair. Concentrates.

The kitchen is big and functional, with stainless-steel sinks and a long scrubbed wood table. The door clicks open and Lorna comes in wearing a shot-silk evening dress. She sits down next to Alan, puts a dictaphone and notebook on the table and starts adjusting Alan's tuxedo collar, lips brushing against his neck.

Alia is still wearing her college clothes, Levi's jeans and a green jumper knitted by her Auntie Yasmine. Sweat trickles from her armpits down her sides. She tries to breathe sensibly, not too fast. At the far end of the kitchen, Kozo is hitting something with a meat tenderiser. She winces at the impacts.

'Mm. Pity. But you still have your cultural foods, yes? Foods are edible social histories, Alia. Japan, for instance, has an ancient tradition of raw fish from the southern settlers, followed by Buddhist taboos on working with dead animals. Then we have the Portuguese merchants arriving with their fritters and egg-tempera painting techniques. Lo and behold, the Japanese create deep-fried tempura. Nowadays they eat beef via America, but they often eat it raw. The traditions are sublimated but they evolve, you see? Lorna, you look ravishing.'

'Oh, thank you.' Alia watches the way the younger woman blushes across her neck and cheeks, crossing her legs. She looks back at the Professor. He is sitting astride his chair, mouth slightly open, small eyes moving from one student to the next. Gauging them for something.

What are you doing here? she thinks. She stops watching him, uncomfortable, while Kozo sets bowls and trays on the table. Angus boosts himself up to look into his bowl. He chuckles. Kozo sits down.

'I will explain to you.' Alia looks into her black lacquer bowl. Inside is a pungent mash the colour of fried liver. She draws back at the smell of it.

'This is called natto,' says Kozo. 'It is the rotten beans of the soya plant. On your trays are soy sauce, yellow mustard and the egg of a quail. Mix in the condiments like this.' Kozo breaks the pebble-sized egg over his bowl and beats its raw gold plasm into the beans. 'Then the soy and mustard. And taste. You see?'

They eat without talking. The natto is delicious. Angus is the last to finish. He licks his chopsticks clean and sits back.

'Very interesting. Perfectly satisfying in dietary terms. But the perfect product is perfectly dull. You have to give a little humanity to bring the food alive. Don't you think? Lorna?'

'Sorry Kozo, but look, even Alia likes it, don't you Alia? And it's her first lesson. What we want' – she leans forward towards Kozo until he begins to move back – 'is something to talk about. Even something we can't talk about. So that when we're trundling into campus on that provincial little Falmer train, we can look at all the first years with their packed Spam, and know that we're better than them. Excite us, Kozo. That's what the World Feasts are about.'

Lorna has let her face sink into her hands, posing. Alia feels a smile playing round her lips. Kozo is staring at the thin blue veins in the blonde girl's eyelids, the thick ink-blacked lashes. 'When Angus was talking, Japanese food sounded so cruel and unusual. Like the people.'

'No. It is Chinese food that is most unusual. Excuse me, please.' Kozo stands up, his chair falling back as he walks towards the work surfaces. Alan stretches out one hand and catches it.

147

'Easy on, tiger!' He stands the chair upright. Alia sits back, quiet. She folds her napkin into a carp, but her movements are jerky in the growing threat of silence. There is a distant sound of police-car sirens through the rear windows. She flattens the carp out, looks up, tries to think of something to say.

'Are you married, Professor?'

She knows it is a mistake immediately. Alan draws back from the table. She stumbles over the words and no one says anything. For a moment she thinks Angus is going to ignore her. Then he rolls his head up and smiles at her.

'Of course. I'd forgotten you were a first year – a fresher, in fact. Any second year knows about my marriage. Well. It was a bloody mess. Ha! Ha!' His laugh is brittle and stagy. 'Bloody and botched. Scenes all over campus, we were like boxers on tour. I haven't seen my wife or children in almost a year, they upped and left. Alan, could you pass the tea? Thank you.' He pours green tea into his own cup, then offers it to Alia. She shakes her head. He shrugs. Leers at her.

'I've still got my kitchen, though. And my personal students. Oh look, Lorna, it's puffer fish. And you've just made the chef so angry, my love.'

Kozo is setting down an octagonal platter in the middle of the table. The surface of the dish is covered with wafers of flesh, cut almost to transparency, mottled, bloody. They are arranged as the petals of a chrysanthemum. Alia feels saliva against her teeth.

'Please.' Kozo motions to the platter, sits down. Lorna cranes forward.

'Well. It's not Spam, anyway. What is it, Kozo-san?'

He grins, a white flash of vindictiveness. 'Cruel and unusual delicacies.' He claps his hands together in prayer, then begins to eat. His eyebrows rise comically. 'Quite safe and tasty. Eat please!'

Lorna sits back next to Alan. Alia watches the way he laughs without opening his mouth. She imagines him with a beard, russet like his hair. 'I thought it was poisonous, puffer fish?' says Lorna.

148

Alan sighs. 'Who says it's puffer fish?'

'It takes years of training. The filleting. Alan.'

'He never said it was puffer fish, all right? Stop thinking and just eat it. Eat it.'

'You eat it.'

'You first. You're the one who got nasty, remember?'

'It's nice,' says Alia. When they stop and look at her she feels the warmth spreading out from her full stomach. The feeling of belonging. There is a mottled piece of flesh speared clumsily on her chopsticks. She chews. 'Really. Not fishy at all. It's not fish is it, Kozo?'

He takes off his spectacles, wipes them clean with his napkin. 'Puffer fish is most specially expensive. Professor Hayter's department would baulk at such expenses.'

'Thank you for thinking of me. Now then. Raw belly of tuna, is it? Good with salt, yes. Kozo? What is it?'

He points: bloody, mottled, purple. 'Heart, tongue, liver. Of horse. A speciality of Hiroshima. Please eat up. The next course is alive and time is a factor.'

'Good,' whispers Angus. 'Very good.'

Alia licks the meat into her mouth and grins. Skin and hair prickles along her thighs; the raw heart of a horse.

Alan laughs, his voice high, almost hysterical. 'What do you think, Alia? Are you hooked? Or out? Alia.'

She picks up her cup of green tea. Drinks without letting it spill. It tastes wonderful. 'I think we must do this more often.'

'I can't believe it.'

Alia lies back on the shingles. They are cold and grey against her hair. The feeling is good, solid. At the periphery of her vision she can see Lorna sitting up on the picnic blanket, pouring champagne. Hair haloed against the sun and seagulls. She leans close, nestles a glass into Alia's hand. Strokes her cheek.

'You have such beautiful skin, so smooth. What can't you believe?'

'You know what. Oh, all of it – what we ate, what we said.'

She pauses. The tide hisses against Brighton West Pier. She can smell sour salt and rust. 'That I enjoyed it.' Lorna lies back next to her. Just the two of them. Friends. Alia wants to laugh and she does, a little.

'Oh well. I know what you mean, though. But just remember the parsnip principle.'

'What's that?' Lorna's hair is curling into Alia's mouth. She pushes it gently away.

'When I was little I used to hate parsnips. Then one day we were at a dinner somewhere and they served this soup and I couldn't get enough of it. So after the umpty-umpth serving my mother leans over and says, You'll never guess, Lorna, and of course it's parsnip soup.' She laughs, head back, shrill as the gulls. 'She was going to tell all the guests and I said Don't, so she made a promise to try everything once and I did. That's the principle. Because you never know what you'll like. You should try everything once.'

They say nothing for a while, listening and drinking. In the distance is the synthesised jangle of fairground attractions on the Palace Pier, the rush of traffic. Somewhere out to sea a tanker hoots. Alia leans up to watch it, wrinkles her face against the sun. Ships crawl against the horizon.

'When did it start? The World Feast?' Behind her Lorna shifts on the blanket, getting comfortable.

'Last June, end of term. We stayed down over the summer break. I suppose we're addicted, really. India, Brazil and Japan we've had, so far, one every few months. We were just a tutorial group, to start with. It was Angus's idea. He is remarkable. But it has become more – well, unusual. That just happened, I think. Just a sort of slippage.' She sits up.

'Angus is cooking next. Then it's your turn, if you like. That doesn't worry you, does it?'

Alia shakes her head.

'No. Angus wouldn't have chosen you if it did. I bet you're a great cook. Are you drunk yet?'

She laughs. 'A bit. Lorna, can I tell you something?'

'If you like.'

She sits up, pulls her knees up to her breasts. 'I was really glad when I met you. The three of you. I don't know what I would have done otherwise. My parents, they moved back to India last month. To be with my aunts and uncles. I don't have family here now. But I wanted to stay.' She blinks back stupid tears. 'It was the best thing. Meeting you.'

Lorna stands up. 'Is that all? God, Alan thought they must have died or something.'

Alia looks up at her; she is brushing off her skirt, slim and meticulous. Suddenly the taste of champagne in Alia's mouth is sour and musty. She tries to stand up, staggers. Lorna takes her arm.

'You are drunk. You are nice, Alia. Come on, let's get you home. It's almost time for tea.'

The first of November smells of gunpowder. A cold mist comes in off the sea and the odour of corner-shop rockets hangs around the clocktower and the grim concrete architecture of the university. Alia works in the library until the lights start being turned off at closing time.

She packs away her books, walks to the main exit. Figures stand outside on the wide steps, dark against the darkness. Students smoking cigarettes, waiting for friends. Alan is sitting on the wall to one side. He shucks away from it, takes Alia's books, kisses her. His lips are cold but his mouth is warm. They walk together to the train station.

'Angus called.'

Alia smiles out a cloud of white breath. 'What did he say? When is the lesson? Is it ready?'

'He said to say that Angus called.'

She grabs him. 'What else?'

They stop. He is laughing with his mouth closed again. 'He said it's ready. He's cooking England tonight. Nine o'clock.'

'Shit! What time is it now?'

'Don't worry.' He points out into the dark. A car is parked at the university entrance, pale and sleek. Lorna is waving to them from the driver's window. They run across the lawn.

The roads around Angus's Kemp Town house are crowded with parked cars. Lorna has to drive round the block three times. She clicks her nails against the wheel, sharp and nervous.

'Oh well. Lucky in parking, unlucky in love, that's what my mother always says. Here we are, anyway.' She eases them into a space. They get out and stand on the pavement while she straightens up. Kozo's face is white against the blackness of his hair and dinner-jacket. Alia takes his hand.

'Are you all right, Kozo?' He nods and pulls away. Alia looks at Alan and he shakes his head, Leave him. The car door slams. Lorna comes round the bonnet, heels loud against the cold ground. Alan walks up the steps to the door, turns.

'Are we ready?'

They go inside. The doors to the kitchen are open. Five Bauháus chairs at the smooth black table. There are objects on the table. Even with the spotlights, Alia can't make them out. She goes closer. Looks into the blood-stuffing of a giant puffball. Strokes the fairground tail of a peacock.

'And do we eat this?' says Kozo. He is at the head of the table. Something stands there, tall and winged, balanced on jointed poles. Kozo looks back at them. 'Is this a funny joke?'

'No, actually it's a heron.' Angus is standing in the cellar doorway. He is holding four bottles of wine by his fat butcher's fingers. Watching them. Carcass freezers hum in the dark behind him. 'Roasted with sandalwood and raspberries, mediaeval recipe. Hell of a time getting hold of it. RSPB, etcetera.'

He lumbers in, filling the room. Alan steps back towards Alia. 'The peacock's imported, so that was easier, but it's a trick to get it back into the skin after roasting. Barely fits, like a swollen foot. Anyway, lovely to see you all, do sit down, let's eat first and talk later, yes? A hungry stomach has no ears. Who'd like a honeyed dormouse?'

Alia sits down. Angus rubs his hands together, cleaning, cleaning. 'Dinner is served.'

*

They never eat with Angus between lessons. They never go to restaurants. Alia is doing well in all her courses, but there are rumours of staff cuts and Angus has no allies on the faculty. The school secretary tells Alia she used to worry for the wife, she was such a small woman. She gives Alia a form to fill in on Angus's teaching. Alia throws it away. It's not something she wants to think about.

She spends time with Lorna and Alan, sometimes with Kozo. The other students seem cut off from them. She dreams of eating – meringues of sea-foam, the bitter metal of knives and forks, anonymous meats – and when she wakes from the dreams, she is always hungry. The campus doctor gives her something to help but the dreams don't go away. She stays at Southover Street over Christmas because she has nowhere else to go. They all do. She plans the next World Feast. She is going to cook France.

It is the day before term begins. They are sitting in the front room, trying to study. The phone rings and Alan takes it, still writing course-notes

'Hello. Yes, it is. Yes.' He sits up, puts down his pen.

'No, no problem. We were just –' He listens, frowning. 'Muscardini. No, I'm sorry. It sounds like an Italian wine –'

When he laughs everyone stops. Alan never laughs out loud. His eyes lock with Alia's. 'Dormice. No, I've never heard anything like that in relation to Professor Hayter. I must say it sounds rather *News of the World*-ish. But I'm sure he'll talk to you himself if you ring him. Mm? Oh, no problem. No. Goodbye.'

He hangs up and dials immediately, waving Lorna away. 'Angus. I just had bloody Animal Welfare ringing me.' His voice shakes. Alia puts her hand on his shoulder. She can hear Angus's voice, distant and tinny.

'Alan! How are you? I never see you these days. When is Alia going to be ready with the next lesson, eh? No, listen. Don't worry about the animal people. It's all taken care of. It just takes a little money. Trust me. This is bound to happen as we explore food cultures in such depth. Next time we'll have something less traceable, won't we? Oh, and don't ring me again.' The line clicks shut.

It takes her nine days to cook and it's still a failure. Alan helps her with the heavy work, the gutting and stitching. They use Angus's kitchen because the table is stronger. They compliment her cooking and eat. Alia feels her pride shrivel inside her.

M. F. Le Maëstre's *Escalopes de langoustes à la Poincaré* with a chopped cockscomb sauce; Louis Kannengieser's *Pains de foie gras à la Française*, with its quarter-kilo of truffles and two kilos of foie gras. Larks enshrouded with pig's lungs and a bouillon invented by Carême. They eat at Alia's creations in queasy silence while Angus talks and talks.

'I was a gastro-nomad at your age. I was fascinated by taboos and pleasures. Not consuming honey or crayfish. Consuming lambs' testicles or smoke. Sex and death and filth – kitchens have it all and people love it.'

He picks detritus from between his molars, twisting one thumb between the canines. It makes him ursine, thinks Alia, the face snarling. 'Some more than others. Met my wife in China, she couldn't stand it, just wanted McDonald's. The boys, too. Quite picaresque, it was. Got all the way to New Britain and back. Excellent soups. They use three different kinds of turtle eggs.'

Alia crumples up her napkin, stands up. 'Forget it. This isn't working is it? Why not? All that bloody work and you all look like you're sitting in – in Pizza Hut.' She spits words at them, angry and scared. What happens next? she thinks, but she pushes the thought back.

'Anyway.' She drops the napkin on her plate. 'I'm going to have a fag. Someone else can do the washing-up.'

Alan calls after her. 'You don't smoke.'

'You don't know anything about me,' she shouts back. Later they make love in her single bed and she bites his shoulders and cries at the taste of it.

*

154

The invitations arrive two weeks later, one for each of them: *Professor Hayter invites you to* THE LAST WORLD FEAST *(Melanesia). Nine o'clock, Leap Day, evening dress.* Lorna collects them up and tucks them next to the sitting-room clock.

'Oh God, I can't wait. Especially after last time – sorry, Alia. You know what I mean. I haven't been able to think about revision, have you? What is Melanesian cuisine?'

Alan stands up, wipes the palms of his hands against his cotton trousers. None of them say anything. After a while Lorna sits down, the breath going out of her in a long sigh.

'I knew really.' She picks a piece of hair off her cardigan. Smiles wanly. 'Actually, I've been thinking about it for a while. Dreaming, sometimes. Are we going to go?'

Alia drags on her cigarette. Waits. Kozo is sitting beside her on the rug, legs crossed, light catching off his glasses. They watch Lorna. She shivers and nods.

'I'm afraid the main hors-d'oeuvre has failed to materialise. Dancing fish, Kozo, specially for you. But they died en route. Which leaves us with the three main roasts. Do you know the story of Vaté, who cooked the royal French banquet in 1671? Killed himself when the fish didn't arrive on time. Imagine. I suggest red wine, but white is not unsympathetic. Alan?'

'Red. Thanks.' His voice is tight but under control. The ovens are still on and Angus's kitchen is hot and wet. The four students sit tight in their seats, coats on. Kozo takes off his glasses and puts them down. They clatter against the dark lacquer of the table.

'Professor Hayter? Where are they from? These roasts?'

'Where are they from?' Angus comes back to the table with an uncorked bottle, begins to pour, pauses. 'Are you sure you want to know? You're not worried about it, are you?' Kozo stares.

Alan shakes his head. 'No. Not really. Should we be?'

He smiles. 'Of course not! We're breaking down taboos, remember? Why on earth should we stop short of this one? How can we stop short now? Besides, it's a very fine meat.

When it's properly basted. People tend to eat it rather plain. As if it were sacred. But there's no shortage, eh? I'm not even sure where these were from, but probably somewhere on the Indian subcontinent, I hope that won't offend Alia.'

He begins to carve. 'And do you know?' He looks up, red-cheeked. 'They have the most marvellous wishbones.' Alia sits back, smooths the linen napkin across her knees. Her stomach growls.

Lorna still writes to her sometimes. Alia can hear her shrill laughter in the letters from airports and airplanes. She writes back short letters about small things. Once she saw a photo of Alan on a paper left in a train. It was the *Financial Times*, his face heavily lined but pink and grainy, so she can't be sure if he looks old or if the photo is just bad. He was one in a group of company directors, shaking hands. The only one not smiling.

Kozo went back to Japan two days after the last World Feast. She never saw him again. She wants to know what happened to him. She would like to know if any of them have ever talked, if they have found someone to listen. Because she never has. She misses them.

And when they are both older, Alia meets Angus on a business trip to Prague. She sees the alcohol before she recognises him, the green wink of absinthe catching the bar lights. He is jealous of her success.

'You look splendid, Alia. Oozing life. Like in the song, remember? No. What do you remember?'

She shrugs. Feels the silk of her dress drag against her skin. 'The feasts. Then you left. They didn't like your teaching methods.'

He leans forward, across the table, until she leans back. 'Oh no. They could sweep my teaching under the carpet, that was all right. It was the kids, you see? They didn't mind my wife disappearing. But they wouldn't stop asking about the kids. Pig-ignorant, porky little piggies. I lied, Alia.'

She stands back, away from the small glitter of his eyes.

'What did you lie about, Angus?' He tips his head sideways, grins.

'What does it matter? One little white porkie pie. Meat's meat. Christ!' He looks at the bar clock. 'Lunchtime already. I must go. The world awaits, eh?'

She moves away from his kiss. She doesn't shake his hand. They have nothing in common. He walks to the bar door and waves. She watches the sunlight rose-pink through his fingers and holds her arms together tight.

Zoo

'Anja? We have to go now.'

However hard she tries, she can never get the smell of animals off her body. She likes that. It's what she takes out with her from the cages and enclosures, into the city where the people are. Today it's the scent of night mammals, the amazed eyes of lemurs and bush-babies. She trusts their closeness. Like an address sewn into a child's clothes.

But she must be clean. Her skin is ruddy with the water's heat. She scrubs at pores and scar-tissues. For a moment the water goes slack and cold and she thinks of prisons, the smell of trapped sweat and cheap soap. Then the warmth comes back. She takes her time. Wrings her hair out into a long, dark rope.

'Anja, we have to go.'

The extractor-fan is jammed open, and through it she can see a crack of evening skyline, canal mist hanging over the squat green turrets of the Elephant House. This is still new to her, the sense of the zoo around her, a place without people. It helps her breathe. There is the sound of gulls scavenging, their drawl and mewl. The distant bellow of the bull oryx near Snowdon's Aviary. Someone calling up for her, calling her name.

She leans out from the shower's spray to see. Alexis is down by the laboratories, a lanky figure in zoo overalls, his voice still echoing along the concrete walls. The wolf keeper is with him, a larger outline, standing back in the half-dark. Anja tries to remember his name. She turns off the water and buries her face in a towel, requiring herself to be ready. Breathing into the smell of furs.

'Hello beautiful girl. Wanna dance?'

She shakes her head, hair still wet against her neck. The music is getting louder. She can feel the beat against her ribcage. There are men in the crowd, watching her, moving towards her and away. It reminds her of shark cages. The brickwork arches of the club shake as a train goes over, east towards Caledonian Road.

She drinks tonic without gin. Next to her at the chrome-topped bar a boy in yellow jeans orders frozen vodka. She can smell it as it melts. Bitter, like traffic fumes. Against her neck she can feel the pendant of her mother's wedding-ring. She is still cold from the streets outside and the plain gold is warmer than her skin. She sits, hands resting on knees, watching the crowd.

The wolf keeper is dancing, she can see his bulk and the way space opens around him. He smiles at her, teeth white through the beard. His name is Shamash. Alexis introduced them in the car: Anja, Shamash, Shamash, Anja. She knows nothing else about him. He looks different outside the zoo, less animal, more like someone who has come from somewhere, a family, a place of birth. She looks round for Alexis but he has been taken in by the crush of bodies and voices.

Anja looks away from the crowd. A draught of air passes over her and she feels a quick wave of nausea at the smell of spilt lager and marijuana. Her muscles shiver with the vibrations of bass music. She wonders how long it would take to get out, if she had to. The crowd is thickest by the entrance, where two bouncers in puffa-jackets frisk down the men one by one. A woman with blonde dreadlocks opens out her pockets onto a side-table. Anja looks round for a fire-escape, but she can see nothing beyond the slow mosh of people. She gags once and then breathes in slowly, holding the bar to keep herself still until the claustrophobia passes.

The boy with yellow jeans isn't drinking. His vodka is almost melted, the last ice like flaws in quartz. She looks down at the glass wrapped in her own hands. The cold hurts her palms.

She makes herself finish the tonic water. Then she pushes gently through to the door and goes outside. From the club entrance she can see Camden Lock, late-night traffic hooting at the junctions and the blue light of the Telecom Tower above them, in towards the centre of London. When she looks up there are no clouds. The sky is dark and she can make out stars. She stands there with her head back, smelling the sour autumn cold. It makes her think of Helsinki, the city she no longer thinks of as home, only the place she came from. Her mother's voice, worrying holes in the dark with its intelligence:

Come on, be more precise, Anja. It's not just rain. What is it? Don't they teach you anything now?

Mother, please. I don't need to know about rain. It's so cold. Can't we watch from inside?

Five minutes. Well. Serein: a fine rain falling from a cloudless sky after sunset. So now you know, yes? Next time you won't get wet guessing.

It starts to rain. Her bladder hurts. There are toilet cabins off towards the road, white trailer cabins on an unlit stretch of car-park. Anja trudges over to them, but the Women's is locked and unlit. The smell of chemicals and human sewage disgusts her. She waits until she's sure the Men's is empty, drizzle cold against her cheeks, then goes in. She sits and reads the graffiti, male and slightly alien: SUPERFLY ARE COMING, SPURS KICK HAMMERS, SCREWDRIVER RULES. She's on the way back out when she catches a glitter of green from the corners of her eyes. Like sequins.

She goes back in, past the urinals. By the wall is a sprinkling of particles, smaller than sequins. Anja picks one up, then another, turning them on the tips of her fingers. The particles are iridescent, finely ribbed, and familiar to her. It takes her a moment to recognise them in this alien place. The feathers of green hummingbirds. She screws up her eyes at the hairline shafts, the texture of vanes. They fall away from the movement of her breath and the passage of air across her hands.

The wolves are watching her. Three of them, like Alsatians but not smiling like Alsatians. Meat-eaters looking at meat. Their eyes are the colour of urine. Anja works with her back to them.

'Look at them,' says Alexis. 'They're bloody watching us. Sleekit creatures.' He leans on his rake and huffs at them, body-warmth condensing in a cloud of white breath.

'Wolves do not attack healthy adult humans. This is a rural myth. There is no proof of it.'

She distrusts her English. Not her competence, but what it reveals. Emotion and accent, the guttural vowels which make people ask questions. Alexis asks few questions. It makes them close in a way that isn't friendship but something less permanent, a relationship defined by privacies.

'Is that a fact?' Alexis is lighting a cigarette, cupping it in his hands. Not really listening. The electric motor of a zookeeper's buggy whines in the distance.

They're up by the end of Wolf Wood, clearing leaves off a steep path down to the Bird Houses. Anja has never seen anyone up here except the pensioners, who come to fall asleep in the warmth and birdsong of the buildings. And the wolf keeper. She looks up for his animals but they've gone, back into the trees, she can't even see their eyes. Parrots scream and tussle on the far side of the incubation rooms.

She concentrates on scraping leaves off the tarmac. The ground is slippery with impacted mulch. Anja keeps her feet spread, leaning into the gradient for support. It's easier than ice, and she is used to ice, her body remembers it. She is sure she won't fall.

'Bird House next.' Alexis talks while she works. She doesn't mind. This is their routine. She is the new girl, so she does the work. 'I never did like the birds, you know? They're a bit ghostly. The way they, you know, fly. God, what a fag-end, arse-end of a day. Did you like it last night, though? What a rave, eh?'

She nods. There is a pattern in the leaves. A serrated heart, repeated again and again. She rakes it apart and piles it up against the wooden fence.

'So. You liked the Wolfman?'

Anja looks up, surprised. Alexis squats on his lanky

haunches, watching her through screwed-up eyes, pulling on his cigarette. She shakes her head.

'You know, his bird and my bird are best pals.'

She can't help smiling. 'I think the only birds you have are waiting for you to clean their shit off the floor.' Alexis gets up, stretches. The path is cleared, wet macadam grey with reflections of cloud.

Alexis slips as they walk down the slope. Anja catches him as he falls. She has never touched him before. He's thin enough that she can pull him up, his arm bony and hot inside the damp overalls. They wait in the Bird House while he catches his breath.

'I'll be OK.' Behind them hornbills creak and hoot in the undergrowth of their cages. 'I think I'm coming down with something, though.'

She sits back, hands in coat pockets. It's not something they've talked about, his illness. Anja only knows what she has noticed. The bruised skin, the way he boils tapwater before drinking. Five weeks ago, the day she arrived, Alexis closed the heel of his hand in a cage-hinge. Anja watched the way he reared away from his own blood, forcing the fist into his pocket to clot. Hiding it from her. Now she doesn't know what to say. She has never been good with people.

The incessance of the birds makes her tired. She closes her eyes, resting them.

'What happens to the feathers?'

Alexis shifts beside her. She can feel him, warm and slight against her side. 'What, hen?'

'From the birds. Condors and ostriches and hummingbirds. Mountains of feathers. Do we burn them? Or do they go to the gift shop?'

'No. I don't know. Who cares?'

He leans against her to push himself upright. She listens to the clank of his bucket and the flutter of panicked birds.

'Aw, shite. What a waste.'

Anja opens her eyes, goes over to him. There is a dead bird on the cage floor, still huddled against the bars. Alexis opens

162

the aviary, lifts the small body out. Anja holds it in both hands while he locks up. She can hardly feel it through her gloves. Its plumage is brilliant as red neon in the half-light.

'Deaths?'

The big zoo kitchen smells of screw-worm, sweet like shrimp. On a chipped blackboard the head keeper is writing *4/11 pelican juv. on Sarah's not foxes*. Through the crowd Anja can see only the back of his head, strands of hair gelled across pale, freckled skin.

'One black widow. Male, healthy, nine months old.'

'Cause?'

'Cannibalism.'

'Sexual?'

'Stress. I think stress.'

Chalk clacks against the board like a typewriter. *It's not a crowd, thinks Anja. These are people like me. They are not at home with one another. They hate the hard intelligence of this language. They want to be out of here. With the animals.*

The man who talks about spiders is smiling down at his Doc Marten's. He has a point of red high on each cheekbone; otherwise his skin is the colour of egg-whites. He lounges against a steel cutting surface, hands folded tight across his chest. Anja knows what he is thinking: he is blaming them. In some way it is their fault, and he would like them to know it. If it brought the spider back, he would make them pay. Anja can see it in the way he stares away from them.

She moves back against the window. The glass is crammed with stickers: WORLD WILDLIFE FUND, BELIZE JAGUAR RESERVATION, ANCHORAGE ZOO.

There are children outside, two Japanese girls and a boy. They stare in at the keepers, pointing and laughing. Anja waves back, pulls a face.

'There was a bird died too. Up in the Bird House.'

She turns back at the sound of Alexis's voice. Someone laughs, an overweight volunteer with a gold neck-chain and grizzled throat.

'Details.'

'A red bird. About so long. Tropical.'

'Order? Genus? Species?'

Anja can see the head keeper's face now. The blood is building up around the dissolved-blue of his eyes. It feels like a crowd around her now, she can feel the bright eyes on Alexis. Like a classroom. She is not good with crowds, and she has never liked classrooms.

She puts up her hand. 'Sir.' In front of her a tall girl in a green army sweater moves away.

'Sex, Alexis? Or were you confused about its sex?' The laughter spreads. An illicit, anxious excitement.

She raises her voice. '*Sir.*'

Now he sees her. His irises look like they have been in water for a long time, thin and blue against the blood. 'Yes? You're new. What's your name?'

'Anja Kivinen.'

He nods once. 'The live-in volunteer. From Finland.'

'Yes. It was a King Bird of Paradise. I found it, in fact. Alexis was also working in the Tropical Bird House.'

He is frowning at her. As if he can't understand why she is talking. Then he shrugs and turns back to the board. 'Cause of death?'

'Age. Lots of the birds in there are old.' The others are quiet now. Anja can hear a radio on in the background, the manic chatter of airtime advertising. 'The indoor cages are a kind of retirement home for them.'

'Good.' Something roars outside. The hot-mouthed boredom of a lion. The head keeper stops writing and looks round. His voice is deadpan.

'Tomorrow will be busy. The sea-water tankers have already left Dover, we'll need people at the Aquarium first thing tomorrow. I want two volunteers on hand up at the Lion Enclosure for the delivery of our first liger, her name is Salar, she'll be on loan for six months from Johannesburg. And the Chinese alligators are going home, the curator of reptiles will need four helpers with that. Night keepers should be ready in five minutes. The rest of you have a good evening.'

Anja is the last to leave. She puts together morning feed while the closing-time klaxon echoes over Albert Road and Regent's Park. Eel and margarine for the otters, ox-hearts and carrots for the kiwis. She likes it when the others have all gone. She feels as if she has won something.

When there is no work left to do she switches off the radio, locks up, turns out the lights. The dark is drawing in outside. She stands still and lets her eyes adjust until she can see Goat Hill, a derelict concrete hulk against the glow of London. When she walks, animals flutter around her in the gloom, eyes like road-studs. Nervous and vulnerable, on the edge of sleep.

In Anja's dream there are animals moving through the trees. Slow with inertia, the way big creatures move, and these are big enough that she is looking up at them through a wicker of branches. She can smell the white clouds of their breath, the whoosh of it like nightclub ventilators. Blood and pine, intimate as the scent of her own skin. She wonders if they can smell her. She flinches in the cold dark of her rented room.

But they are almost past now, herded away between the cold pines. They're moving towards something, a sound of – what? A voice? Like wind across a bottle's mouth.

It's important to make it out. She pushes through the wings of firs. A glitter of feathers falls around her, fine as ice particles, itchy against her bare skin. There is a sound of cars, the slow sigh of distant traffic. And someone is crying through the trees.

She can almost see him now, but she has to brush the feathers off her thighs, her skin is green and gummed with them. When she looks up again there is only stupendous sunlight, the sound of bells from St Mark's Church, the birds of prey screaming for their six o'clock meat.

The tank is full of dead branches and the green coils of ferns. Hanging from the branches are two household air-fresheners.

A sticker on the glass in the public gallery says VENOMOUS SNAKE TEMPORARILY REMOVED.

'Yes. Lovely new skin. You can hear it. Can you hear?'

Anja turns round. The curator of reptiles is sitting on a swivel chair, too low for the laboratory table. He is skinning a dead snake lengthways. It sounds like a zip opening. 'Yes. Can you find the cast-off in there?' He smiles quickly up at her without seeing. 'Good girl.'

The ferns are dense, pushing condensation against the glass. Anja can see the undersides of fronds, stippled with seeds.

'There are no more snakes in here?'

She isn't scared; she asks because people make mistakes. Especially people who look without seeing.

He laughs, a dry hiss. Alexis says he eats screw-worm. Alexis says people can spend too long with the animals they love. 'I should think not. Why not use long forceps? They're around here somewhere, by the skins, possibly? Got them?'

She pushes between the fractals of leaves. There is no old snakeskin in the tank, only odd arrangements of mouse bones, digested or disgorged. The smell of pine freshener reminds Anja of the dream. She pulls her head away, snaps the tank-top shut. 'There is nothing in here.'

The man at the workbench looks up again. Striplight catches off his glasses, glaring and surprised. 'Not again. Are you sure, really? Oh well. Zoo gremlins.' He is concentrating on the dissection, rambling. 'It may turn up, that happens too, sometimes. For the moment we'll blame it on the gremlins, shall we? Never mind.'

He lifts the new skin away in his hand. The scales are burnished, graded from bottle-green to the blue of deep water along the scrolled length. Anja touches her fingers against its cool smoothness.

'It's beautiful,' she says, and the curator of reptiles nods, pleased. 'It is, isn't it? I'm so glad you like it. Yes.' He sighs, takes off his glasses. His eyes are almost hidden under draping epicanthal folds. 'It is a very beautiful thing.' They smile together in the prison-grey laboratory. There is no sound except the chirr of locusts in their long, bright tanks.

'Shamash. It's a nice name.'

The wind catches at her voice. He doesn't say anything, doesn't even look up at her from the half-open crates of sprats. The sunlit whitewash of the Penguin Pool hurts her eyes.

'It's not Arabic, is it? Is it Sanskrit?' She feels a tug of feeling when he doesn't speak. Just a little hurt.

She leans her head back; the sky is cloudless. Airplanes wink in the high atmosphere. Seagulls criss-cross, closer in. They loiter in the trees and on the penguin slides. The breeze pushes at their feathers as they wail for feeding time.

She sighs and looks back down. The wolf keeper is watching her; now he looks away. Scatters a handful of fish. 'How do you like it?'

'What?'

'The zoo.' She feels an easing in herself at the small irrelevance of his question. *This is not simple for him either, this talking,* she thinks.

'I like it very much.' She reaches into the crates. Cold fish the colour of tin slip between her fingers. She can't think of anything else to say. Around the pool penguins waddle for fish-heads, clumsy on the walkways, streamlined in the murky water. Seagulls glide between them, lean and hungry.

'I didn't know you worked down here.'

'Sometimes.' He nods at the gulls. 'Look at them.' She leans on the wall and peers down. Two big herring gulls squabble in mid-air. The penguins wait, lazy and aloof. The wolf keeper leans beside her. She looks at him. 'So?'

'The whole zoo is like this. Seagulls eat the penguins' food, herons steal what we give to the pelicans. Starlings steal everything and shit on the rest. The mice eat what's left and the kestrels eat the mice.' His voice is accented, a slight lilt. Anja thinks it is something Middle Eastern. 'Foxes come in and kill newborns. Rats eat the eggs.'

He smiles at her. Like the other night. His teeth are very

white. 'You see how it is. We think we're here to keep the animals in, when all we do is try to keep them out.' He looks away, breath clouding slightly in the cold air. 'It's ironic. If nature is outside trying to get in, what do we have locked up in the cages?'

'Did you know someone steals snakeskins?'

He looks at her without expression. Waiting. She turns right round to look at him. Keeps her voice down. 'It's you. Isn't it?'

'No. It's the feather man.' He doesn't smile.

'Who?'

'The feather man. He takes what he likes. Usually it has been feathers. Sometimes snakeskins. Nothing alive. Mostly at night. He never does any harm.'

'Have you seen him?' The wolf keeper shakes his head, no. 'Is he real?'

He smiles. 'I think so. Or it could be the zoo gremlins. What do you think?' She stands there, looking at him. He waits, smiling, while the seabirds wheel around them.

'Truth, dare or promise?'

'Truth, dare, *kiss* or promise. Duh.' Through a mist of afternoon drizzle comes the grieving of a donkey from the Children's Zoo. 'Dare.'

'I dare you to put your hand in there.'

'No.'

'Chicken.'

'No.'

'Chicken. Buk. Buk-buk-buk.'

Laughter. Spider-monkeys hang upside-down from the cage roof, five-limbed, watching. The boy looks up at them through thick glasses and then away, wretched. Anja leans on her broom and smiles back when his eyes fall on her. But he doesn't notice; she's too far away. Or his eyes are too weak. She prefers to think that she is too far away. The second boy laughs again, high and cocky.

Someone grabs her arm from behind. She twists out of the grip and round. Her fist is tight against her side, ready to hit out.

It's Alexis. She shrugs away from him. He snatches his hands back, jeering, like the boy. 'Hey! Hey. It's me, OK? I'm not going to eat you and I don't want a shag.' He holds out one hand again, palm up. 'Smell: no blood, no pheromones.'

She tries a smile. It's not an apology. She has nothing to apologise for. 'What is it?'

'I want to show you something. Are you coming or not?'

She goes with him. The character of the zoo changes as they move away from the public paths, back into the service areas and laboratory yards. Room-sized wooden boxes are piled against walls, airholes punched in their sides. There is a faint smell of incinerators. Behind the back of the Aquarium is a mountain of pale yellow sand, crusted with rain.

'It's in here. Anja.' His voice is dull with hurt. She turns away from him and peers up through the drizzle at the squat, grey building. It looks like a weapons silo. There is a winch-hook on the third floor, heavy and rusted. The sign on the wall says HAZCHEM LABORATORY R1 (FELINES). Outside is a skip full of broken caging and orange plastic bottles.

She sighs. 'What are we doing here, Alexis?' For a moment she feels like the boy by the monkey cage. Wretched with her own fear. Alexis touches her arm again and she lets him, relaxing as they go in. She is surprised that the door is unlocked. The corridor and then the room are full of people.

There is a monster lying on the operating table. Anja can't take her eyes off it. Its face hates her and loves her, like the wolves, massive and carnivorous.

'God. God.' She is talking to herself. Alexis is whispering in her ear, shrill and excited, but she can't hear what he's saying. She pushes gently through the crowd, wanting to get near.

The feline body is too long for the table, more than ten feet, so that the bearded, maned head is lolled back towards Anja. Upside-down the jaws leer open, fangs stained lurid kidney-reds and arterial blues. The smell of half-digested meat and formalin makes her want to retch. She turns away, voices whispering around her.

'Look at it. Head like a bloody dustbin lid.'

'What happens now? What? But something has to happen. Animals don't just die –'

Another voice, the head keeper, unfamiliar with stress. 'Well for Christ's sake, I can't see a thing wrong. This morning she was behaving perfectly, she looked wonderful. Butter wouldn't melt in her mouth.'

'It won't now, anyway. She's been dead for almost four hours.'

Anja looks up. The lab zoologist is walking round the table, hands moving across the liger's barred fur. Pushing against internal organs. She stops in front of Anja and stands back, next to the head keeper.

'They want her back at Jo'burg for analysis. We may be liable or not. She's not young, she's zoo-born, and she's a crossbreed with reduced life expectancy. But I can't find out for certain without opening her up. What do you want me to do?'

They go on talking, quiet and urgent. Anja can recognise faces in the crowd now; the white-faced man from the Insect House, the volunteer with the gold neck-chain, bulky in a hooded parka. *The whole zoo is here*, she thinks. *Everyone except the animals*. Then the head keeper is shouting into her face. Ordering them all out.

She stays as long as she can, a matter of seconds, just to look. To keep it in her mind. The eyes are almost closed, orange crescents set deep into the lids and fur and sockets. She feels a tug of greed, a wanting to possess. The fur is banded with diffused lights and shadows.

Then the crowd is pushing, pulling her along. Alexis is waiting outside. It's already getting dark and the rain has stopped. They walk back towards the Monkey Houses.

'What do you think happened?'

He shrugs. 'Animals die. It's no big deal. This time next week no one will give a toss.' His voice is dull, hoarse with too many cigarettes. Macaws scream at them for attention from beyond the dried-out Seal Pool.

'So why did you show me?'

He sighs in the dark. She can't tell if he sounds angry. She can't see his face. 'I thought you'd like it.' In the far distance now is the sound of cars, the shudder of lorries.

She takes his hand. 'I liked it.' They walk on as the closing-time klaxon begins to sound.

Her room is full of books – dictionaries of Faroese and state Norwegian, a Dutch East Indies guide to river-fish, some poetry but little fiction. They are her vice, that is how she thinks of them. There are too many volumes, they are too heavy and mismatched. The way she carries them from one rented room to the next makes no sense. Most of them she will never read again. But she will not let them go. Therefore they are a physical addiction. She is happy to admit it. She loves them more than alcohol.

Her favourites are stacked neatly in one corner, by the kettle. She sits down on the floor, waiting for the water to boil. Grey morning light comes in through the window opposite. The sky outside looks like concrete.

The wall is hard and cold against her back and head. Anja yawns, picks up a volume from the top of the pile. Opens it, cradling the spine.

It is Knut Hamsun's *Mysteries*, the first English translation. On the flyleaf is the loping handwriting of her father: *To Anja my daughter on her university entrance. Good luck with the animals and all their mysteries – Dad.*

The message always seems unfinished to her. Broken off. She turns the pages, not reading, wondering what he was trying to say with the halting words; with the book. Maybe there was nothing else to buy in the offshore stores. She remembers Edith, flicking through pages, snarling *Such a fool he is, the stories of a Norwegian Nazi, what has this to do with you?* But Anja liked it, this tense, self-obsessed writing. She imagined her father in the glare and dark of the oil-rig, reading by naval warning-lights. The hollow, white noise of the sea.

She closes the book. Her father is dead, her mother is dead. In thirty years she will be older than them both. It will never get easier, the remembering of them. She feels the sadness coming across her in a long, slow wave that darkens the room.

She leans forward, kneading the heels of her hands into her eyes, then drags hard fingers back through her hair. The skin pulls taut against her scalp, forcing her eyes open. She stares out at the sky. When she is ready she breathes out, stands up, gets ready to go.

'Good morning. You look tired.'

'Yes.' She sits stiffly by the fence, wanting to hear him talk. She can smell snow coming, a sourness in the air. Wind catches on the cage-links.

He holds out raw meat in his hands. The wolves snap at it, worry it apart, lick his fingers clean. He talks to her over their eager, narrow faces.

'You know a lot about animals. You studied them, maybe.'

'I dropped out.' Her teeth chatter and she shuts her mouth tight, leans forward against the cold.

'You're Finnish. Karelian blood?'

'Some.' She keeps the surprise out of her voice. She remembers her mother's father, small and almost Mongol-featured. His endless, halting stories of Karelia, Finland's lost eastern isthmus; the taste of Karelian salmon, the Russian soldiers with their farmyard uniforms, easy to kill but numerous, overrunning the land, stubbornly cruel. Anja remembers the slant of his eyes and the way he cried when he drank. She touches the braid of her black hair, pushes it away from her face.

The sadness comes at her again, slow and quiet. She looks round for anything, anything she can do. An action which will take her out of herself. Her leg muscles tense with the need to run.

The largest wolf barks for attention. Once, twice. The keeper hushes him, whispers instructions.

'I worked up in Oulu for a few months. At the university. They were counting the wildlife – these.' He slaps the animals back with a handful of offal, grins up at her.

'Why did you come here?'

He shrugs. 'I got lonely for the big towns.' She laughs; the lie is blatant to both of them. He has no love of people. She understands that. Love of people is something she can only imagine or remember.

'How about you?'

She doesn't answer for a long time. He goes on feeding the wolves, not looking round at her. After a while they trot away towards the trees and sit, tall on their haunches.

'I had to get away. No more people. I just had to get away.'

Her voice is quiet. He stands watching her. When she doesn't move he comes over to the cage fence, puts his hand through, touches it against her cheek.

She reaches up without thinking, holds the warmth of his palm against her. His fingers are rusted with blood from the meat. He smells like iron. She closes her eyes and leans against him. He is cradling her head. No one says anything. She can hear his breathing, wind in the park trees, the distant city chorus of sirens.

The sirens come closer, a rising panic, joining up discordantly in the network of approach streets. Anja opens her eyes. Her pupils have contracted in a moment, hard and small. She pulls back. Looks up at the wolf keeper.

'The police. You didn't know?'

She stands up, folds her arms tightly across her chest. 'Didn't know what?'

He frowns and moves his hands, a clumsy gesture of embarrassment. 'Then I should have told you. Something happened. Maybe last night. The liger is gone.'

It begins to snow, light and bitter. She brushes its cold feathers away from her face.

'Close the door, please. Sit down.'

She sits down. The chair and the voice make her think of prison; hard, cold, plastic. She feels a wave of claustrophobia and leans back against it, requiring herself to relax.

'And your name is –?'

'Anja Kivinen.' The policewoman is over six feet tall, broad-shouldered, masculine. She frowns down at her checklist, makes a tick. Smiles back up. Her eyes are very beautiful, the irises almost grey.

'How is your English, Ms Kivinen?'

'My English is well, thank you.' It's dark in the small zoo-keepers' room, the police haven't turned on the lights. Snow flurries against the window and funnels away. Anja wonders if the dimness is intentional.

She flinches at a noise outside in the corridors; metal falling, laughter. The policewoman is still smiling, a tension of facial muscles. 'Great. Do you know why you're here?'

'The Johannesburg liger. The body has gone missing.'

'Yes, that's right, I'm sure every keeper in the zoo knows that.' She crosses her legs, sits forward. 'My name is PC Phelps. I'm here to find out what else you can tell me. Plural you. No need to be nervous, you're just –'

'Helping with your enquiries.'

Phelps laughs shortly between her teeth. It sounds like paper tearing. 'That's exactly right. You'd know, of course. I noticed you helped the Finnish authorities with their enquiries for eighteen months, yes? So.'

She looks down at her papers again, reading. Anja unzips her jacket. She doesn't take it off. It's hot in the small room. She thinks of the wolf keeper. His hand, warm against her cheek. She concentrates on that.

'So?' Phelps is looking at her again. A big, soft-featured, sharp woman. 'What did it look like, this liger? Tell me about it.'

'You must have photos from Johannesburg.'

'Well. You tell me. You're the trained zoologist.'

Anja shrugs. 'Ligers are the product of lion–tigress impregnation. They're zoo animals – unnatural. In nature the parents would never meet. Lions and tigers are two versions of the same idea, evolved on different continents.'

The policewoman nods, only half-listening. Anja watches the wallclock as she talks, the blank movement of its face. It's already past noon. She makes herself sit back, hands loose in her lap.

'The animal that died yesterday was fairly typical – darker and larger than either parent. Probably infertile. Very large.' She remembers the yawning leer, the orange crescents of the eyes. 'Heavy. How was it moved?'

'Electric car.' Anja imagines one of the zoo buggies whining through the deserted dark, the flurry of panicked animals.

'There are security cameras. It must all be on tape.'

Phelps stands up without answering. Walks round the desk. Wind whistles outside. She frowns out into the snow. 'Ms Kivinen. You do fairly menial work here, don't you? And on a voluntary basis. What is a scientist like you doing in a job like this?' She smiles back into the room.

Anja sits without moving. 'I needed somewhere to live.' They watch each other in the underlit room. 'Also I am only half-trained. No use. Like a doctor who can cut but cannot sew. I never graduated.'

They are close together now. Phelps has stopped smiling. It makes her look kinder, younger. 'Why?'

'My parents died. Nothing exciting.' The policewoman nods. The papers are exposed and white in her hand. 'A car crash. You must have details. I didn't want to stay in Finland.'

'I'm sorry.' Phelps's voice is soft. Anja wonders if she has been trained in emotional awareness. For a moment she feels like crying anyway. 'Anja. I don't care about your record. I just want to finish this job. If this liger stays missing, your zoo could be liable for a lot of money. But you're the one who cares about it, not me. Help me. Don't you want to do something?'

Anja stands up. The chair legs grate away from her on the linoleum floor. The need to act rises up in her like happiness. 'It's a big place. Things go missing all the time. One dead cat more or less makes no difference.' She zips up her jacket. 'Now I would like to go.'

Phelps leans against the desk. She sighs, leafs through her papers. 'Of course.' Quite suddenly she looks bored, the eyes going listless with exhaustion. 'Send in the next one, please.' She doesn't look up when Anja leaves.

The security guard is called Les. His breath smells of pickled herring and smoked mackerel. He leans over Anja to rewind the video, hand painfully heavy against her thigh.

'Mickey Mouse is good, that's got all puzzles in it, not just shooting and stuff like in Doom. Doom's seriously diabolical. Here.' He stops the tape and presses Play. Smoke from Alexis's cigarette curls into Anja's eyes. She sits closer to him anyway. The wall is full of televisions.

'Raz – his mum's Indian he told me, not corner-shop Indian though – it was him what was up here last night. He's in a bit of trouble, as it goes. For not noticing. He'll keep his job, though, definitely. Definitely. It weren't a living animal or nothing.'

The nearest screen comes on in a wash of white static and noise. Les adjusts a dial. On the ranked monitors are images of the zoo in grainy black and white: the turnstiles, the members' gate, a roundabout with moulded goldfish and giraffes. Anja knows every scene, but the camera-angles make them oddly alien. Child-faces in the afternoon crowd look up, wave.

'Does your head in at night. All the screens. I play Doom, only just to keep my eyes open. The adrenaline buzz. But Raz, he sleeps mostly. Crashes out. Give us a fag, Alexis. Cheers.'

A new picture blinks on. It is distorted by static and sharp contrasts of light. There is a skip full of broken caging, a drab laboratory entrance, the tail-end of a sign: R1 (FELINES). Shadows of caging criss-cross the doorway. An electric zoo buggy whines in from the left and coasts out of sight behind the skip. The movement leaves after-images on the close-circuit screen, soft and grey.

There is something coming out of the shadow, standing. Big in the bone, but full of small movements – head cocked, listening, hands touching the skip, the cages.

Anja feels a rush of emotion that leaves her smiling. *There – he's real, he was here*, she thinks. She looks round at Alexis, wanting to share her exhilaration. But his face in the dark is white and twisted with something. Fear or repulsion.

'The feather man,' says Les. His chair creaks in the dark.

'Don't be a wuss. It's just some sick bastard, you can see it in his face. Do you not see his face?'

But she can't see his face. The light picks out nothing except the sheen of a head, almost hairless. The figure lumbers round the side of the building. Two minutes later it comes out of the entrance door with a black plastic bag under one arm. It goes back in, moving with the huge oil-suppleness of a bear. When it comes out again it is crouched, dragging something down the lab steps, briefly into the light.

It is a roll of plastic sheeting, some kind of floor covering or a shower curtain. On the bottom step a massive forepaw catches and pulls against the ground. The figure looks back. The camera's digital readout flashes *3.09 a.m.* across the abstract black-white face. There is nothing visible except a circle of darkness, the distorted socket of an eye.

The picture cuts without sound to a long black hall, lit with rippling light. The Aquarium. The juxtaposition is disturbing; Anja takes a quick breath, feeling the rhythm of her own heart muscle against her lungs.

'What happened?' Her voice sounds raw and angry. The figure turns in her mind, face obscured, half-animal in the half-light. Anja wants to find him. She feels she would recognise him anywhere. She feels Les shrug next to her. The chairs smell of old cigarettes.

'It switched. Different camera. That's what close-circuits do.' She pushes back her chair, walks to the window, pulls open the blinds.

Outside the snow has stopped. A heron flies low over the building, bow-necked and reptilian. Anja bites her knuckles, staring out at the hunchback skyline of aviaries and concrete mountains.

'Anja?' Alexis's hand is fragile against the hard leanness of her shoulder.

She thinks of the wolf keeper. His voice, the smell of iron on his hands. But most of all she thinks of a figure in the dark, clumsily shaped but moving with grace. The green dust of hummingbird feathers. She wants to touch and talk to them, the people who have brought her here. It has been a long time.

'She all right?'

'Sure, she's fine. I'll see you, Les, yeah?'

'Yeah. Later.'

She turns round. 'I'm fine.' But Alexis is already out into the corridor and Les is putting on headphones. There is no one here for her. These are not the people she is looking for.

She walks along the canal path towards Camden Town. The backs of houses and undersides of bridges are scrawled with black graffiti. It reminds her of the video, shadows of caging against white concrete walls. Harsh in the throwback of arclights.

There are children in Chalk Farm Road, running between the traffic-lanes. The screech of tyres disturbs Anja; she forces her hands hard into their pockets, walks with her head down. The children are screaming laughter. 'Slow snow! Look, slow snow!' Cars hoot and flash their lights in the four o'clock gloom.

Anja looks up, surprised out of herself. The snow has begun again without her noticing, fine white flakes drifting down. She can measure the sky in them, looking back and up until it makes her dizzy and she leans against the market wall. She can hear the children, but already they are out of sight.

Camden Lock Market is deserted. Anja walks through the rambling warehouses and alleyways towards the railway line. The early darkness makes her think of the Scandinavian winters, havens of bright music and electric lights and drink. She wants a drink so much.

The railway looms ahead of her, brick archways rising up over shut-down weekend market-stalls. There are signs nailed to the crumbling brick: FRIDAYS = GRUNGE NITE + CLUB DJ MISTAH KIPLING. Arrows pointing to the last arch, the end of the market. Anja follows the arrows. The entrance to the club is painted in psychedelic orange and green swirls, locked-up and unlit. Anja comes to a stop outside, the momentum going out of her. She doesn't know what to do next.

She turns round, looking for the toilet cabins. It takes her a few minutes to find the place they were parked, halfway between the club entrance and the road. The ground is slightly discoloured with motor oil, less littered.

She kneels down. Gravel grinds against her knees. The snow hasn't settled, but the light is going. In thirty minutes there will be no colour left to see, only the unnatural neon-blues and greens of restaurants and late-night shops. And colour is important now. Anja concentrates on the red of an impacted Coke can, the yellow sheen of a McDonald's carton. Her eyes are good, she trusts what she sees. Taking small, straight steps, she begins to cover the ground.

It takes quarter of an hour and she finds nothing. Her knees ache when she stands. She looks around but the market is still deserted, no one is watching. There are lights in the condemned houses along the railway, but Anja can't see people there. She is sweating inside her jumper despite the cold.

She's running out of time. Squatting down, Anja begins to search again, moving out towards the club, the road, the derelict houses and warehouses.

There is a feather caught under a broken wedge of breeze-block. Sharp and slender, long as her thumb, the colour of egg yolk. She gives a short shout of laughter as she picks it up. Two fire-engines go past on the road; she holds the feather up against the glare of their siren-lights. It is exotic as saffron in her hand.

The lights pass. The laughter goes out of her. She turns, looking off towards the dead-ends of brickwork and the blank windows of empty houses. She knows what she knew days ago; he was here. She has learnt nothing. The yellow feather is useless, it leads nowhere.

Anja holds it tight in her fist. Tomorrow she will be back to look again. She grins, walks. The air outside the market gates smells of street-food, sweet and sour. Her stomach growls. She crosses the road, towards the shops, moving carefully between the hard momentum of cars.

There is nothing sharp enough to gut with except the bread knife. Anja uses that. She cuts open the turbot on its blind side, reaches in for the intestines, cleans it out. She grates the white root of a horseradish into a bowl of green mustard and dill. Crushes fresh green peppercorns. Water simmers on the cooker. She melts butter, brushes the fish-skin. Scrubs black mineral earth off the silvery skins of new potatoes.

The kitchen windows are cladded with condensation. Passers-by outside would see nothing except her movement, his motionless bulk. And there is no one outside. Mist comes off the Grand Union Canal, drifting between animal cages.

She is cooking for the wolf keeper. It has been a long time. Eating has become a private thing. Privacy is all she has. She works with her back to him. They talk a little.

'All this.' He clears his throat. 'It looks expensive.'

'I have money.' She cuts smoked salmon and smoked sturgeon into glass-thinness, folds them on rye bread. Scatters them with chives, drips them with the juice of limes.

'You don't need to work. Here, in the zoo.'

'No.' The flatfish cooks, turning from translucency to opacity, the skin crisping. She opens the fridge, takes out the wine from its bright glare. 'I don't need to work anywhere.' She opens the first bottle, pours. Two long glasses. They frost instantly. 'I told you why I'm here.'

'To get away.'

She turns to him. Holds out a glass. 'Yes.'

'You didn't say from what.' His eyes are lucid, pale brown. Canine. She takes a long drink, letting the alcohol warm her. For a moment the taste makes her nauseous, so that she stands, waiting for it to pass. Then there is only warmth. She shakes her head.

'Later. First let's eat.'

The food is good. She enjoys it and the way he works at it, head down, face open with concentration. When there is nothing left he leans back against the wall and grins, easing the weight off his stomach. They sit on the floor of her room, between the uneven piles of books. Traffic passes on the Outer Circle road. She watches the red glare of tail-lights crawling across the ceiling, fading out. For a while they don't talk. It feels good.

'You went looking for the feather man.'

'Yes.'

'But you didn't find him.'

'No.' The pale yellow wine seeps into her bones. She leans back against the side of the bed, cradling her glass, eyes half-closed.

'It might not have been him. The liger. There is a market for that kind of carcass.'

She opens her eyes. 'So the feather man needs money. Did you see the security video?' He watches her for a moment, then away. He nods.

She remembers the ligerskin, barred with light and shadow. 'It was him. And the animal was beautiful. Another beautiful thing.' The wolf keeper nods again.

'Why do you want to find him?'

She doesn't know what to say. She doesn't know. He holds up one hand, taking the question away. Leans forward to pour out the last of the wine.

'I am here because I killed my parents.'

She wants to say it very quietly, so that she doesn't have to hear. He looks at her as if she has shouted into his face. She stops watching him. Some time soon he will start to swear, try and attack her. She tenses her crossed legs, ready to hit back. Swills the wine in her glass.

'We drink a lot in my country. Not this, though. Wine is too fine. But you've been there, yes? So. Do you know why we drink in Finland?'

He puts down his glass. She keeps talking. Fast; she is getting out of breath already. 'We drink to get drunk. Crayfish season, midsummer, midwinter – especially winter. Because it cheers us up. Because we miss the light.' Her left eye is stinging with tiredness. She kneads it with her fingers, leans against the hand.

'It's a long season to go without light. Drinking made it better. For me. Without drink, I couldn't do anything. When I was drunk, I could remember what summer was like – the fenlands, the field-flowers. All the colours. In winter everything was dull. The sea was the colour of coal. Blue-black under the ice. When I was small I thought it was all that colour, like handfuls of ink. But my father brought me some back from the rigs. Norwegian sea. In a plastic bottle.'

She looks up at him, as if this is important. It isn't important. It's just that she doesn't know where to begin. Nothing is more important than anything else.

'It was only black from a distance. My mother taught me why. The rules of light. Diffraction and diffusion.' She sees sky over Edith's house. The sky is blue from distance. It is the colour of flags snapping taut at Helsinki South Harbour and Tar Island.

'My father brought me things. My mother taught me the rules. Now you know my parents. He bought me a beer, she taught me to drink. He bought me a car, she taught me to drive.'

She sits with her mouth slightly open, past talking. She goes over it in her head. Later the wolf keeper's arms are round her, he is whispering in her ear, something. But now there is only

the smell of blood and pines. It makes her want to vomit. She can taste vodka, the clean abrasion of it coming up from her guts. She is hanging from the seatbelt.

She is hanging from the seatbelt. The catch is on the ceiling. It takes too long to find it (too long for what?). She releases the belt and falls onto the hard car roof. The interior metal is slithery with frost. Glass crunches into her hair, she can feel it, cold pain against her scalp.

She opens the door and pulls herself out flat. The hill up to the road is steep and she lies back against the car, looking up at the firs, the white-green wood shining where they have been broken. Her father was telling a joke but she can't remember the punchline. Only laughter, the steering-wheel moving under her lax hands. Anja wishes she could remember the punchline.

The smell comes to her again. She retches but nothing comes. It is already too late to stand up, she knows. She stands up anyway. The car creaks, it rolls away from her. Down the hill, into the green trees.

She follows it down. Now the car looks right again, only the windows are broken. Her parents in the back of the car. They are holding hands. They are sprawled together – no. They are making love in the back seat. Anja can't see their faces. She looks away. They make her bored.

She tries to remember where they were going. Was it home? It is important to remember. For the police and the ambulance to know. Drunk drivers go to prison. Every Finn knows the law. It must be important to know where she was going, where she was coming from.

There is no noise, the hiss of the engine has died. Sometimes snow falls down from the wings of firs. It sounds like breathing. Anja imagines sirens. Sometimes it is the ambulance to take her parents away. Sometimes it is the police coming for her.

There are no sirens, only the sweet-mint smell of blood and pines.

She can't breathe. She crouches down against the car and vomits alcohol. She isn't very drunk any more. In winter she is always a little drunk.

She wipes her mouth. It is very hot against her hand. Now she can see where the sky ends and the road begins; the sky is darker. She gets into the car again, to keep warm.

Warmth becomes the most important thing in the world. She can feel where it ends, in her limbs, the points where the blood no longer circulates heat. Cold grows inwards, cell by cell. Like ice on a lake's surface.

The air congeals in her lungs. She wants to stop breathing, to keep the air out. Her teeth are chattering, then after a while the chattering dies away. It feels good when it stops. Easier. She wants to ask her parents how they are, but her mouth is hardening and the words won't come.

They keep quiet. They are waiting for the sirens. There is no sound. Only the smell. Snow comes in through the empty windows and settles against their skins, gently as feathers.

She feels a sharp line of pleasure. When she opens her eyes the wolf keeper is there. Very close, very warm. She can feel the hair and skin of him against her under the sheets, his hand between her legs. She moves against him. Kisses the corner of his mouth, feeling her breath quicken. Her eyes are adjusting to the dark, widening.

She wants to know what he knows, what she has said. When she tries to talk he kisses her mouth. He lets nothing out of her but the sound of her breathing. His hand has found a rhythm, not fast, building slowly. It brings her back into herself with a quickness that shocks her. The crash, the frozen cell of the car – it clicks off like a loop-tape. Now there is nothing except the dark bedroom, his neck softer than her mouth, his knuckles grazing gently against her.

It has been so long. After she comes the first time he holds her still for a while. Tightly, the way a parent holds a child that might hurt itself. When she is ready she takes his arms away, kneels over him, takes him in.

'Anja.'

She is awake instantly. Her mouth is numb, greasy with old alcohol, and her head hurts. The bedroom is bright and cold with electric light. The harsh bell of an alarm grates the air from somewhere nearby. Inside the zoo. She sits up. The wolf keeper is already half-dressed, pulling on shoes.

She has never heard a zoo alarm at night. Animals chitter and scream, traumatised out of sleep. Something roars in the dark. She stands up, trying to remember where her clothes are, where he undressed her.

He is by the window, peering out. Turning his head, ear to the glass. Gauging distance and direction. He is already zipping up his jacket.

'Wait.' She shrugs on her bra, sits to pull on leggings. She can feel his eyes on her. She turns away. 'Did you know the alarms would be on?'

'Yes.' He is waiting by the door. His voice is controlled, patient. 'But you didn't feel like telling me. The stupid foreign

184

volunteer.' Bitterness rises up in her, but she keeps her voice down. He shakes his head. It could mean anything, the gesture. That she is wrong, that he is innocent. She yanks at the buttons of her quilted shirt. Her hands are clumsy with sleep and hangover. 'It's him, isn't it? How did they know he'd come back?'

'It might be him. He has always come back. He had no reason to change. It was just a matter of time.'

The alarm stops abruptly. There is shouting outside, a martialling of people, the maddened flutter of wings. She recognises the expression on his face, the claustrophobia. She waves him away. 'Go. Go! Get out.'

'I'll meet you there.' He is already out of the door, his voice muffled. When she is dressed she goes to the window and looks down. The zoo is spotlit, shadows of people and animals thrown grotesquely against walls and cages. There is a mill of movement by the main gate, through the trees.

She turns out the light. At the lodge entrance she begins to run, her trainers skidding on the frozen tarmac. The condors hiss down at her from their high cages. Mantling their wings, faces like old men.

There is no one at the main gate. She stands by the ticket booths, listening to the shouts of security guards and night keepers echoing through the Monkey Houses and subway tunnels. From the distance comes the headkeeper's voice, distorted by a megaphone, cold and mechanical.

There is no traffic along the Outer Circle. She wonders what time it is but there is no clock and she has forgotten her watch. She turns slowly, looking for escape routes. The gate, Reptile House, Aquarium. The mouth of a subway.

Anja jogs towards the subway, looks in. Light sheens the mock-cave paintings and the snow crystallising against tunnel walls. There is a hoar of frost on the sheltered ground, blackened and smudged with footprints. Someone is standing at the far end. Thin shoulders in a green denim jacket. Anja can see the small glow of a cigarette.

'Alexis.'

He flinches back, dropping the butt. His face is red with cold. 'Anja, is that you? Jesus, you move quietly. I thought you must be him.' He trudges up the tunnel towards her.

'Have they found anyone?'

'Don't be silly. He's probably long gone. Fucking necro.' He coughs up phlegm, hawks it out.

They turn back. Alexis gets out another cigarette. 'It's really freezing, you know. Really.' Lights up. 'Listen. There must be a warm place we can look for him.'

She isn't listening. They are standing outside the Aquarium. The building is hooded with the moulded concrete mountain enclosure. White paint peels from clapboard. Anja walks up the slope to the entrance, presses her hands against the wood. It is perspiring slightly, warm against her cold skin. The door has been left half-open.

She looks back at Alexis. He smiles broadly at her through a pall of smoke and condensed breath. 'Great, great. No problem.' They go in.

The entrance room is dark. Alexis finds a light switch, clicks it on. The walls are painted turquoise and the air smells of water, sweetish and dank. On the wall is a sign, FRESHWATER HALL, and a map of the building: engine rooms, service tunnels, underground reservoirs. There is nothing else to see. Alexis swings open the inner doors and goes through.

Anja catches the doors before they close. She stands still, listening. There is darkness, the echoing sound of water, the rippling of tank-light. Alexis is faceless against the bright cubes of exhibits. When Anja moves, the doors swing shut behind her.

Her eyes adjust. She can see the waterlogged lengths of catfish and electric eels, motionless in their narrow tanks. Almost immediately she walks into a bench, the cast iron grazing her legs.

'Anja? Are you OK? Where are you?'

'I'm fine. It's nothing. You go on.' She sits down, waits for the dark to clear a little. Her breathing is too fast; she forces it slow. There is blood, warm against her calves. Not too much.

Swing-doors whisper against the floor, up ahead. She can't see Alexis anymore. She sits back, yawns in the dark.

The hall is full of small sounds, amplified by water, like a public swimming-pool. Now she can see black pillars between the benches, empty tanks between dim occupied light.

There is a sound in the dark. A connection of surfaces. Anja gets up and moves towards it. Not fast, but walking quickly, arms outstretched. She is aware that her eyes are wide, nocturnal, searching for movement.

She pushes through swing-doors to the Sea Hall. It's darker here, she feels it against her eyes like a weight. There are sounds everywhere, submarine creatures moving against thick glass. She can make out the caffeine-black eyes of sharks, the pent-up collisions of leatherbacks.

The air is becoming hotter. There is a sign on the doors ahead: TROPICAL HALL. Anja is aware of a constant background noise; a muttering, the tanks silvered with bubbles. She frowns, head down, but there is no sound except the oxygen feeders. Through the swing-doors she can see the next hall, an exit sign lit green at the far end. Alexis is going through, the fire-bar swinging shut behind him. Anja feels cool air on the nape of her neck. She looks back.

There is a stepladder in the second hall, half-hidden between pillars. Anja walks back to it, puts her hand out to touch the fourth step. It sits steady and flat. The wood is slightly damp, and cold. She looks up.

The Aquarium ceiling is low and black, so that at first she doesn't see the trapdoor. The cover is skewed half-open. There is a draught coming down from above, Anja can feel it against her face. No sound. The cold makes her shiver involuntarily.

She remembers the green glitter of hummingbird feathers. The zoo echoes around her, an institution of locks and bars and plexiglas. She wants to leave for the first time, and it feels like joy. She starts up the ladder.

The darkness above the ceiling is larger than the hall below. There is a sound of dripping. External light from high windows catches the sides of metal tanks, reservoirs suspended between girders. Anja puts out a hand to pull herself up. The beams are pillowed with dust, her hand sinks in and comes away coated with a grey talc.

She stands up, disoriented. Gusts of air catch at her, hot from below, freezing from the roof above. It makes her feel feverish, so that she leans back against a pillar. She thinks of going back for Alexis, but it is too far. There isn't time.

There are rungs set into the pillar. She goes on up slowly, off-balance, swaying in the gloom. In the roof is a manhole cover. An old Chubb padlock swings heavy and broken on its clasp. The cover barely moves. Anja sets her shoulders against it. Pushes out into the open.

She is on a mesa, eroded smooth and bare of vegetation. All around is London, glittering and cold in the night. Mice skitter away from her across the steep, icy concrete. The freezing air catches at her breath and drags it away. She stumbles, almost falls. There is a pyramid of light, distant, floating in the sky.

'The tower. It's the tower.'

The sound of her own voice brings her back. Altitude lights wink on the pointed summit of Canary Wharf, miles away. There are other towers, closer; a mosque, the metal gridwork of a construction crane. She has come out onto Goat Hill. The abandoned enclosure still smells of mammals, their hair and faeces. Directly below are the Bear Pools, drained and overgrown. To Anja they look like inner-city landfills. She can see piles of rubble and buddleia silhouetted against the bright emergency lights. The zoo's southern edge is close, a soft stasis of fog across Regent's Park.

Voices shout, shout back, far off towards the Gibbon Cage. Anja sits back on her haunches, lowering her centre of gravity, testing for balance. The path down is sheer-edged, spiralling artificially from the peak like a seaside helter-skelter. The concrete rock face shines dully with frost. Anja's left foot starts to move and she digs down with her calf muscles until it stops.

The spiral of the path looks too steep. She closes her eyes against vertigo, imagining the perspective from ground level. When she opens her eyes again, she notices that there is no frost on the path. *At least he didn't fly*, she thinks. The frost hasn't had time to grow back. She tries to smile, the cold sclerotic in her muscles. Her breath coalesces, floating out towards the fog.

She rolls onto her front and starts to slide, gaining momentum too quickly. Against her face the concrete smells of goat-piss. She grips with her whole body, hugging the cold. Cave entrances loom in the rock face, their entrances locked shut behind cage doors. Her jeans against the path sound like sandpaper. She feels pain in her calves where she grazed them in the Aquarium. Something bright flickers past her face. She cries out, throws out her hand towards a cage door. Holds herself there, one hand around the cold iron of a cage bar. Turns her head to see.

It is a fish-scale, frozen to the path. Anja turns her head, trying to recognise the species. The surface is bright silver, fading to steel-blue at the base. Large as a thumbnail, shed from a big creature. *Yes. This is also beautiful*, she thinks. It feels like an agreement. The water on the scale is already frozen, but still translucent.

Her hand hurts. It doesn't matter. She lets go of the bar and slides down the last shallow turn towards the Bear Pools. There is a scum of rainwater in the darkness below, frozen around an empty oil-drum. Anja stops herself going over the edge. She kneels, head down, angry at the pain in her hands and legs. Her calves are bleeding again, she can see the frost pinking around her jeans.

'*Sisu.*' She is talking to herself in the abandoned dark. The word means what she loves in herself: single-mindedness, stubbornness, isolation. The rest of her she hates; she would cut it right out, if she could. She feels like crying and grits her teeth against it, snarling. Stands up.

Someone is running away through the fog, quite silently. The park lamp-posts throw back a shadow, a giant projection on the mist. For a moment it seems to be looming closer, and Anja has to stop herself stepping back into the half-empty Bear Pool.

Then she is moving, down the walkway, pushing through

the bushes to the rusted perimeter fence. She hauls herself over and begins to run. Eyes wide open, watching the movement of shadows on the prisms of fog.

She moves easily now. Her balance is good. There is a path ahead, running along the zoo perimeter towards the Outer Circle road. Anja can see isolation cages through the fence, grey metal and concrete, shapes huddled in corners. A zoo reduced to its base components. She crosses the deserted road and keeps going.

The fog surrounds her. Now it is no longer static, she can see currents, turbulence. The peripheral movement disorients her and she stops, listening, trying not to breathe. There is still no sound, only the hulking movement of shadows ahead. Eddies of water vapour move back towards her, past her.

The path splits, a switchback going downhill to the Grand Union Canal. Now she can hear something, a rhythm, already fading. Footsteps on the hollow concrete of the towpath. Slow, barely running, moving south-east to Camden and King's Cross. Anja is almost too close. She makes herself wait, leaning against a tree. Her ragged breathing eases, smoothes out. She tries to remember how far it is to the next towpath exit. When she can't wait any more she walks down the slope. Her legs are shaking. They ache where they have bled.

The mist is thicker over the water, rolling under bridges and aviaries. The bottle-green water is half-frozen, floes of ice moored to narrowboats. Anja stays near the wall, one hand trailing against the damp brick. Undergrowth brushes against her wet jeans. Her teeth chatter once before she shuts her jaw tight against its own movement.

There is a sign on the bridge ahead, DEAD SLOW SHARP BEND in fluorescent red lettering. Anja remembers it from yesterday, the walk to Camden Lock. She has left the zoo behind, without noticing. The canal widens towards the lock, fog thinning under the hot lights of shops and bars and traffic islands.

She walks into clear air. The emptiness of it makes her naked. She wants to go back into the vapour, where she is invisible, where she can follow turbulence and shadows. Up ahead, a figure climbs the path to the main road. It has a black plastic rubbish sack cradled in its arms. Anja can see it breathing in the still pre-morning air, horse-clouds of breath. She wants to shout out an order or a warning.

She starts to run. It turns to face her and turns again, out onto the street. A truck horn blares up above, discordant with parallax as it passes. Anja pounds her feet against the cobbles, making friction. Her legs hurt again. She doesn't slow down.

The road is deserted. Traffic whispers in distant streets. Lamp-posts pick out coronae in the residue of mist. Vapour hangs faintly around the shop-signs, BAR BRAZIL, BIK CHIEF. Anja walks into the middle of the high street. From the white line she can see the curve of Chalk Farm Road, heading north.

A red car comes down past Marine Ices, tyres complaining on the salted asphalt. It hoots at her as it passes. She steps back into the road behind it. Paper skitters in the gutter. Telephone wires move with the small tremor of an Underground train. There is a creak and clink of padlock chains. Anja turns to look. It is the gate to Camden Lock Market. The high metal doors have already stopped moving.

She starts to run again. Her feet go from under her. The impact of the road against her shoulder thrusts the breath out of her lungs. She lies on the white line, curled up, waiting for the pain to go. It is hard to get up again.

The cold is back, settling in her limbs. She can feel the extent of her body-warmth. The point where it ends. She walks to the gates, stands close, looks in.

There is a security window off to one side. Blue light dances across the face of a guard. Sunken young eyes and lethargic, pouted lips. On the TV Claude van Damme is fighting two men on a mirror-top drinks-bar. Anja can hear the synthesised punches through the small window. She puts her hands on the gate. Pulls herself up and over clumsily, not looking at the guard. It takes too long, but her hands are numb, the metal speartops feel warm against her fingers. Then she is down, the dirt ground chuffing against her shoes. She walks without looking back.

There is an alley between the blackened backs of two buildings, high and narrow. Damp soot brushes Anja's shoulders as she walks. At its far end the alley widens to join a path of arches. The railway. Anja follows it round.

Outside the club is wasteground, rough grey gravel stretching to the road. Anja walks with her head down, looking for the place where she found the yellow feather. The gravel is the same everywhere, so that she keeps recognising angular rocks and formations. She sighs and stands back, looking around.

The club lights and music are synchronised. Dub rhythm echoes in the alleyways and lights up the walls of empty buildings. A train clacks past overhead, goods carriages grey and windowless. Anja watches them, silhouetted dark against the sky. It is almost morning.

She turns back to the derelict buildings. There is a terrace of them along the market wall, overlooking Chalk Farm Road. Cracked windows held together with grime. Dead wires trailing out to pylons. Dirt hangs from the wires in clumps.

Anja walks to the third derelict. Looks up at the wires, pulling her hair out of her face. The accumulations of dirt are regular, tough fronds unfolding from stamens, trails of roots. Vegetation growing out along one wire. The pylon is festooned with airplants. Anja remembers the zoo nurseries at night, greenhouses illuminated like long, dim light bulbs. Her eyes travel back along the wire, to the third house.

The rotting brick is cracked with subsidence, step-fissures opened in the mortarwork. There are creepers hidden in the cracks. Anja puts her hand out, trying to recognise the fine, sharp leaves. Pale yellow buds hang from the stems, dead with frost. In the sunken front garden Anja can see their roots, branching out like buttress trees. The front door is boarded up but there is a gaping hole in the basement wall, a window smashed or booted in. Anja lowers herself down, feeling soft mulch under her feet.

She looks into the cellar. It is full of greenery and warmth, succulents crowding up to the windows. She takes a breath of the hot, wet air. Holds it inside her. She climbs in without falling.

The room smells of mushrooms and orchids, dark and sweet. Anja can hear a whirr of electric fans. She shivers when the warm air touches her face, a spasm of muscles. Her hands begin to ache dully, the cold blood hurting in its veins. She gnaws at her knuckles, trying to control the pain.

The ceiling creaks. She snaps her head back, arms out to support a roof beam or plaster. Nothing falls. Her lips are still pulled back against her teeth. She feels sweat on her face as she moves through the plants. The air cools it across her forehead and cheekbones.

There is a stairway, half-hidden behind growths. The bannister has fallen away and she climbs with her hands against the wall, feeling for support. The window at the top of the stairs has been painted black. She turns round. There is a computer on the floor, filling space with the rippling light of a screen saver. The room is full of feathers.

It is a mosaic of green, metallic blue and gold. Condor wing-flights hang down, massive as oars, the colour of dried blood. She starts to laugh, softly at first. The feathers laugh with her, dancing away from her breath.

They are all over her, a hot insulation. She tries to push them away but the floor is covered. Soft grey-green down eddies up towards her like fog. She can't breathe, feathers catch on her sweaty skin. The ceiling and walls are disturbed by her motion. They move like sequins on a glitterboard. In front of her is an arc of brilliant red. *King Bird of Paradise*, Anja thinks, and cries out, on the edge of panic. She backs away, falling against the stairs. Holding on, not going down.

'How long have you been here?' She is talking to herself. As if the feather man is inside her, a parasite. Her voice is the wheeze of an asthmatic, dried-out with avian dust. Her head sags with exhaustion. She leans back against the wall, closes her eyes. Shouts, 'How long have you been here?'

Her voice has no echo. The feathers baffle it, moving and

193

settling. A bus groans outside, changing gears. Distant as sound heard through water.

She walks back into the room. Carefully, keeping her motion to a minimum. Feathers rise and fall around her. Hummingbird down glitters against her torn clothes. She turns her head like a sleepwalker. Behind the computer, the wall is barred with ostrich plumes. Anja draws in breath through her nose. Blows gently towards them. The plumes swing back into space.

She pushes through. There is a second staircase, unlit, loose feathers adhering to a worn-out carpet. A sour, pungent odour of alcohol. *A zoo smell*, Anja thinks. She frowns in the dark, trying to match it with a cage or an enclosure. She thinks of the liger, its head yawning back on a laboratory table.

There is a landing at the top of the staircase. Empty fishtanks are stacked beside an empty doorway. In the gloom Anja can make out a kitchen, dust collecting on cracked white tiles. On top of a broken cooker is a portable gas stove, water boiling in a pan. One plate, one cup. A freezer hums in the corner, enamel bright white. There is a black rubbish sack in the chipped sink.

The knotted plastic is too tight for her fingers. Anja pulls the polythene apart. A black mass spills out across her forearms and she pulls away, not crying out. The kitchen fills with the stench of fish. She leans forward. The sink is full of caviar, a sturgeon's roe-sac breaking apart as it oozes free of the plastic.

She begins to shiver again. The spasms won't stop. It is a question of control. What she has lost, what she can keep. Her teeth begin to chatter. There is a door in the far wall. Anja makes herself stop, listening. There is nothing to hear. The door isn't locked. She goes through.

Before she sees anything there is the sour odour of formaldehyde and she doubles over, retching. Anja remembers the liger, school laboratories, the slit eye of an ox. The smell clogs her lungs. She backs away coughing, looks up.

The room is jammed with Formica café tables, shopping trolleys, plastic beer crates. Fishtanks are packed close together on every surface. There are shapes frozen in the tanks, suspended in liquid. Anja goes closer. The room is quiet as a museum. She can see an armadillo, curved like an ammonite in a box. A gilthead fish, round and flat as a pot lid, eyes mildewed white with preservative.

A dead zoo, she thinks. *All the beautiful things*. The animals peer back at her, eyes whitened or sunken away. *It dies with them. There is nothing here that isn't monstrous*. There is window light in the next room, falling across bare, dry boards. She can see it through the open doorway. She wanders in.

The tank is head-on to the doorway. At first Anja can see nothing but the liger's head, huge and savage against the glass. Its beard and mane are tangled in the formalin, and the eyes are already misting with vague cataracts of preservation. Anja walks round towards the window. The liger's torso is wasting, the belly visibly shrunken. Violently grotesque. She thinks of the Sea Hall, leatherback turtles colliding in their confinement. The tunnel-vision of sharks.

She presses her hands against the glass. It is cool and solid on her skin. There is slight movement in the tank, beyond the great cat's bulk. The feather man is standing on the far side, distorted by the liquid. Watching her. The carcass floats between them, talons extended. Blue and yellow ivory.

'This is not right.' Her voice is calm. 'I thought it would be – not like this, something wonderful. But –'

He smiles with his mouth, not with his eyes. Shakes his head, raises one hand to his ear and turns it away. Anja can see the wizened texture of his skin, the washed-out blue of his old eyes. She mouths at his deafness through the glass. *This is not right. Not right*.

He doesn't move, his mouth still smiling a little, muscles not yet returned to laxity. Anja steps back, the light of the window behind her. She punches the glass hard, knuckles clacking against the surface.

He watches her, hands at his sides. She can feel blood running down her knuckles to the fingertips. She clenches her fist. 'Look what you've done.' She whispers it. Shouts, 'What have you done?'

She runs back into the adjacent room. The café tables are round, iron under the Formica. From the nearest table a lemur gazes back at Anja with white owl-eyes. She kicks its tank away, gagging as it hits the ground in a wash of glass and formaldehyde solution. Picks up the table by its legs. The alcohol is already on her skin, she can feel its itch and liniment burn.

He is still waiting. She watches him as she swings the table back. 'What were you making? Is this a zoo? A dead zoo, is that what it is?' He is shaking his head, puzzled or dazed. She grunts with effort and hauls the table forward by its legs.

It clangs off the glass. The tank booms like a drum. The liger moves slowly in its liquid, head keeling to one side. Its paws move lightly, the way dogs dream of running.

The feather man lowers his head away. Anja wants to bring him to her. Make him hear. She rolls the table back with both hands, feeling the strain on her shoulders. Groans as it swings forward against the glass.

It cracks easily as eggshell. Anja closes her eyes against the expulsion of formalin. It washes over her, a cold oil against her skin. She gags and kneels forward, pulling her arms across her hair and face, trying to clean herself. There is nothing she can do. She can smell the rot and alcohol on her skin. Sickly sweet, like blood and pines.

She doesn't see the liger fall. It collapses bonelessly, forepaws folding across her. She feels her ribs snap, hears them inside. She opens her mouth to scream but there is no air, only wet fur. She breathes in on it instinctually, wanting to force air through the meat. Her diaphragm shudders with the effort.

The dead weight is killing her. She slaps at it, pushes frantically. It reminds her of childhood anger, hitting against her mother or father. Their immovability. She giggles. Livid spots bloom on the insides of her eyelids.

The air comes back to her. Wonderful, stinking of formaldehyde, stinging her throat and sinuses. The liger has gone. *Back to the zoo*, she thinks, and laughs again. Her ribs grind together and she opens her eyes wide to shout.

Her head is level with the floor. The liger is sprawled against one wall, jowled face staring back at Anja. She can see formalin soaking down between the floorboards. Glass is scattered like broken pond ice.

She turns her head. The feather man is sitting on his haunches beside her, rocking slightly. He is picking glass out of her clothing. She can feel his hand, close but never touching. His arms are wet with preservative from the liger's skin.

'We have to take the liger back. To the zoo.' Her voice is a whisper, oddly distorted by broken bones. She is trying to see his face but he is half-turned away. The corner of his mouth grins like an animal's: a gibbon, salmon, dog. She's not sure if he's smiling. She reaches out, thinking he hasn't seen her lips move. Wanting him to read them.

He moves towards her. His hands are fast and wider than her face. She remembers the feel of suffocation and flinches back. He lifts her easily, like feathers, and starts to walk. The ribs move grudgingly inside her and she bends into herself, struggling for a place where the pain is lessened.

He is walking between tables. She can hear the slide and crash of tanks, the hiss of formaldehyde on electric sockets. In the kitchen she can smell caviar and burnt metal, the water boiled dry in its pan.

The pain is a caul across her face. She is foetal, curled up around her hurt, protecting it. Part of her is trying to remember how formalin burns. She thinks it burns well. She can feel the poison vaporising on her skin.

They are moving through a mire of feathers. Liquid drips through the ceiling and trails down the walls, dragging down the ostrich plumes and condor flights into a drab sludge.

There is a voice talking quietly in the background, like a radio. Anja knows it must be hers. She can't make out the words. She reaches down towards the ruined feathers. The room is full of bitter plastic smoke, the computer humming ragged and dangerous in its corner.

They are going down into the plants. Now she can hear her

voice, louder than the whicker of fans. She is saying sorry, to everyone, over and over again. The house crashes around her like a car. The wings of firs catch at her face as she falls.

She is not falling. The feather man has lifted her up, out of the basement. Anja is lying on open ground. She cranes her head round to see him. She waits for him to come out.

He doesn't come. Anja calls out for him, but her voice is weak. She waits a little more, lying on her back. The sky is grey and bright. *It looks like rain*, she thinks. Condensed fog hangs in droplets from the airplants and telephone wires.

Anja tries to remember what is happening next. The house, the feather man. The way formalin burns, the gas stove's tight blue flame.

She gets to her knees, stands slowly. The pain is bearable if she bends forward, like an old woman. She shuffles to the edge of the sunken yard. She wants to call down but she doesn't know his name and she knows he won't hear. She calls anyway, just words, trying to bring him out. There is no one at the dark hole of the window.

There is no way back down except to jump. Anja tries to guess if it would kill her, or how long she would pass out for. She doesn't think she has much time. She shuffles round, looking off into the deserted market ground. The gates are open, early morning traffic moving slowly beyond them.

She walks towards the gates. Formaldehyde burns in her nostrils and against her lips. It takes a long time to reach the road. There is a telephone shelter on the opposite pavement. Anja goes across, not waiting for the cars to stop. They hoot and shout at her.

She has money. The line clicks and whirrs as junctions connect. The number rings for a long time before someone picks it up.

'The Zoo.'

'This is Anja Kivinen. I need to speak to Shamash the wolf keeper.'

'The Finn. You should be here. Where are you?'

It is the head keeper. Anja crouches forward against the

hood of the telephone shelter, supporting her body. 'Please. I need the wolf keeper.'

'Wait.' The phone clicks onto hold. There is music on the dead line, a full choir singing *Stille Nacht*. She starts to cry. The tears hurt her raw skin.

'Anja? Where are you?'

She presses her cheek against the receiver and the calm of his voice. 'Shamash. I've found him.'

'Where are you?'

'Camden Lock Market.' She smiles back the tears. 'He's in a derelict house, it's not safe but I can't get him out. I need your help. Can you come?'

'Where is the liger?'

'In the house. He had all these animals in formalin. Like a secret zoo, and I' – her voice is fading to a wheeze – 'I broke it all. Was that right?'

His voice is a steady monotone. It doesn't pause. 'Yes. You were right.'

She doesn't believe him. She starts to cry again. Gritting her teeth so he won't hear.

'Anja, we don't need it.' His voice is still calm. Clumsy, giving away nothing. Not truly clumsy. 'The liger. Johannesburg say she was old. The zoos agree it was a natural death. So. We don't need it any more.'

She feels a wave of dizziness. 'The feather man. He's still important. It has saved me, Shamash, his zoo, it was wrong but good came out of it – and he saved my life! He – But I can't get him out now. Please, there's very little time. Will you come?'

The line sighs like a shell. She can hear whispering. Crossed lines, the head keeper and the wolf keeper. When the voice comes back it takes a moment for her to recognise the head keeper. 'Anja. When can I expect to see you back here?'

She doesn't understand. 'Where's Shamash? I need –'

'He's doing his job, which is caring for animals. Not people. Not people who steal dead animals. Do you understand?'

There is dead air again. She thinks of late-night radio stations. 'Anja. We are zookeepers. This is where you belong now. You know that. Hang up. Call the police. Then come back. Come back soon.'

She steps away from the telephone. It swings on its steel wire. When she looks back at the market there is already a thin plume of smoke where the derelicts stand. It fans out high above in the grey air. No one has noticed yet.

She goes back towards the road, the gate. Each step takes time and an acceptance of pain. There are people there before her, two teenagers in puffa-jackets, watching the thickening trunk of smoke. There is a sound of glass pinking and falling. Someone comes out of the security guards' office. They are shouting at her to get back. She ignores them. She can feel the heat of the burning house on her face. When it starts to hurt, she stops.

The fire is breathing, she can hear it, gusts of movement inside the house. A big animal in a small cage. It is trying to get free, moving out along the lines of creepers and telephone wires. It roars in the chimneys and staircases. It throws itself against walls and Anja steps back, knowing she won't be able to run. It warms her and she feels good. Alive with it.

There is a sound of sirens, lost in traffic and distant one-way streets. Anja looks back at the crowd. They huddle against the gate to see. The roof is burning away, blue flame running crisscross between roof beams.

The smoke glitters. Feathers rise in the intense heat. They ignite, burning cupric green and alcohol-blue. In the high air they spread, erupting and vanishing over the tenements and car parks. Someone in the crowd starts to clap. The fire-engines wail closer.

Anja puts out her hands. Shafts and vanes float against her, charring into nothing. They are beautiful; they disgust her. She wipes them away. They cover the ground in a black snow. She leans her head back and looks up. The sky moves with the small, quick lives of feathers.